Fatal Hunt

by

Michelle Godard-Richer

Fatal Hunt

Cover Art by *Diana Carlile*

The Wild Rose Press, Inc.
PO Box 708
Adams Basin, NY 14410-0708
Visit us at www.thewildrosepress.com

Publishing History
First Edition, 2022
Trade Paperback ISBN 978-1-5092-4486-7
Digital ISBN 978-1-5092-4487-4

Published in the United States of America

Jessica's limbs weighed a ton. She forced her heavy eyelids open. After a split second they shut on her again. She lay on something soft, and an engine droned around her. *Where am I? What happened?*

Then she remembered her fruitless struggle in the hospital room. Willing her head to the side, she forced her eyes open again. Her kidnapper sat in a chair across from her reading a newspaper.

He looked over the top of his paper and smiled. "You'll be groggy for a while longer. Go back to sleep."

Too tired to fight, she gave into the void sucking her down.

Praise for Fatal Hunt

Dedication

To my husband, my partner in all things, and our amazing children. I love you. And to all the writers on Critique Circle who helped me realize my lifelong dream.

Chapter One

Jessica Kent coasted along Main Street with her son Bryce, foot on the brake pedal as they skidded on the icy road. They passed brownstone buildings housing gift shops, an art store, and a photography store, among other local favorites. In the sunny backdrop stood the Rocky Mountains, white from top to bottom after a fresh snowfall. A postcard-perfect day in Lewistown, Montana.

Spying a coveted parking spot in front of the Rising Trout Cafe during the lunch rush, she signaled and pulled in.

Bryce unclipped his seatbelt. "I don't see Dad's truck anywhere."

Jessica gazed into the rear-view mirror at her son, the most precious gift she'd been given, and massaged the tiny bump on her stomach. "Don't worry. He'll be here soon. You know him and those cinnamon rolls." She climbed out and slid open the back door of her minivan. "Take my hand."

He frowned. "I can get out by myself."

Jessica sighed. Her eight-year-old little boy wasn't so little anymore. Since being kidnapped the previous summer and escaping on his own, Bryce had become independent. But she didn't want to give him his own space. She wanted to hold onto him and never let go. She'd couldn't fathom someone taking him away again.

"I know. But there's a patch of ice here."

"I'll be fine, Mom." He sat on the floor of the van, took hold of the grab handle, and climbed out, avoiding the ice. "See? Told you." He ran ahead, wrapped his arm around one of the black iron lampposts lining the sidewalks, and looped around it.

A cold wind whistled through the cracks in the buildings, stinging her cheeks. She zipped her parka to her chin, then crossed the sidewalk to the cafe. Pulling the glass door open, she hollered, "Come on, buddy."

"Coming." He jogged past her into the warmth of the small space and made a beeline for the desserts in the display case.

She followed and stamped the snow off her boots on the welcome mat. The scents of cinnamon, chicken, and onion mingling together churned her stomach. *Oh no. Not again.*

Whoever named morning sickness had been mistaken. The nausea hit anywhere, at any time, without warning. She held her breath, caught the eye of Lydia, working behind the counter, and pointed to the restrooms.

Lydia set a pan of cinnamon rolls on the counter. "Go ahead. I'll keep an eye on Bryce."

Jessica jogged to the bathroom, swung the door shut behind her, and kneeled in front of the porcelain throne seconds before her breakfast made a comeback. She groaned. *Hope this is the last time for a while.*

Earlier that morning, her obstetrician had prescribed medication for the nausea. Those pills had been her salvation during her first pregnancy. She held her stomach and waited for the heaving to stop. Once her stomach muscles unclenched, she rinsed her mouth with cool water, then dried her face with a paper towel.

She returned to the dining area and scanned the room for Bryce. He sat at a square red table in a wooden chair with a coloring book and crayons. And he wasn't alone. Her heart thumped in her ears. *A stranger!*

A middle-aged man in a grey three-piece suit sat across from Bryce. After seven months of living in Lewistown, she recognized most of the locals on sight, and none wore suits.

She strode across the room, stood behind Bryce's chair, and held his shoulders. "Hello, sir. I see you've met my son." Out of the corner of her eye, she glimpsed her husband, Jon, through the window. His dirty blond, grey-streaked hair poked out of his favorite dark brown cowboy hat. *Oh, thank God.*

The stranger stood and smirked. "Good afternoon, Jessica. What a fine young boy you have here."

How does he know my name?

He turned his back to her and ambled toward the exit. Jon entered the cafe, stood in front of the door, and looked the stranger in the eye. They spoke, but conversations happening at other tables drowned out their words. The man exited the shop. Jon stared after him before heading their way.

Jessica squeezed Bryce's shoulder gently. "Who was that man?"

Bryce shaded a dinosaur with a blue crayon. "Don't know. He didn't tell me his name."

"What did he say?"

"He asked me stuff."

"What kind of stuff?"

"He asked me where my parents were and where we lived."

Jessica's stomach churned again. "What did you tell him?"

"I told him I live on a farm with you and Dad. I didn't give him our address or names. I know better."

"Good job. I'm proud of you."

"Thanks." Bryce glanced up from his drawing. "Don't worry. He didn't seem like a bad guy."

Jon kissed her cheek and fist bumped Bryce. "Sorry I'm late. How did your appointment go?"

"Okay. I got some pills for the nausea." The creases in Jon's forehead betrayed tension. "Do you know that man?"

Jon shook his head. "No. Never met him."

"What were you talking about?"

"He asked for directions to a hotel. I told him if he wanted something fancy, he'd best head to Great Falls. Why?"

"I had to use the washroom. Lydia was supposed to be watching Bryce, but when I came out, the man was sitting beside him. He asked Bryce questions about who we were and where we lived."

Jon patted her hand. "I understand why you'd be antsy after what we've been through, but I think it's logical to ask a child sitting alone who and where his parents are."

She yanked her hand away. "I'm *not* overreacting. He knew my name, and he didn't get it from Bryce."

Bryce glanced up from his coloring book. "I didn't tell him our names, Dad. I swear."

Lydia came around the counter. "Sorry, I couldn't sit with Bryce. I got swamped. What can I get you folks?"

"We're fine, Lydia. Don't worry about it." Jon

ruffled Bryce's hair. "What do you want to eat, buddy?"

"One of those big chocolate chip muffins and hot chocolate."

Jon chuckled. "I should have known. What about you, sweetheart?"

Jessica's tummy garbled and churned at the mention of food. "Chamomile tea is about all I can handle."

"Sorry you're not feeling well again." Jon kissed the top of her head. "I'll have my usual, Lydia. Turkey club and a cinnamon roll."

Lydia asked, "Want your order to go?"

Jessica nodded. "Thank you." She needed them home, behind a locked door.

****

As he followed Jessica home in his Dodge Ram, Jon scrolled through his contacts and pressed Sam's number. Since Jon had retired from the FBI three years earlier, Sam had transferred from the field office in Washington, D.C., to the Criminal Investigative Division. From his new position at the bureau, Sam would be able to help them.

The man at the cafe had asked about hotels, but that wasn't what he came to find in rural Montana.

Sam answered on the first ring. "Hi, Jon. How's it going? It's been a while."

"Not good. I have a problem."

"What kind of problem?"

"About ten years ago, I went deep undercover in Kansas City. Remember?"

"Yes, and?"

"Someone told Hugh Jones where to find me."

"All traces of you were wiped in Lewistown after you resigned. Your employment file at the bureau is classified, and Kent is such a common name, it would be virtually impossible for him to find you."

Jon glanced in his rear-view mirror on the lookout for followers. "Yet he did."

"When? What happened?"

"I'll need recent photos of his associates to be sure, but I believe one of them followed Jess and Bryce to the cafe about half an hour ago. He questioned Bryce while Jessica was throwing up in the bathroom."

"Is she okay?"

"She's pregnant. Ten weeks along."

"Congratulations."

Jon took a right turn. "Thanks. I wish we'd waited. I can't tell her about this. The stress might cause her to miscarry. But I can't *not* tell her. She hates lies."

"A no-win situation. I think you should put off telling her for a few weeks. She might get angry, but she'll get over it. Did you rent out the house across the street from your ranch?"

No, Sam. She won't just get over it. She'll skin me alive. "No."

"Good. I'll send an agent to keep an eye on Jessica and Bryce. He'll be discreet, and he's one of my best. Trent Cooper. His family owns a ranch in Texas, so he'll blend in with the locals."

"If I'm lying, I may as well go all in." Jon shook his head at the deceitful thoughts crossing his mind. "I'll hire him as a ranch hand. It'll give him a reason to be around my house, and we can communicate without suspicion. Any number of unsavory characters may surface in Lewistown now."

"I'm not so sure. Jones is controlling and vindictive. He'll want to kill you himself. He won't risk anyone beating him to it by spreading word of your location."

How reassuring. "Maybe. I assume there's still an open investigation into the Kansas City mob?"

"Yes. I'll let the special agent in charge of the field office in K.C. know we need to accelerate the investigation."

"I know I'm retired but…"

Sam cut in. "I'll get you the file on the Kansas City mob."

"Thanks. I'll start paving the way for Trent's arrival." *What have I done?*

Chapter Two

Jessica stood in the kitchen scrubbing the last dirty plate in the sink. Overcome by a yawn, she leaned on the cabinet beneath the sink and waited for it to end before rinsing and setting the plate on the dish rack to dry.

Jon wrapped his arms around her middle and gently rubbed her stomach. "You're tired, sweetheart. Why don't you take a nap?"

"What about Bryce? You're usually out working with the ranch hands during the afternoon."

"They'll be fine without me. Speaking of ranch hands, I got a response to the ad I placed for the rental across the street. Turns out he was looking for work as well, so I hired him. His name's Trent. I couldn't pass up someone with his experience."

"But you're fully staffed."

"With the baby on the way, I figured it'd be nice to have more free time to spend taking care of you."

She dried her wet hands and wrapped them around his arms. "That's sweet." She yawned a second time, and her ears popped. "I'm taking you up on that nap." She kissed his stubbly cheek instead of his lips. Even the smell of food on someone's breath was enough to set off the nausea.

"Need me to bring you anything?"

"No, I'm fine."

Jessica padded along the carpeted hallway to their

bedroom and climbed into bed. She yanked the duvet to her neck and shut her eyes. The stranger's face flashed in her mind. His presence in town bothered her, and so did Jon's reaction even though he'd explained the situation away.

Am I being paranoid?

****

Jon sat on the black, leather sofa in the living room as Bryce raced cars around his battery-powered track. Jon's thoughts spun like the wheels of the cars. Trent coming to stay was a good first step, but more needed to be done to fortify the ranch.

A draft from the floor to ceiling windows chilled him to his bones. Jon kneeled on the floor and crumpled paper underneath the hearth in the fireplace. He stacked some kindling on the grate and lit the paper. Once the kindling caught, he added two thick logs, and set a black cast iron screen in front of the fire.

The flames danced, and the wood crackled, warming the room. His phone pinged. The file Sam promised had arrived. Jon retrieved his laptop from the coffee table. He clicked on the file and shuffled through reports until he came to images of Jones' known associates.

One face stood out. Jon covered his mouth to hold in a string of curses. The stranger from the cafe was Anthony Greer. Jon memorized the faces of everyone known to be involved in Jones' operations. He refused to be taken by surprise again. Jon clicked on the app linked to the surveillance system surrounding his ranch, ensuring every camera and motion detector was online and set to alert if someone trespassed.

Dammit, I can't believe this is happening again.

The one vow he'd made after retiring from the FBI

was never to be responsible for another death. He'd broken it once when he shot David Hayes, a serial killer, to protect Jessica. Now he'd have to break it again. If these mobsters walked onto his land, he couldn't let any of them leave.

No matter how hard he tried to escape them, evil and darkness wove their tendrils around him and squeezed with all they were worth.

*****

Jessica sat up in bed disoriented, then recognized the furniture in the primary bedroom she shared with Jon. In the dream she'd woken from, she'd been adding a seasoning packet to browned ground beef in a frying pan at her house in Cochrane, Alberta. The one she'd been forced to flee last summer. She hadn't given it a second thought in months. *What a weird dream.*

The harmonious aromas of chicken and root vegetables permeated the air. She shut her eyes and inhaled deeply. *Yum.* Those smells belonged together, and Jon's skills in the kitchen exceeded her own, though she'd never admit it. Her tummy rumbled in anticipation. Maybe those pills had kicked in. And maybe her subconscious mind had scented out dinner and brought on the random dream.

She glanced at the clock and scrambled out of bed. *I slept four hours!* No wonder her bladder was about to explode, and Jon had started dinner without her. After freshening up, she scurried down the hallway to the kitchen.

Bryce stood on a step stool with Jon behind him at the kitchen counter, both covered in white flour. Together, they pushed a rolling pin across a ball of dough. Her heart warmed. Jon could never replace

Adam, her deceased husband and Bryce's father, but he filled a void in their hearts. The loving relationship they shared as a family continued to blossom.

She wiped flour from Jon's cheek and kissed him. "What are you working on?"

"I'm showing Bryce how to roll out pie dough. He asked if we could have apple pie. I told him he'd have to pitch in."

She ruffled her son's hair, dislodging more flour. "You're doing a great job."

Bryce glanced over his shoulder. "Am I done helping yet?"

Jon chuckled. "Sure. Wipe your hands on this towel, and you're free to go."

Bryce cleaned his hands, hopped off the stool, and made his escape.

Jon set the rolled dough on top of the pie, brimming with apple filling. "Feeling any better?"

Jessica swept the remaining flour off the counter into her hand. "Dinner smells amazing. That's a good sign." She wiped the flour off her hands into the trash. "I had a dream about my house in Cochrane."

"Makes sense. You lived there a long time."

"I need to go back to Cochrane to pack the rest of our stuff. Put the house on the market before the baby is born."

Jon placed the pie on top of the stove. "How long do you think it will take?"

She shrugged. "Don't know."

"Once Trent is settled, maybe we could go together."

"What about Bryce? And school? I can handle it on my own."

Jon leaned against the counter beside her. "Why go alone?"

"Well, I would miss you two a lot. And my parents and sister would be thrilled to see us all. But Bryce needs to be in school."

Jon rubbed her stomach. "If we wait until the end of the school year it'll be harder. You'll have more appointments and less mobility."

"You have a point."

"Besides, a few weeks off won't hurt Bryce."

Jessica said, "We could get the school to give us his work."

Jon opened the oven and removed a sheet tray full of chicken thighs, carrots, and potatoes. "Great. It's settled. We can leave this weekend."

Jessica stared at Jon's back. He seemed eager to leave town. Pretty convenient timing with the stranger showing up. "Why the rush?"

He turned to face her. "There's a lot less to do around the ranch in January during the dead of winter."

"That's right. In a few months, once the hay starts to come in, it'll be a lot busier." *Why can't I shake the feeling something's off?*

The back door swung open, and Jessica's aunt came into the kitchen.

"Hi, Aunt Debbie." *Shoot! I totally forgot about inviting her to dinner!*

"Hi, Jess, Jon. Dinner smells great." Debbie hung her puffy coat on the hooks by the door, then slipped out of her snowy boots. "Anything I can do to help?"

Jessica ran water inside the kettle and set it on the base to boil. "No, thanks. Jon took care of everything. Should be delicious. Tea?"

"Yes, please. I'll get the mugs out for you, dear."

****

A rapping sounded on the front door halfway through dinner.

Jon stood before Jessica could. "I got it. Probably the new guy." He hurried to the foyer and swung the door open.

A sturdy cowboy over six feet tall with dark features smiled and tipped his hat. "Howdy. I'm Trent. You must be my new landlord, Jon."

Jon stuck out his arm. "Yes, that would be me. Nice to meet you."

Trent shook his proffered hand. "Good to meet you, too."

"Come in and meet my family."

Jon locked the door while Trent kicked off his cowboy boots on the welcome mat. "This way. We were just having dinner. You hungry?"

Trent's stomach growled in response. "Reckon I am."

"Here we are. Have a seat. I'll fix you a plate. Trent, meet Jessica, Bryce, and Debbie."

Trent nodded. "Howdy, ma'ams and young sir."

Bryce laughed. "You talk funny."

Jon bit his lip to keep from laughing. He glanced over his shoulder as he placed chicken and vegetables on a plate. Jessica's cheeks flamed red. Debbie also had her bottom lip in her mouth with laughter in her blue eyes. With their dynamic as a family being somewhat new, he left the admonishments to Jessica.

Jessica managed about a stern a look as she was capable with her gentle nature. "Not everyone sounds the same. Trent is a Texan. That's how people from Texas talk. It's not nice to say someone sounds funny. Apologize."

Bryce looked down at his plate. "Sorry."

Trent grinned. "It's okay, ma'am. Kids his age are honest."

"Thanks for understanding. Please, call me Jess."

Jon set a plate in front of Trent. "Dig in."

****

After dinner, Jon led Trent outside and locked the front door behind them. "I'm grateful you got here so quickly." Jon glanced at the older truck parked along the gravel lane. "Nice touch."

"Sam said to blend in and suggested I play up the Texan drawl for your family and staff. He sent me a file on Hugh Jones and the Kansas City mob. Nasty characters."

Jon led Trent around the outside of the house to the outbuildings. "Yes. That they are."

"May I ask you a question?"

"Shoot."

"Why are you staying? I know your wife is in a delicate condition, but you're taking an awful risk. The FBI could move your family into a safe house."

"I have my reasons." Jon led Trent into the stables to his favorite horse's stall. He unhooked a brush and ran the bristles through Daisy's dark brown hair. Trent stood outside the stall with his hands in his pockets.

Jon pointed to a stool in the corner. "Pull it up and have a seat."

Trent placed the stool in the open doorway of Daisy's stall and sat. "What reasons?"

"Jessica and Bryce only arrived seven months ago. It wasn't a planned move, and I'd rather not uproot them again. Ask Sam to send you the file on David Hayes. Read it and you'll understand." Jon hung the brush on a hook. "Jessica gave me a way to get her out of town. We're leaving on the weekend."

"How long will you be gone?"

"I'll keep her in Cochrane as long as I can. Jones' people will figure out we've left eventually. When they do, chances are they'll find us there, but one step at a time."

"Who's in charge of the ranch when you go?"

"Chip is my right hand. I'd like to keep him in the loop, so he'll follow your orders while I'm gone. But I'm not telling him where we're going. The rest of the staff can't know anything."

Trent nodded. "Most definitely. These mobster types love to torture for info. Who else could Jones use to get to you?"

"My brother can take care of himself. My mother, Sally, I worry about. She's dating Sheriff Hank, but it's casual. Jessica's Aunt Debbie can also take care of herself."

"Really? She's so laid back and friendly. I would've never guessed."

"Oh, yeah. She's a sweet lady, but she's brave as hell and an excellent shot. Debbie chased a serial killer off her farm all by herself. She even shot him in the leg."

"Good for her. And don't worry. I'll keep an eye on them while you're gone."

"Thanks." Jon gave Daisy a pat and led the way outside. "Later girl."

They drove Trent's old truck across the street to the rental house, then lugged suitcases and a load of firewood inside. Once Trent was settled, Jon headed out.

He didn't want to leave Jessica and Bryce for any length of time after the incident at the cafe.

Shoving his numb hands in his pockets, he trudged through the hard-packed snowdrifts. The night was silent save for his boots crunching in the snow. He lifted his head to the full moon and stars shining above him in the clear black sky. In the secluded Montana countryside, he'd mistakenly believed the darkness couldn't touch him.

It's here. And today is only the beginning.

Chapter Three

Jessica's emotions warred with one another as Jon pulled up to her house in Cochrane. Being home and seeing family should be comforting, but memories of what had sent her packing clouded her joy. Dusk had given way to dark, and darkness evoked shadows of the worst night of her life. All it took was one glance at the driveway next door for the horror to replay in her mind.

David dressed in black from head to toe, dragged something long, sagging, and cylindrical wrapped in a tarp across the asphalt. He hoisted the bundle over his shoulder and shifted it onto his truck bed. A bloody arm came loose from the tarp revealing an identifying purple and blue butterfly tattoo.

Jessica's friend Sarah had been murdered by her own husband, David.

A hand on her arm jolted her to the present. "Sweetheart, you okay?"

She shifted her gaze from the empty driveway to Jon's face. "I'm fine."

"Bet you and Bryce made happy memories here."

She clasped Jon's hand. "Yes. I'll focus on those."

"Let's head inside and make some more. I'll get the luggage."

Jessica slid open the back door of her van. "Coming, buddy?"

"Yep. I missed this house." Bryce jumped into the

snow piled beside the driveway.

Jessica dug into the side pocket of her purse and retrieved her keychain. "Maybe we can order pizza for dinner. Up for that?"

Bryce ran up the steps to the front door. "Pizza. Awesome! But no yucky anchovies this time."

Jessica chuckled as she placed her key in the lock and opened the door. "We'll order Dad his very own pizza. I don't like them either."

Jon deposited their suitcases inside the door. "More pizza for me. I'm game."

Bryce took off down the hall to his room while Jon returned to the van for the rest of their things. Jessica stepped out of her boots, wandered into the living room, and flicked the switch to turn on the gas fireplace.

Leaning on the mantel above the dancing flames was a large, framed photograph of Adam in his dress uniform. She'd taken the photo at his graduation ceremony from the police academy fourteen years ago. He wore a special smile reserved just for her, and the sun twinkled in the golden flecks of his warm brown eyes.

Resting her fingers against the glass, she wanted nothing more than to travel through time to that moment and hold him again. The love she'd shared with her first husband endured, as it always would.

Jon stood beside her. "Bring it home. He was a big part of your life. I know how much this picture must mean to you."

She wrapped her arms around Jon's middle, leaned her cheek against the flannel of his plaid shirt, and took in his natural musky scent. *Is it weird that I love them both, guilt free?* "I would really like that. Thanks for being so understanding."

"Of course, sweetheart."

"Why don't you have a picture of Cynthia anywhere?"

"I have pictures of her in my dresser. It hurts too much to look at them."

She sighed, wishing she could take on his pain for him. With the mysterious circumstances surrounding his first wife's disappearance, he may never move past the grief.

****

After Bryce settled into bed for the night, Jon grimaced at the flames in the fireplace while Jessica leaned against his chest. Although it threw good heat, a gas fire wasn't the same as a burning log of wood dissolving into coals.

At least his family was safe. For now. With any luck, the FBI would put Hugh Jones behind bars before his people tracked them down. The amazing woman in his arms, his first love, would then never have to know about Hugh Jones.

Dark, yet miraculous forces had brought them together after they'd parted ways before college, and after they'd both been widowed. Jessica didn't know it, but she'd saved his life.

Her eyes shut, and a few minutes later her head drooped.

He rubbed her arms. "Ready for bed?"

She yawned. "Definitely. The massive dust bunnies are in check, we have fresh bedding, and full tummies. Time for sleep."

"Mind if I have a quick shower first? My back is aching from the long drive."

"Of course."

Jon kissed Jessica goodnight and headed for the bathroom. He set his phone on the counter. It pinged and the screen lit up. Jon touched the screen. He had a message from Trent.

—*Anthony Greer is still in town asking about you. I don't think anyone told him anything. We haven't spotted him around your property yet. You got out of here just in time.*—

Jon responded.

—*Thanks for the update. I trust you'll handle it.*—

Bubbles appeared on his screen followed by a reply.

—*Not much I can do unless he does something illegal.*—

Jon ran his hands through his hair and tugged at the ends. He stared at his hands and rolled his eyes. *Damn nervous habit.* If only he could be in two places at once.

He turned the spray on hot, set his watch and wedding ring on the counter, then stripped down and stepped into the shower. He rested his palms on the tile wall and leaned forward until the hot water landed on his lower back.

A chill sliced through the hot, steamy cloud of moisture in the air, giving him goosebumps. Jon peeked around the shower curtain expecting to find Jessica and an open door. But the door remained shut and the bathroom empty. He turned off the water and dried himself with a bath towel.

Without explanation, the air grew colder, yet he hadn't turned on the exhaust fan. Where was the draft coming from? *Maybe I'm coming down with something.* A squeaking noise made his teeth tingle. Jon turned his head toward the mirror. Letters appeared on the glass. *Tell her.*

The hair on the back of his neck prickled. He'd faced off against cold-blooded criminals, wildlife, angry women, and irate supervisors. But nothing could prepare him for this. Only one possibility made any sense. Adam. Jon had never believed in ghosts, but those words and the cold weren't something you could explain away. Jessica's deceased husband had sent a message of disapproval from the beyond.

Jon picked up his phone and snapped a picture of the writing on the mirror. Physical proof would give him faith in his own sanity later when he questioned his memories.

He cracked open the bathroom door and glanced into the bedroom. Jessica's eyes were shut, and her chest rose and fell slowly. He closed the door and addressed the ghost in the room. "No. I'm protecting her. She's *my* wife now, and it's my decision."

Jon exited the bathroom, dumped the towel in the dirty clothes hamper, then climbed into bed beside Jessica to warm up. He debated asking her in the morning if she'd had any creepy experiences in this house before, but that would mean admitting to his own. Her quiet breaths calmed his racing pulse, and eventually he drifted off.

****

Jon sat at the round table in Jessica's kitchen. *How did I get here?* Across the table, the bank of cabinets and the coffeemaker appeared out of focus, like a poor resolution photograph. A mist formed in the air and gradually took shape. It settled in the chair across from him gaining color and resolution until it became crystal clear. The man from the picture above the mantel stared back at him with furrowed brows.

21

Jon shut his eyes. Maybe the scene in front of him would be different when he opened them. *Nope.* Adam's angry expression continued to burrow into him. "Ah, hell. Can't you take a hint? Jessica's an amazing woman, and I understand why you love her. But I love her too. She's mine to protect now."

Adam leaned forward invading Jon's space. "Get your head out of your ass. This house is listed under Jessica's name. You're no safer here. The people that hunt you *both* will be here soon. Bryce and Jessica are *my* family. You're putting them at risk. If I was alive, I'd beat the snot out of you."

Jon blinked again. *Impossible.* Adam died eight years ago. "How are we even having this conversation?"

"You're dreaming. I've been trying to reach Jessica and Bryce through dreams but couldn't figure out how. Turns out strong emotions like my anger for you are the key. Now that I've figured it out, I'm issuing an ultimatum. Either you tell Jessica the truth, or I will."

"It won't work. She'll think it's a weird dream. I wouldn't believe this if it wasn't for you spying on me in the shower."

"Nope." Adam grinned. "She feels my presence and talks to me all the time. But you didn't know. She keeps those moments private. Our souls are connected."

"She's carrying my child. It's early. She might miscarry."

"No, she won't. But you're jeopardizing her and your unborn child's survival."

Jon leaned back in his chair and crossed his arms. "How can you know?"

"I'm privileged to some information on the other side."

"If you've crossed over, how are you here?"

"That's not for the living to know."

Jon pinched himself.

Adam laughed. "You're not waking up. I've got a hold on your subconscious."

"Let's compromise. If I get a whiff of danger, or warnings from the feds, I'll tell her."

"No deal. You've been warned. There are more enemies at work here than you know. Beware…"

Jon jolted to awareness, and his eyes flew open. Jessica lay in the bed beside him, still fast asleep. Faint shafts of light filtered through the edges of the blinds. Not enough to be daylight. Jon raised his head to read the alarm clock on Jessica's end table.

4 a.m. Thanks for the rude wake-up call, Adam.

Jon had never experienced the paranormal, and he'd always thought himself as a sane person, but the vividness of the dream unsettled him.

Jon climbed out of bed and rifled through his suitcase for jogging pants and a sweatshirt. Clothed, he made a beeline for the living room. He switched on the lights and stared at Adam's picture over the mantel. In his dream, Adam had appeared older with crows-feet around his eyes and a few grey hairs, in keeping with a man in his mid-thirties at the time he died.

I couldn't have created that in my subconscious. Could I?

Jon brewed coffee and sat in the same spot he'd occupied during his otherworldly dream. Wait, Adam had tried to warn him about something before the dream cut off. *More enemies. Who else could be involved?* "Damn it all. I'm going to have to tell her."

"Tell me what?"

He turned his head. *Oh no.* Jessica approached and sat across from him in the chair Adam had occupied during his dream.

Her gaze bored into him. "Well?"

"Want a cup of coffee or tea? I'll get it for you."

"Stop putting it off, Jon. Spill. Something's been off since the man in the cafe. You rushed us out of town for a reason."

Time to face the music. The kids would have a hard time pulling one over on her. Jon sipped his coffee. "Listen, at the time, I wasn't sure who he was until I got in touch with Sam. I thought it best not to tell you in your delicate condition."

Her brows furrowed. "Who was he?"

"Anthony Greer. He works for Hugh Jones, the head of the Kansas City mob. I put a lot of his men in jail about a decade ago. Hugh's sleazeball lawyers greased the judge to throw out the evidence I had on him."

She leaned forward in her seat. "How could you not have told me? Are you insane? I can't be on alert without understanding the threat."

"You were protected."

"Let me guess. Trent. He's FBI, isn't he? Sam sent him."

"Yes."

"Why are you confessing now? Did something happen? Did those mobsters find us here?"

"Relax, sweetheart. No one found us. As to why I'm telling you now, I'm not sure you'll believe me."

She hissed, "Try me." Her eyes shot daggers his way.

"Remember that shower I wanted?"

She nodded and pursed her lips.

24

He pulled up the picture of the writing on the mirror and handed her his phone. "Adam wrote this. Then invaded my dream."

Her eyes widened, like one of Bryce's cartoon characters.

"You believe me?"

Jessica said, "Yes."

"He was telling the truth about you sensing him."

She crossed her arms. "At least *someone* understands the concept of honesty. I wish he would've visited my dreams and told me himself."

Ah, heck. This isn't going well. "He said he couldn't figure out how. Apparently, his anger toward me made him strong enough to get into mine."

"I can't believe you lied to me, *again*. I warned you not to after you figured out David was in town and didn't tell me. I can't trust you, *at all*. If it wasn't for this baby and Bryce, I'd kick you to the curb, Jon Kent."

"Sweetheart, please calm down. I was going to tell you once you were a few more weeks along. I was terrified you'd lose the baby from all the stress."

She wrung her hands. "I am sick of everyone treating me like a porcelain doll. I don't want pity. All I've ever wanted from you is honesty, and you *knew* that." She stood. "I need to lie down. Move your stuff to the guest room. You aren't welcome in my bed."

Jessica stormed off.

Jon leaned his head in his hands and sighed. The one threat to his marriage he never anticipated was Jessica's husband reaching out from the grave to interfere. And after the events of that night, one burning question niggled.

Why hasn't Cynthia reached out to me from beyond?

Chapter Four

Four years earlier, Cynthia Kent had hummed as she'd skipped to her car in the driveway, smiling so wide, her cheeks hurt. Jon was finally home for good. No more undercover assignments taking him away for months at a time, and they were starting a family. Soon, she'd be pregnant with her own child to nurture. She loved her special-needs students, professional detachment be damned, but her own child? *Magical.*

She climbed into her Honda Civic, set her purse and briefcase on the passenger seat, then turned the key in the ignition. The engine purred to life. At the same time cold, hard metal pressed into the back of her head.

A man's voice said, "Where's your phone?"

I don't want to die! She stared into the living room window, willing Jon to see her and run to her aid, but he'd been about to do the dishes at the opposite end of the main floor minutes earlier. *Don't panic. Stay calm. Think.* "It's in my purse. My wallet's in there, too. Take whatever you want. Please don't hurt me."

She snuck a glance in the rear-view mirror. Her assailant wore jeans and a plain tee with a black baseball hat and sunglasses. He was Caucasian and clean shaven with a generic face. No distinguishing scars or marks. The hat and sunglasses hid enough that she'd have a hard time describing or recognizing him.

"I won't hurt you unless you give me no other

choice." He reached a gloved hand into her purse and retrieved her wallet and her phone. "Drive to the park and pull over."

With a gun at her head, she didn't have much choice. She put the car in reverse, then backed out.

"I'm putting my gun on the seat beside me. No funny business, and it'll stay there. Understood?"

"Yes." She drove around the crescent to the community park and stopped at the curb.

He lowered the passenger window and launched her phone into a grassy field. "Drive to the airport. Speed limit the whole way."

Her heart sank. With her phone gone, no one would be able to track her location. Her voice trembled. "Why are you doing this?"

"I'm here under orders from Hugh Jones, an extremely resourceful, rich, and powerful man. My assignment is to kill you and bury your body where it'll never be found."

Tears filled her eyes blurring the road in front of her. "But-but you said if I listened, then..."

He interrupted. "I don't plan on following orders, but the choice is yours. I don't spare many, but I don't want to punish a woman who's dedicated her life to disabled children. You aren't responsible for your husband's actions."

"Oh, thank you. Thank you." *What could Jon have possibly done?* Jon refused to divulge any details about his work saying it was better she didn't know. But he was a kind-hearted man who wouldn't hurt another unless he didn't have a choice.

"Don't be so quick to offer gratitude. You have two choices. The first, I kill you with one bullet to the brain.

The second, I give you a new identity with similar credentials. You get to start over and continue your noble work, but you can never contact Jon or any of your family ever again. I'll be staying in touch and making sure you live up to your end of the bargain."

How can this be happening? "Is there no other way? I love my husband and my family. I can't imagine life without them."

"I'm sorry, but no. Hugh Jones wants you dead to punish Jon. If he finds you, he will kill you, and then he'll come after me for lying about killing you. This is the only option."

Her dreams, within reach, after so many years of waiting while Jon served his country. Gone. "I don't know if I can live that way."

"You can. You're still young and beautiful. There are plenty of fish in the sea. Much better than Jon Kent. If you knew the half of what he's done in the name of justice—trust me, you wouldn't want him."

Living without Jon and her family would be hard, but maybe in time, she'd find a way to get her life back. This man and the other one, Hugh Jones, if they went to jail, she could reach out to Jon.

She wiped her tears with her sleeve. "I'll go with option two."

He tossed a brown envelope on the passenger seat. "Cynthia Kent is dead. Your name is Meredith Green. You have no family, but you do have fifty thousand dollars in your bank account. You'll find a wallet, burner phone, plane ticket, passport, social security number, driver's license, and resume in that envelope. The references listed on the resume will check out as will your identity."

"How?"

"That doesn't matter. I'll check in with you once a week. Please don't break the rules and make me kill you. Remember, I'm your angel of mercy. Without my protection, you'll be dead. If you don't believe me, google Hugh Jones."

She pulled into the airport parking lot. "Who are you?"

"It's better you don't know."

At least I kissed you goodbye, Jon. I love you. I'll do whatever it takes to get back to you.

****

Hugh Jones removed his platinum cuff links and placed them on his dresser. The pretentious part of his day was over. His criminal empire lay hidden beneath legitimate businesses, primarily his casino. Maintaining a positive image and connections with other wealthy businessmen and government officials in Kansas City consumed his days. The nights were his. A time when he could be himself without scrutiny.

His phone pinged.

—The tip you got on Kent's location was good.—

Hugh pumped his fist in the air. "Yes. I've got you now, Jon Kent." He typed his response.

—Start surveillance. Find his weaknesses.—

The betrayal from a decade earlier still stung. Operations had ground to a halt when the FBI stormed Hugh's mansion on a Saturday night, arresting everyone during a party. Of course, Kent was arrested to keep up appearances, but he never surfaced in jail. Hugh bought his way out of trouble the following day, and the charges against him were dropped. The day after that, Hugh's private investigator had informed him the man he'd thought of as family was an undercover federal agent.

Revenge would taste so sweet. *Finally, he's going to pay the price for crossing me.*

His elderly butler, Chuck, stuck his head in the doorway. "Sir, your limousine and companion are waiting out front."

"I'll be down in a few minutes."

"Yes, sir."

Chuck's dress shoes scuffed the floor as he shuffled down the hall. Hugh's father had hired Chuck fifty years earlier when Hugh was born. Back then, Chuck's steps were sure and quick. He'd slowed down over the past decade, but the man refused to retire, and a more loyal employee could never be found.

Hugh pulled on a plain white dress shirt with buttons, foregoing cuff links, and tucked it into his black pants. He slung his matching suit jacket over his arm and headed outside to meet his date for the night.

He'd never wanted to settle down with one woman. Wealth afforded him the opportunity to buy as many high class, beautiful women as he liked. It saved him from the song and dance of flirting, dating, and wooing to get laid. Besides, he was too old for such nonsense anyway.

His limo driver opened the car door.

Hugh climbed in and accepted the martini offered by the blue-eyed, blonde-haired, big-chested babe he'd ordered. "Thank you, darling."

She batted her long dark eyelashes and picked up her own martini. "You're welcome, Mr. Jones."

He settled in the seat across from her to admire the view, and what a view it was. Her little black dress clung to her curvy body, and the black high heels on her dainty feet accentuated her long legs. *What a bombshell.*

Sure, he was old enough to be her father, but the hunger in her eyes said she didn't care. The hours spent in the gym maintaining his physique and stamina would be well worth it later when she joined him in his California king.

Chapter Five

Jessica sat up in bed alone, lips pressed into a tight line. To avoid Jon, she'd made the excuse of being tired to escape to her room. A few days had passed since his confession, but she couldn't yet move past his lies.

And the irony of the dangerous situation in which she found herself trapped was it could've been avoided. But if she'd heeded the warning letter left at her hotel door on her wedding day, she'd have lost her first love again. Even though she'd burned the letter before walking down the aisle, she remembered every word.

Dear Jessica,
I wish you and Jon all the happiness in the world. You both deserve nothing less, but beware. There are those who wish to make Jon miserable. His double life will always come back to haunt him and those he loves most. I know this better than anyone. This is your last chance to walk away. Once you become his wife, you and Bryce will have targets on your backs.

The tone of the letter was matter of fact, neither kind nor unkind. *It must be connected to Jon's first wife, Cynthia.* Had the sender known Hugh Jones was close to finding Jon, putting her and Bryce at risk?

If only she hadn't burned the letter. She'd never told Jon about it. In a sense, that made her a hypocrite. But a letter was a small thing in comparison to knowing a mobster was sniffing around town for them and not saying anything.

Jon's heart had been in the right place, wanting to protect them, but she was a grown woman, not a child. She deserved the truth from her husband. What stung the most was the broken promise. Was the man capable of being open with her?

Danger had also become an issue. How could she stay married to someone with many enemies and a propensity for covering up threats? Sure, she'd known when she married him he'd made enemies as an FBI agent, but she never imagined they'd come so close to her and Bryce.

Every day she'd need to be on the lookout for bad people who meant them harm, unable to rely on Jon to warn her of threats. The loving connection she shared with Jon was unique, but this was no environment to raise children in.

Tears trickled down her cheeks. She swiped them away with her hands. The only thing she envisioned in her future, after this latest crisis ended, was divorce. A return to single motherhood with two children to raise instead of one. She glanced around the room. *Bryce likes it here. Should I try to get past the nightmare that happened next door? Send for our stuff?*

If she kept her distance from Jon, maybe the man hunting him would leave her and Bryce alone. Jessica lay down and pulled her quilt to her chin.

****

Coldness clutched Jessica's fingers. She turned her head and opened her eyes. Adam lay facing her, holding her hand. His head was propped up on his elbow in a typical Adam way, and he wore a plain white tee and jeans, his usual home attire. The sun streaming in the window shone on the golden highlights in his dark brown hair. *My love, finally.*

"Adam? You're really here?"

He swept a strand of her long blonde hair away from her forehead. "Yes, baby. In your dream."

His deep, familiar voice reverberated through her soul. She rested her palm on his hard chest. Despite the dream state, his skin was like ice. "I miss you so much."

Sadness flickered in his gaze. "I miss you, too. Sorry for leaving you hanging with a brand-new baby. I caused you so much pain. Seeing you alone in this room, night after night, so sad, like you are now—it's hard to swallow."

"It's not your fault. You got shot being a good cop and a good man."

"Jess, I don't want to see you like this anymore. You need to move on and be happy."

She sighed. "I tried. Look where that got me. Pregnant by a man with enemies chasing him."

"But you love him the way you love me, and he loves you. I see the way you are together. He's a good man. I peered into his past. He risked his life working undercover to keep drugs and weapons off the street. Sure, he has enemies, in the same way I gained a few, putting bad guys behind bars. You can't hold that against him."

"He lied to me, thinking he's protecting me."

"But he did protect you and Bryce. The feds hid his location well. No one should have found him."

Adam's form flickered in and out of focus. Jessica glimpsed the dresser behind him through his body.

"You're breaking up."

"Seems I'm not allowed to tell you specific information about what I know. I lost the connection with Jon the same way."

"Don't tell me anything then. I'd rather have you here, beside me."

"Do me a favor, baby. Give Jon one more chance. He agonized over keeping the truth from you. I believe he's learned his lesson. Remember the good he's done."

"Okay, I'll give him one more chance. For you."

He held open his arms. "I can't maintain this much longer. Come closer. Let me hold you before I go."

"Gladly." She scooted over to him and wrapped her arms around his cold middle, miraculously her dream let him be solid.

He kissed her forehead and pulled her against his body. "I love you, baby."

"I love you, too." Shivering, she closed her eyes and breathed him in.

The pine scent of his aftershave enveloped her. For eight years, she'd prayed for this moment. A chance to connect with Adam again. Too soon the sensation of his strong arms gradually faded away.

She clung tighter to what was left of him. Her arms passed through air. "Wait, I'm not ready for you to go."

"Don't worry. I'll visit again."

Jessica opened her eyes. Darkness surrounded her, illuminated by the numbers on the alarm clock beside her bed, and the little bit of light creeping in through the shut blinds. "Adam?"

Silence greeted her in response. Tears brimmed in her eyes, then stained her cheeks. *What a bittersweet dream.* She'd gotten to speak to Adam and hold him again, but he was dead. Nothing would ever bring him back. Her shoulders shook, wracked by loud sobs. She smothered them into her pillow.

Her door swung open. Jon came in the room and shut the door behind him.

He climbed into bed and pulled her into his arms. "What's wrong, sweetheart? I sure hope I didn't cause these tears."

She clung to him and breathed in his musky scent. His warm body contrasted sharply with Adam's chill. Adam was right, Jon at his core was a good man.

Her tears subsided. "It isn't you. Adam visited. It was the most vivid dream I've ever had."

Jon rubbed circles on her back and leaned his chin on the top of her head. "What did you talk about? You don't have to share if you don't want to."

"He apologized for his death." She chuckled. Adam had defended Jon after scaring him half to death. "Would you believe he told me to give you another chance?"

"He did? Will you give me another chance?"

"Yes. One more. Honesty is the one thing I value most. You know that."

Jon brushed her lips with a feather soft kiss. "I know. I won't lie to you ever again. I love you too much to risk chasing you away."

Jessica's forehead creased. She leaned back on the headboard. "Adam started telling me something else. He couldn't finish explaining because he almost disappeared. But he did say the feds did a good job of hiding you. He said no one should have found you. What could that mean?"

"That concerns me. The last thing he said to me was there were more enemies at play. I wish Adam would have given one of us a name."

"You said we were safe here, but for how long?"

"I think a few more weeks before they find out about this place. We can fortify the ranch, or Sam can find us a safe house. I'll let you decide."

"I hate the thought of a strange place, but a safe house seems the best option. I think we're pushing our luck by staying here. The sooner you can get us out, the better."

Jon's brow furrowed. "I agree. If we are going to uproot our family, there's no point waiting. I wish I knew how close Jones is on our tail."

"I have a nanny camera in my closet from when Bryce was younger."

"Did it display times on the feeds?"

She handed him her phone. "This is the website. See for yourself. The camera activates when it detects motion and provides dates and times."

"This is great. If someone breaks into the house, we'll know exactly when they were here." Jon sighed. "I wish we weren't in another country where I don't have connections."

"You never talk about what you did as an FBI agent. I've left it alone, but I need to know why Jones hates you so much. This seems to go beyond you being the arresting officer."

He lowered his eyes to the quilt and ran his finger along a line of stitching. "Sweetheart, I don't want you to know me as that guy. I'm not that person anymore."

Lifting his chin, she guided his eyes to meet hers. "I love you. The work you did was in service to your country. Tell me. It won't change how I see you."

"Oh, boy. I'll tell you about Jones, but that's all I

can handle sharing. Okay?"

"Okay. I'll take what I can get."

"While I was young, I did undercover work. Younger agents have an easier time assimilating into the culture of criminals." Jon chuckled. "Picture Sam trying to infiltrate a drug operation with his grey hair and holier-than-thou facial expressions."

Jessica laughed. "I can picture him in a leather vest with a bandana tied around his head."

He ran his hand through his hair. "Anyways, I was assigned to infiltrate Jones' operations. He smuggled drugs, weapons, women—you name it, he moved it."

She shivered and tugged the quilt to her chin. "Women? Is that what he'd do to me?"

"Don't think that way. I'll never let him harm a hair on your head."

"Okay, keep going."

"One day in the early spring, I showed up at Jones' casino in Kansas City. A front for laundering his dirty money. I gave a fake name and convinced him I was the illegitimate son of one of his deceased cousins.

"He let me into his organization bit by bit starting with menial tasks like fetching lunch. Eventually I was sent to collect debts. I had to commit all kinds of crimes and pretend to be unaffected to earn his trust until I became a member of his inner circle. By then, I had gathered loads of evidence against all the key players, and they were arrested."

Jessica swallowed around a lump in her throat. *No wonder he has enemies.*

****

Jon struggled to fall asleep long after Jessica's breaths slowed. He lay on his side facing her and bunched his pillow under his head. The strawberry scent of her shampoo and the rise and fall of her chest usually lulled him to sleep. But not tonight.

Western winds tunneled through the Rocky Mountains, whistling and shaking the windows in their panes. He shivered and yanked the quilt up to his ears. Windstorms were nothing new. They happened in Montana all the time, and he slept through them fine.

What kept him awake was Hugh Jones. Rehashing his time undercover stirred up memories and images he'd pushed to the back of his mind with good reason. One horrific incident stuck with him no matter how hard he tried to forget, playing like a movie reel in his mind. The agonized screams, the snapping of bones, and the blood, so much blood.

****

A decade earlier, Hugh Jones had ordered Jon to track down Francis Hennessy and bring him to a warehouse near the port. Hennessy had borrowed fifty grand at Jones' casino and gambled it away on horse races and craps. He'd failed to repay his loan, and Hugh was done waiting to get his money back.

Sweat trickled down the back of Jon's neck as he waited for the traffic light. He loosened his tie and launched it into the backseat of the old Cadillac. The air conditioning was broken, and even though the sun had set an hour ago, the heat built up in the concrete jungle of downtown Kansas City hadn't let go. His head ached from the exhaust fumes wafting in his window.

The light turned green, and Jon stepped on the accelerator. He pulled into the parking lot of the only casino he hadn't checked and went inside. Being a degenerate gambler, chances were high his man would be at a craps table somewhere, blowing his paycheck or someone else's money. By the grace of God, no woman or children depended on him for their survival.

The slot machines chimed and beeped as they sucked people dry, occasionally flashing for the lucky few. As Jon came upon the craps tables, he spotted his mark. Frank Hennessy was never hard to miss in his suits from the disco era complete with bell bottoms. Today's powder-blue ensemble was incomplete without the usual thick yellow gold rings on every finger and the peace sign necklace dangling in his dark chest hair. Likely he'd hocked them at the pawn shop down the road on his way to the casino.

Frank blew into the dice he cradled in his hands before letting go. They rolled the length of the table, then paused on a five and a six. He jumped up and down and cheered as chips were stacked in front of him.

Jon placed a hand on his shoulder and whispered, "I need you to cash out and come with me."

Frank, a mere five and a half feet, craned his head to meet Jon's gaze. "Who are you? You don't look like security."

"I work for Mr. Jones. He wants a word with you."

Frank's face paled as he shoved casino chips in his jacket pocket. "I-I'll have h-his, money by the end of th-the week."

Jon's gut twisted, but if he didn't bring Hennessy in, Hugh would send someone else and view Jon's failure as a reason to cast him out of the inner circle. "You can tell him yourself."

Frank's shoulders slumped as he cashed out and trudged toward the exit.

Jon led him to the old Cadillac, and Frank climbed

in and fastened his seatbelt without a fight. Most men, after discovering they had an upcoming audience with Hugh Jones, either fled like they were being chased by a hungry lion or tried to sock him. Jon wished Frank had kicked him in the balls. The more despicable his marks were, the better. The nice guys haunted him.

Maybe Frank's winnings would buy time and save him some pain. That was a big maybe. Few men walked out of the warehouse after they went in.

Frank didn't utter a word until Jon parked behind the warehouse and killed the engine. "Wh-what are we-we doing here? I th-thought you were t-taking me to Hugh's office at his casino."

"This isn't that type of meeting."

Downtown Kansas City smelled like a sewer this time of year and the closer you got to the Missouri, the worse it was. Bile crept up Jon's throat as he hurried around to the passenger side and opened the door. Combined with his headache and guilty conscience, it took willpower not to hurl. "Let's go."

Frank climbed out of the car and followed Jon inside the pitch-black, sweltering, two-story brick warehouse. Aware of what came next, Jon hung his head as he bolted the door behind them. *So much for serving and protecting with honor.*

The overhead fluorescent lights came on, illuminating an almost empty warehouse save for Hugh Jones and his enforcer, Raymond Sands. Plastic sheeting covered the concrete floor to make clean up easier.

Raymond stood in the center of the room behind the only piece of furniture, a metal chair. His command echoed. "Sit."

Frank looked over his shoulder at Jon, eyes bugging

out of his face. Behind all the flamboyance was a timid and gentle man who'd lost himself to addiction. Sure, he owed Hugh money, but he wasn't a criminal, and he didn't deserve this fate. No one did.

Jon pointed to the chair. "He means you, Frank."

Frank stood in place, shaking and unresponsive. Circles of sweat moistened the fabric under his armpits.

I'm going to hell for this. Jon took Frank by the elbow, dragged him across the floor, and plunked him down on the chair.

Hugh said, "You know what to do. Tie him up."

Raymond used zip ties to fasten Frank's wrists and ankles to the arms and legs of the chair.

Frank said. "Pl-please d-don't. I-I've got f-five thousand. T-take it. I-I'll get t-the rest b-by the end of t-the week."

"It's too late." Hugh said, "I gave you three chances to pay back my money and you didn't."

"P-please, sir. Just o-one m-more."

"And let you make a mockery of me? Make me look soft? No. People need to know what happens when they don't pay up."

Frank's gaze dropped to his lap as big, fat tears rolled down his cheeks.

Raymond rolled his eyes and shook his head.

Hugh said, "Hammer."

Jon clenched his fists, nails cutting into his skin as he struggled to keep his expression neutral. He couldn't show weakness or disdain no matter what they forced him to witness.

Raymond pulled a hammer out of his tool belt, swung it like an expert carpenter about to hit a nail, and crushed Frank's right pinky finger. Crack!

Frank screamed and writhed against his bonds. The zip tie cut into his wrist and blood trickled down his hand joining the blood spurting from his pinky and pooling on the plastic beneath the chair.

Jon held his head as Frank's screams reverberated around his skull and the coppery, metallic scent of blood penetrated his nostrils.

Hugh put a hand on his shoulder. "You look like you're going to pass out."

"Bad migraine, sir."

"We have this under control. Get yourself some pills and a drink in my limo."

"Thank you, sir." Up until this night, Jon had forced himself to stay and watch as penance. He never administered the beatings himself, but he brought the lambs to slaughter. But with his head aching like it'd been jammed in a vice grip; he couldn't do it.

"Raymond will fetch you when it's time to clean up."

As Jon strode to the back of the warehouse, Frank's screams and the cracking of his bones shattering faded away.

Hugh's empty black limousine idled in the delivery bay. No one would dare steal it for fear they'd wind up like Frank. When Raymond was done with him, every bone in his body would be obliterated and his face would be unrecognizable.

In an hour and a half— because these things had to be drawn out according to Hugh Jones to maximize pain—Raymond, dripping in blood, would fetch Jon and they'd tie metal chains around Frank and dump him in the Missouri River.

Jon climbed in the back of the car and sank into the

plush, cold leather seat. He reached in his shirt and pressed the stop button on his wire. He hadn't cried since he fell as a child and broke his arm. But surrounded in comfort he didn't deserve; his shoulders shook as sobs wracked his body.

****

Jon rested his hand next to Jessica's on her pillow. What would she think of a law enforcement man who'd watch gangsters beat men to death and did nothing about it? Closing his eyes, he prayed she'd never find out because he couldn't bear to lose her.

Chapter Six

Jessica started breakfast while Jon set up the nanny camera. She lined a sheet tray with strips of bacon in a neat row, then stuck it in the oven. After a good night's sleep, the decision to go into hiding still seemed like the best one. This time around they had a head start. The monster wasn't nipping at their heels.

She made a mental checklist of what they needed to do. They'd brought cash, but they'd need quite a bit more to avoid leaving an electronic trail and burner phones. Despite laws preventing it, she was sure Jon had brought weapons. He'd used his FBI identification at the border crossing rather than his driver's license, to avoid searches and questions.

"The camera is set up and working. Time for coffee." Jon rested his hand on the small of Jessica's back on the way to the coffee machine. "More tea for you?"

"Yes, thanks."

"Why don't you sit when I'm done getting drinks, and I'll finish making breakfast."

Boy, he's laying it on thick. "Okay."

After accepting a steaming mug from Jon, she sat at the round table in her eat-in-kitchen and propped her feet on the chair across from her. "Any idea how long until that package from the FBI arrives?"

Jon stirred eggs in a pan on the stove. "At least a day

or two. It takes time to produce good identification and pick the safest location."

"Should we stay here and wait? Or should we go to a hotel near the airport just in case?"

"Moving to a motel might not be a bad idea. We'd want somewhere that accepts cash."

She grimaced. "Gross. We can bring disinfectant spray and fresh bedding."

"Or we can stay here for the time being. I brought guns."

"I kind of figured."

Running footsteps thumped down the hallway to the kitchen.

Jon set a plate in front of Bryce's usual spot at the table. "Right on time. It's bacon. Your favorite. I'll get you some milk."

"Thanks, Dad."

The danger almost didn't seem real during such a normal, everyday, sweet moment in her kitchen. But life threw twists and turns in your path. Her stomach churned as she pictured giving birth alone in the middle of chaos, in a strange place, with a strange doctor. *Don't let yourself go there. This will be over by then.*

****

Hugh Jones sat wrapped in a silk robe in his four-poster bed, with Angel wearing a matching robe beside him. In front of them on trays, lay a spread of Hugh's favorite breakfast foods—scrambled eggs, bacon, sausages, ham, fried potatoes, fresh berries, and croissants.

A few days had passed since their first meeting in the limo, and he still couldn't get enough of her. Something about Angel set her apart from the others. Not only her prowess in the bedroom either. She was intelligent and driven. He sensed she viewed being an escort as a steppingstone to something bigger and better. Without ambition, there could be no progress. A most admirable quality.

"Isn't this the life, my angel? A mansion, breakfast in bed, silk sheets, servants, money galore, what more could you want?"

She bit into a chocolate-dipped strawberry. "It's fancy."

"Fancy?" His phone rang. The name Greer appeared on the screen. Hugh touched the green icon. "How are things progressing?"

"There's no sign of Kent, the woman, or the kid. I think they skipped town."

Hugh gritted his teeth. "Tell me you know where they went."

"The woman owns a house up north in Alberta, Canada. They might be there."

"Might be? Not good enough. Find a contact in Alberta to confirm and get your hands on someone close to Kent."

"Yes, sir."

"If you can't get the job done in twelve hours, it's your ass on the line. You hear me?"

"Yes, sir."

Hugh disconnected the call and set the phone aside. "Minor complications. Where were we? Ah, yes. Fancy?"

She nodded. "Uh-huh. You're so much more interesting than all the stuff your money buys."

"Interesting, how?"

"You're powerful. Everyone's afraid of you. Power

is attractive in a man."

Hmmm. Perceptive. "Why don't you stay longer? Quit your escort service and work for me exclusively. I'll pay you double an hour. You'll live in the wing across from me. I'd require you to make yourself available to me, including social outings."

She kneeled beside him and held a strip of bacon to his mouth. "That's an offer I can't refuse."

He took a bite, chewed, and swallowed. "That's my angel. And remember, exclusive. I don't share."

She caressed his cheek and giggled. "Ah, that's sweet. I like a faithful man. Be right back. I need to freshen up."

He grinned, as she strutted across the room. She turned, winked, and blew him a kiss before turning the corner to the adjoining bath. *This is the life.*

****

Jessica dried dishes as Jon scrubbed. She didn't want to leave dirty dishes in the dishwasher since they'd be hitting the road the minute their passports and destination details arrived. Her plates had never seemed so heavy before, and her arms throbbed as she lifted them into the cabinet.

Jon's phone pinged.

Jessica handed him the dish towel to dry his hands. "Here you go." She leaned against the granite countertop.

"Thanks, sweetheart." He picked up his phone and swiped the screen. "Damn."

"What?"

"It's a message from Sam. We need to clear out of here. Greer found out about this place."

Oh, no! Adam was right. "Bryce! We're leaving."

She touched Jon's shoulder. "Crappy motel by the airport, here we come."

"Too predictable. By the time we get our new identification from the feds, we could have watchers at the airport, train, and bus terminals in Calgary. We need to move cities. Where's the next closest major airport?"

Her mind traveled in a bunch of different directions all at once. Impending doom, things they couldn't forget, and a sense of urgency to vacate her house. *Focus, Jess. Think. Closest big city.* "Edmonton, about two hours north of here."

"Too close."

"Regina, Saskatchewan? It's a bit far. Eleven hours east."

Jon opened the cupboards and pulled out granola bars, cookies, and chips. "Far is better. Farther off the grid. Good thing we didn't unpack much." He handed her a plastic bag. "Mind bagging this stuff while I pull the van into the garage?"

"No." The box of wafer cookies shook in her hand. The tremors she'd fought off seven months earlier returned. Disgusted with herself for letting the fear take over, she lowered her head and shoved the items into the plastic bag. She despised showing weakness. It led to pity from the people around her which she hated even more.

Jon kissed her forehead. "It's okay. I'll keep us safe."

"I know." She took a deep breath and forced her thoughts to relax. The tremors stopped allowing her mind to work again. "I'll get Bryce moving and wheel our suitcases to the door."

"Good. We'll be out of here in five minutes, tops."

Jessica jogged up the stairs to Bryce's room. "Bryce! Come on. We need to go. Road trip time again."

He crossed his arms and huffed. "We're going home already? I don't want to go. We just got here. I miss my friends."

She sat beside him on the floor of his room. "Not home. A trip. You could say an adventure."

"No. I want to stay."

She sighed and tugged him by the arm. "I'm sorry, buddy. I wish we could, but we can't. We need to leave right away."

"Why?"

Since being kidnapped, Bryce had become more aware of the world around him. He would keep asking until someone answered. *I can't shield him from the darkness any longer.* "It isn't safe here. A bad guy your father investigated found out we were living in Lewistown, and now he knows were here."

"Where are we going?"

"Saskatchewan for now." She placed his suitcase on the bed. They filled his suitcase with the few things he'd unpacked.

"We better hurry. Let's go."

She crouched in front of him and ruffled his dark brown hair, Adam's hair. "We're fine. Dad's a superhero, remember? What name did you give him again?"

"I named him Captain Commando Jon."

The garage door banged shut. Jon's voice carried up the stairs. "Coast is clear. Let's head out."

Jessica took Bryce's hand. "See? With Dad protecting us, we'll be okay."

Jon loaded the luggage as Jessica settled Bryce in

the back with his tablet. Jessica climbed in and hit the lock button on her door, sealing them in from the outside.

Jon backed out of the garage and headed out of the neighborhood. "It feels good to be getting out of here. We'll be safe soon, guys."

Jessica stared into the side mirror, spotting a white van behind them as they turned off Highway 22 onto the TransCanada Highway. "A white van, a few cars back, has been behind us since we left the house. A man travelling alone."

"I know."

"This is the only direct route to Regina."

"We'll stop at the next exit and see if he follows again. That would be a big red flag for me."

"If he does?"

Jon clasped Jessica's hand. "We'll take a trip in a different direction and lose him."

She placed her faith in Jon. They'd been followed before, and he'd never had problems losing people in the past. So why did she have a bone-deep, ominous feeling about the situation?

Chapter Seven

Trent sat on Main Street in his old blue pickup truck. Bundled in a black parka, boots, and gloves, he waited for Anthony Greer to emerge from the diner a few blocks away. With his cowboy hat on, Trent blended in with the locals. Greer hadn't taken notice of him on his tail all day, or the GPS tracker now placed on his silver sedan. After Sam's latest update, Trent refused to let him out of his sight. No way Greer would get leverage on his watch.

His phone pinged with an incoming text message.

—*It's Meredith. Any news?*—

He didn't recognize the number, but he did recognize the sender. She'd switched to a burner phone to disguise her location, meaning she'd left their home city of Boulder, Colorado.

Trent typed a response.

—*Jones' men found out about the house in Alberta. They're on the run until the FBI gets them new IDs and settles them in a safe house.*—

He waited for her to reply. After five minutes passed with no response, he sent another message.

—*Where are you?*—

She didn't respond to that one either.

For the most part, their friendship was one-sided since he took her under his wing. Because of her situation, she wouldn't let anyone get too close for fear something awful would happen to them. He'd had to tear down the wall she put up brick by brick, but he hadn't managed to break through just yet. He wouldn't give up. Meredith was worth the effort.

He'd taught her everything he knew including things he shouldn't to help her survive. He'd taught her how to disguise her movements, how to defend herself, and investigative skills. He'd wanted to empower her by giving her the control she so desperately craved over her own life again.

The irony of having been sent to watch over Jon Kent hadn't been lost on him. Perhaps he hadn't been careful enough and someone at the bureau figured out who Meredith was and told Sam. But if they had, it would stand to reason that someone would've told Jon.

****

Two years earlier, after Trent had spent ten hours questioning a suspect and getting nowhere, he had stuck him in a jail cell for the night and had called it quits for the day. A night in the slammer often worked to loosen tongues. On his way home, he stopped at a coffee shop a few blocks away from his condo for a caramel frappuccino.

While he waited for the barista to make his drink, he glanced around the mostly empty room. A woman sat alone in a corner working on her laptop. The evening sun streamed in the window next to her, reflecting golden in her straight, shoulder-length light brown hair, making it look as if she wore a halo. The white sun dress she wore under a light-colored denim jacket completed her angelic look.

Maybe some good could come of his day after all. She didn't look up as he approached her table, focused on her screen. She had typed, *Hugh Jones*, in the search engine. *Why look up the name of a mob boss a few states over?* "Excuse me."

She turned to look at him. "Yes?"

He lost himself in the melted chocolate of her kind eyes. *What was I going to say again? Oh yeah.* "How do you know Hugh Jones?"

Those eyes grew wide, and she shut her laptop. "I don't."

She does. And she's frightened. Great pick-up line, Casanova.

He handed her his badge. "I didn't mean to alarm you. I'm Agent Trent Cooper. I work for the FBI. Maybe I can help. I've come across that name before."

She gestured to the chair across from her. "Please, sit. My name's Meredith."

He squeezed into the booth across from her. "Nice to meet you."

"Are you talking to me in an official capacity?"

"No, I'm off the clock. I find you attractive, so I came over to talk to you."

Her cheeks glowed red. "Okay, so would whatever we talk about stay between us?"

"I can keep a secret."

She clenched her coffee cup, bending it in the middle. "If you know who he is, then you know he's a dangerous man."

"Yes."

"How is he not in jail?"

"The FBI is trying to put him there." Her questions stirred up many of his own. He asked the most important one first. "What did he do to you?"

Meredith took a sip of her coffee, then went silent for a few minutes. He waited. Pushing wouldn't work.

She gazed into his eyes. "I don't trust you enough to say. We just met."

"I'm an officer of the law. If you can't trust me, then who?"

"You don't understand the stakes. It's not just my life in the crosshairs."

Whoa. Whatever it is, it's bad. "What if I promise that no matter what you tell me, I'll never tell another soul without your permission?"

Meredith glanced around the coffee shop, then took a deep breath and faced him again. "I haven't been able to talk to anyone about this, and it's eating away at me, so I may as well tell you. My name isn't Meredith. Hugh Jones sent an assassin after me, but rather than following orders, the assassin spared my life and gave me a new identity. I had to promise never to contact anyone from my old life ever again."

"So, you're thinking that if Hugh Jones goes to jail, you can get your life back. Who was the assassin?"

"I don't know. He's always refused to give me his name. Every few weeks, he calls from a different number and says he's keeping tabs on me. I've tried to get more out of him multiple times, but he keeps refusing."

A lightbulb flickered on in his brain. The hair and eyes were different from the missing person's report. *I wonder.* "Your real name is Cynthia Kent, isn't it? You're Jon's wife."

Her eyes widened like saucers. "How?"

"When an agent's wife goes missing, and foul play is suspected, it makes waves. Your picture was sent to every active agent in the country. Don't worry. The contact lenses and hair color change are working. I only realized who you were when you mentioned the identity change."

Her face relaxed. "Good. You scared me. I was Cynthia, but not anymore. Cynthia is legally dead and needs to stay that way. I can't risk going anywhere near Jon or any of my family. If they ended up dead, I'd blame myself. Both Hugh Jones and the mystery assassin would have to be in jail or dead for me to risk contacting my family again."

"I'm going to help you. First things first, we'll figure out who this assassin is. Give me your number. I'll bring you a picture lineup of suspects from the database at work."

"We can try, but I don't think I'll be able to pick him out. He was average and plain looking and wore sunglasses. I could narrow it down maybe."

"That would be a start."

What he'd intended to be a casual conversation leading to a date, had morphed into something darker and more serious than he could've imagined when he spotted the pretty girl sitting in the corner. Her life was in danger, serious danger. A mob boss wanted her dead, and she was being monitored by an assassin. But none of that curbed his interest. If anything, her courage made her more attractive.

****

A black sedan parked a few cars up from Trent, and a large, slightly rotund man dressed in a suit and wool coat climbed out and headed toward the diner. As he walked, his jacket strained revealing the outline of a gun in his pocket.

Trent grabbed the file on the Kansas City Mob. He pulled out a stack of photos and rifled through them until he came across a photo of the man. The name listed on the bottom was Raymond Sands, his role in the organization, an enforcer.

Is he here to help Greer or kill him? Maybe both.

Greer and Sands emerged from the diner and walked toward the silver sedan. Trent turned the key in the ignition. The lights came on, but the engine stayed silent. Of all the times for the battery to go when it showed no signs of being sluggish before. *Good thing they took Greer's car with the tracker on it.*

Trent hopped out, ignoring the blustering frigid wind, pulled down his tailgate, and prayed booster cables were among the junk back there. No one drove old trucks, especially in colder climates, without them. He pushed aside old work gloves, clothes, then something yellow caught his eye in a box near the back.

He moved around the side of the truck, reached in the box, and pulled out booster cables. "Yes!"

A hand touched his shoulder. "Need a boost?"

He turned and discovered a short, older woman with grey hair wrapped in a black fur coat from her neck to her ankles.

"I sure would appreciate that, ma'am."

"Pop the hood, sonny. Get those cables ready."

Chapter Eight

Debbie rocked in her favorite, chocolate-brown chair in the living room of her old farmhouse. Her best friend since childhood, Sally Kent, sat on the sofa across from her. They couldn't be more opposite. Debbie dressed in jeans, cotton shirts, and sneakers or loafers, all practical and comfortable. She wore her hair in a bun, kept her nails trimmed short, and cared nothing about current trends. Sally, on the other hand, always dressed fashionably in bright colors, with scarves and cute shoes, nails always freshly painted. Yet despite their outward differences, they shared similar values and viewed the world in the same way.

Sally sipped her tea. "When was the last time you talked to Jess? Is she feeling better?"

"Better? I talked to her about a week ago. She's in Cochrane now with Jon and Bryce. She didn't say anything about being sick."

"I stopped by the ranch about a week and a half ago to drop off cinnamon rolls. Jess took them from me, then bolted to the washroom."

Debbie placed her mug on the end table and leaned forward in her chair. "Do you remember if she was cooking? Did the house smell like any other foods?"

"I'd have to think about it." Sally tapped her fingers on her mug and pursed her lips. "Wait. Now I remember. She had some sort of soup simmering on the stove.

Makes sense if she felt ill."

Debbie pumped her fist. "Woohoo!" She laughed at Sally's raised eyebrow, and the inquisitive look in her eyes.

"I don't get it."

"She wasn't sick. She's pregnant. You have another grandbaby on the way. Must be early if she hasn't told anyone."

"How can you be so sure?"

"Jess has iron guts. But when she was pregnant with Bryce, mixed food smells sent her running to the bathroom every time."

Sally's eyes widened, and she smiled. "I love my grandsons, but I sure would enjoy a granddaughter to dote on. Better not get our hopes up. Could still be the flu."

"You're right. Hard not to though."

Sally looked over her shoulder. "Did you hear something?"

Debbie held still and tuned her ears to her surroundings. *A faint grating noise.* "Sounds like metal on metal."

"Yes, coming from your back door." Sally rifled through her purse and pulled out her phone. "I'll call Sheriff Hank."

Debbie ran to her back door and pressed her eye to the peephole. "There are two men trying to break in."

The doorknob turned. They'd picked the lock. Debbie positioned a kitchen chair under the knob to stop the door from opening then ran to her closet and pulled her rifle off the shelf. She removed the safety and positioned the rifle over her shoulder.

A hard pounding shook the door on its frame.

Debbie took a deep breath and willed her body to remain calm. She peered through the sight post of her rifle focusing on the door. "Get down to the basement and lock yourself in the cold storage. It's the safest spot."

"Not without you. Robbers carry guns too."

Debbie groaned. "I've never run from a fight in my life, but you're making sense. Let's go."

"Hank's not answering. I'll call 911."

Debbie shoved open the basement door and flipped on the light switch, illuminating an old, wooden, narrow staircase with short steps. Debbie sprinted down the stairs with Sally behind her. She killed the lights, grabbed Sally's hand, led her into the cold storage, and turned the flimsy lock on the doorknob. "Help me pile potatoes in front of the door."

Sally pointed to her phone. "Oh, someone's answering."

"Okay. You talk. I'll get the potatoes."

"We need police at 5 Camden Road right away. Two men are trying to break into Debbie Johnson's house. Hurry. Yes, 5 Camden Road." She hung up the phone and took the other end of the fifty-pound bag of potatoes Debbie dragged across the floor.

"Did they say how long they'd be?"

"Ten minutes."

"Shoot. That's a long time."

They hefted two more bags in front of the door. The incessant pounding upstairs stopped. Wood splintered. Heavy, fast, footsteps thudded directly over their heads.

Sally grabbed Debbie's arm, shaking so violently from head to toe, Debbie shook too. She whispered, "They're in the house already."

Debbie took a deep, shuddering breath. Sally needed

her to be the strong, level-headed one. She patted her hand and whispered, "Keep it together. Help is coming. Let's hide behind the rest of the potatoes."

They tiptoed across the bare concrete floor and climbed into the narrow space between the foundation wall and the stack of potatoes.

Debbie kneeled and stuck her rifle between the brown paper sacks of spuds. Never had she been happier to be a farmer with an ample supply of her favorite russets. The footsteps moved to the upper level. Maybe they'd take her jewelry box from the master bedroom and split.

Sally crouched beside her with her head between her knees.

Debbie touched her knee. "You, okay?"

"Bit dizzy and faint. This is helping."

"Deep breaths, Sally. You're probably in shock. It's already been two minutes, and they've gone upstairs. There's nothing of value down here. The basement is unfinished. Bet they'll make off with my jewelry and the television and move on."

"I wish Jon was in town."

"Me too. But I'm a good shot."

Sally peeked at Debbie from between her knees. "How are you so calm?"

Debbie shrugged. "Mind over matter. I won't let myself give into fear."

"I'll try it. I'm starting to feel better."

The basement door at the top of the staircase creaked open, and the light clicked on.

A man's voice carried down the stairs. "Those old ladies have to be down here somewhere. Anthony, check behind those boxes."

Anthony said, "We gotta hurry. They might have called the cops."

Debbie huffed and pressed her eye to the sight post. *Old, my behind! Bust through this door and I'll show you what an old lady can do.*

The door to the cold storage area shook.

"They're in here. It's locked. Help me break it down."

With each hard blow, the door shook in its frame, but the potatoes held it shut. Debbie glanced at her best friend. Sally was hunched over into her lap with her eyes shut. *Oh no! Sally!*

Debbie crawled over to Sally and placed a hand on the base of her neck. She had a pulse, and her chest was rising and falling. *Phew. She only fainted.*

Debbie kneeled and took up her post. The bag of potatoes resting on the top of the pile in front of the door, shifted with each blow. Four blows later, the bag fell off the top and landed on the concrete floor with a thud. Three bags of fifty-pound potatoes remained in place.

A male voice from outside the door said, "did you hear that? Something fell in there. She's put something in front of the door."

"Get out of the way."

A much louder blow shook the door, then light streamed through a new crack along the middle of the wood.

Keep your breathing slow. Focus on the target. Then squeeze that trigger.

The crack widened as an elbow splintered the door. An arm reached through the opening toward the lock on the handle. Debbie squeezed the trigger and braced herself for the kickback.

Her bullet pierced the flesh on the man's hand and blood poured out of the wound.

He wailed, then yanked his hand out of the opening. "That bitch shot me!"

Debbie smiled. *Serves him right. Maybe they'll get the hint and leave.*

"Here, Ray. Wrap your hand in this."

"Dammit. Why couldn't you take care of your own shit? Let's just leave. I'll vouch for your efforts with the boss."

"Jones gave me twelve hours. He doesn't give second chances. I need hostages now. Stay here, and make sure she doesn't escape. I'll check the barn for something to widen that hole."

Hostages! Well that changes things. Time to go on the offense. Debbie pulled her rifle out of its hiding spot, tiptoed over to the door, and peered through the hole. The one she'd shot, Ray, a massive man in a suit and pea coat stood with his hand wrapped in a handkerchief facing the staircase. She angled the rifle through the hole, took aim, and debated pulling the trigger. Shooting a man's hand was one thing but killing him while he was looking away would make her a cold-blooded killer. But what would happen when his friend returned? She'd be outnumbered.

Shifting the rifle lower, she aimed for Ray's knee, to disable rather than kill, and pulled the trigger.

Ray screamed and fell backward onto his butt while clutching his knee. Turning his head in her direction, he said, "You're going to pay for that, bitch."

"Pay? I believe I'm the one with a rifle pointed at your head. You broke into my house. Remember? The police are on their way."

Ray twisted his arm in an awkward angle and

reached into his pocket.

"Don't move. You take your hand out of your pocket, and I'll blow your brains out. I spared your life once. I won't do it again."

Anthony called down from the top of the staircase. "I found an ax."

Debbie raised her voice. "Drop that ax or your friend is dead."

Ray lunged and rolled out of her sight. "Get down here with that ax. Quick."

Debbie angled her gun toward the staircase. Anthony ran down the stairs, clutching the ax. She anticipated his arrival halfway down, gauged his position, and squeezed the trigger.

He screamed as the bullet pierced his calf rather than his knee, but she'd hit him, nonetheless. Anthony's leg went out from underneath him. He plummeted down the remaining stairs onto the concrete floor landing face first. His body went still, and the ax flew into the back corner.

Bile rose in Debbie's throat. She swallowed it down. *I sure hope I didn't kill the bastard.*

Another man's voice rang through the air. "Debbie Johnson! Agent Cooper, FBI."

She yelled, "I'm in the basement with Sally Kent. There are two men wanting to kidnap us. One is conscious. Probably has a gun. I think I might have killed the other by accident."

"You okay?"

"For now."

A large hand pulled her rifle farther through the opening.

Wood splintered into Debbie's hand, but she held on

with all her might. "He's trying to take my rifle."

Footsteps bounded down the stairs. A shotgun cocked. "Let go of the rifle. Face down on the floor. Now!"

The pressure on the rifle ceased and Debbie fell backward. She let go of the rifle, bringing her hands back to break her fall. The rifle flew a few feet away, landing harmlessly on the concrete floor.

She got up, then scrambled on her hands and knees for her gun. A gunshot rang through the basement.

"Agent Cooper?"

"I'm fine, ma'am. It's safe to come out now."

Debbie dragged the potatoes away from the broken door and swung it open. She covered her mouth with her hand to suppress a gag. Brain matter and blood covered the floor and the nearby wall. Ray lay on the floor with the top of his head missing.

Trent held a cell phone to his ear with a shotgun slung over his shoulder. "Yes, I'm calling from 5 Camden Road. We need an ambulance right away. One female is unconscious." He glanced at Debbie. "Is she breathing?"

"Yes, good pulse and breathing. I'm getting her a cold cloth."

"Yes, ma'am. The female is breathing, strong pulse. We also have one male deceased and another unconscious, shallow breathing, bleeding from a head and a leg wound. He's lost a lot of blood."

Debbie stepped around puddles and clung to the railing as she climbed the stairs. *He might be alive after all. I'm not a murderer yet.*

She soaked a dish towel in cold water from the tap.

"Debbie. You, okay? Where's Sally?"

Debbie turned from the sink to find Sheriff Hank standing in her kitchen. Sirens wailed on their way up her gravel laneway. "I'm fine. Sally fainted. She's in the basement. Agent Cooper called for an ambulance."

Hank bounded down the stairs two at a time. "Sally? Sally?"

"Wait. It's a mess down there."

He ignored her and continued.

Debbie hurried to catch up. "She's in the cold storage behind the potatoes."

Trent knelt beside Anthony. He'd tied his belt around his leg and was tying a makeshift bandage around his head with part of the man's dress shirt. He glanced up at them. "Sheriff Hank, I'm Agent Trent Cooper, FBI. I'm part of a team investigating the Kansas City mob. These two are known members."

Hank breezed past him into the cold storage. "Secure the scene. I hear my deputies coming in now. We'll talk later."

He kneeled beside Sally and pulled her head into his lap. "Hand me that cloth."

Debbie gave it to him.

Hank dabbed the cloth around Sally's face. "You wake up now, baby. You hear?"

He patted her cheek. "Sally."

Her eyes fluttered. "Hank? Where's Debbie? Is she okay?"

Debbie sank to the floor on her knees beside them. "I'm fine."

Sally sat up and leaned into Hank's chest. "What happened? The last thing I remember is someone trying to break down the door."

Debbie sighed. "Ready for my statement, Hank?"

"Yes."

Debbie took a breath, then told them what happened.

Hank rested a hand on Debbie's shoulder. "Your quick thinking kept you and Sally alive."

"You aren't going to charge me with anything? I shot two men with the door still standing between us instead of waiting for the police."

"Debbie, those men were here to harm you. The minute someone forces entry into your property, you have the right to shoot. Either way, it's self-defense."

Trent stuck his head around the door. "Scene is secure. Paramedics took Anthony Greer away to the hospital accompanied by one of your deputies. The coroner is on his way for the other. Another ambulance is coming for Sally."

Sally said, "I'm fine. Cancel that ambulance."

Hank's face reddened. "What is it with you feds thinking you can just come to my town, and do whatever the hell you want without informing me?"

"It was sensitive information."

Hank's voice raised. "Sensitive? You could have gotten these women killed. Talk. *Now*."

Debbie stood, wobbled, and leaned on the wall for support. "Let's go to the living room. Get comfortable. The smells from all the gore are getting to me."

Trent wrapped an arm around Debbie's shoulders. "Let me help you up the stairs, ma'am. We'll get you and your friend settled, then I'll tell you everything."

Chapter Nine

Jessica glanced in the side mirror at the white van following them as Jon took the next exit off the TransCanada Highway. The van signaled and followed.

"He's still there, Jon."

"I know. I see him." He turned into a combination gas station and convenience store, then parked at a pump.

The van drove past them. "That's a relief."

"Not necessarily," Jon said. "I'll watch for it to double back."

"I better hit the restroom." She glanced over her shoulder into the rear seats. "Got to go, Bryce? Could be the last stop for a while."

"No. But can I have a slushie?"

"Promise you'll ride out the sugar rush in the van without complaining about being bored?"

He grinned. "Promise. You're the best mom ever."

"Uh-huh. I bet. Want anything, Jon?"

"Might as well grab a few burner phones. We don't want to be unreachable for any length of time."

"Good point. Will do."

Jessica hummed along to the country music playing inside the convenience store while she filled a cup for Bryce.

A man brushed past her, knocking her purse off her shoulder. "Sorry, ma'am."

"No worries." She brought the drink to the counter.

"Two of those burner phones, please."

"Sure." A sleepy-faced, tall and lanky teenager swiped his long blond hair out of his eyes and rang up the drink and the phones, placing the phones in a plastic bag.

In a round mirror mounted in the corner of the ceiling, Jessica spotted a man standing in the back of the store staring toward the register. *Probably stealing.* She made eye contact with the boy, pointed toward the mirror, then left with her stuff.

She slid open the van door and handed Bryce his drink. "Are you sure you don't need the bathroom? Last chance."

"I don't need to go."

"Okay. Let us know when you need to *before* the last minute. There aren't many places to stop between here and Regina." She climbed in and handed Jon one of the phones. "Any sign of the van?"

"No." He ripped open the packaging and plugged the charger into a USB port on the dash.

Jessica ripped the other one open and did the same thing. "Now we get to tell our family we're on the run. Delightful." Jessica retrieved a sheet of paper from her purse. "I'm sending out a group text to everyone letting them know to contact me on this number."

"Good idea. Can you do the same for me when you're done?"

"Sure."

****

Goosebumps rose on Jon's arms as he drove toward the entrance onto the highway. *Something's not right.* The van passing by didn't reassure him at all. If he was tailing someone, he'd continue straight and wait out of sight near the next exit onto the highway. He signaled left, made a U-turn back toward the city, and floored the accelerator to get through a yellow light.

Jessica stopped typing on the phone and looked up. "Where are we going?"

"Back to the city. We need a decoy. I'm not convinced we weren't being followed."

"A decoy?"

"Yes. We'll get a rental."

Jessica set her new phone aside and picked up Jon's. "There's a problem with that. You need a credit card to rent a car. That leaves a trail."

"It does. But these companies have secure systems that take time to hack. Also, by the time anyone got the information, we'd be long gone, and they wouldn't have any leads as to where. If we shake our followers, we'll be fine renting."

Jessica's phone pinged. "Your mom says she needs us to call her. It's urgent. Oh, and she knows about Trent and the mob."

"For her to say it's urgent, it can't be good. Something's wrong. Text and ask for more info. Explain we're driving all day and we won't be able to call until late tonight."

"I will. I'm worried, too. Sally isn't one for drama."

While he waited for more information, he maintained his watch on their surroundings. Diligence was a must with Jones coming at them from every angle.

****

Jessica's phone came to life a few minutes later with a page long reply. She gasped. *None of us are safe.* Jon wouldn't take the news well either. At least Bryce was wearing headphones. He didn't need to hear the message she needed to relay.

Swallowing hard against the lump in her throat, she said, "Sally and Debbie are okay, but they had a serious incident. Two men, Greer and Sands, broke into Debbie's house while her and Sally were having morning tea. Debbie killed Greer accidentally, and Trent killed Sands."

Jon gripped the steering wheel. "They might be physically okay, but you and I both know the mental wounds are worse. Your aunt especially must be traumatized." A vein in his neck bulged. "Trent should've stopped those men before it came to that."

Boy did Jessica know about psychological wounds. Tears filled her eyes. Poor Aunt Debbie, a widow in her sixties, had endured far too much in the past year because she happened to be related to Jessica—having her barn lit on fire, getting shot at, and now having to kill another human being.

Jessica wiped her tears with a napkin from the glove compartment.

Jon held her hand. "I should have kept that thought to myself. I'm sorry."

"It's nothing that hadn't crossed my mind. Now what? Will Jones send more men?"

"Probably. He's warped. And he won't be impressed that things didn't go his way." Jon relaxed his grip on the wheel. "Can you ask where they're staying?"

"I'll ask. Although clearly, my aunt can take care of herself."

"Debbie is a force of nature. Not many older ladies could take on two mobsters and come out unscathed. Bet she saved my mom."

Jessica's phone lit up with a response. "Hank has

moved everyone into his place."

"Good. So far, I don't see any sign of that white van. If he was following, we lost him."

"We probably weren't being followed after all. How would Jones get people here so quickly?"

"It wouldn't be hard. His organization is well established and far-reaching. He's probably still smuggling women up here, giving him allies."

She shuddered. "That's creepy. You have no idea who they'd be, do you?"

"Unfortunately, no."

"I'm not sure there's an advantage in going all the way to Regina anymore. If we were followed, they'd expect us to go east. Maybe we should head north instead. There are a few more routes off the beaten path to Edmonton and major centers in between. Plus, way more cars on the road to blend in with."

Jon said, "I agree. With a rental vehicle on a populated highway, we'd blend in. Edmonton's the capital, isn't it?"

"Yes."

"Population?"

"A million. It's more condensed than Calgary, and it's usually bustling. I think we'd be better off staying in Red Deer. It's about an hour and a half south of Edmonton. We could drive in last minute for our flight."

"Sounds like it could work. How big is Red Deer?"

"About 100,000 people."

"That's plenty big enough to blend into. I don't think they'd look for us there."

She peered into the passenger side mirror. "I haven't noticed any followers. You?"

"None, yet."

****

Jessica powered up her laptop while Jon went inside the car rental shop. She connected to the free WIFI to check on the nanny camera. She logged into her account, then a live feed alert flashed on the screen.

Her front door hung sideways, and two men with guns clomped up the carpeted staircase with their dirty boots on. They disappeared from the view of the camera sitting on the mantel of her fireplace.

Her breath came in short pants, and her pulse raced. *If we hadn't left when we did...* She breathed in deeply, forcing her lungs to open. "I can't faint. I need to call the police."

She picked up her burner phone, then dialed the direct number for the RCMP detachment in Cochrane. With her finger over the send button, she paused.

A woman wearing a black balaclava on her head, crept through the front door with a gun. She followed the men up the stairs and out of view. The men hadn't worn a disguise. The woman couldn't be with them, so what was she doing there?

Jessica hit send and put the phone to her ear. While she waited for someone to come on the line, two loud blasts came out of the speaker of her laptop. The woman dashed down the stairs and out the front door. Jessica hung up the phone and stared at the screen to see if the men would follow. If they did, she'd call the police right away. If they didn't, she'd give the woman a chance to get away first.

Jon climbed into the driver's seat with keys and paperwork. "I showed them my badge, and they're going to take the plate off your van and park it on the lot."

She turned the laptop so they could both see it. "You

need to watch this. It's a live feed."

"Okay, but we need to move."

"This is important."

"But I don't see anything."

She restarted the feed. "The woman must be a fed. Don't you think?"

"I don't know. Feds don't usually disguise their face. We'll call the police once we're on the road. You'll want those bodies out of your house before they start to stink." He opened the door. "You guys wait here. I'll move our luggage over to the SUV."

Jessica's stomach churned. She forced the image of the two men lying dead, bleeding on the beige carpet, out of her mind. The important thing was two fewer men would be after them, but who was the mystery woman?

****

An hour and a half later, Jon pulled into the parking lot of a small, dilapidated inn. It offered apartment-style rooms each having its own exterior door and windows. The shabbiest lodgings in town, and the least likely choice for a family. Hence, the safest option.

Jessica had dozed off halfway there, likely a result of the pregnancy combined with the shock of what they'd been through.

He shook her shoulder gently. "Wake up, sweetheart. I found us a place to stay."

She opened her eyes, stared straight ahead, then grimaced. "I forgot the disinfectant spray."

"Sorry. But it's only until Sam couriers us passports and flight tickets. These kinds of places take cash and don't usually care about names. There's a drug store across the street. After I grab a room, we'll run across and get supplies."

"Makes sense. We'll figure it out."

Jon locked Jessica and Bryce inside the SUV, then jogged inside the office.

He rang the bell on the cracked, worn desk. "Hello. Anyone there?"

"Just a minute."

A man around Jon's age came around the corner. His well-groomed short hair and creaseless clothes said former police or military, and he might be sympathetic to their plight.

The man leaned against the desk and touched his mouse, stirring the old computer screen in front of him to life. "Can I help you?"

"I need a room." Jon pulled his old FBI badge out of his jacket. "I'm Jon Kent. A retired agent. I chose your establishment because I was hoping you'd take cash no questions asked. Can you help us?"

The man nodded. "I'm Sean Harris. Former PPCLI."

"Infantry?"

"Yes." He plucked a key off the wall. "This place isn't much to look at, but it's clean. I'll take cash, and if anyone comes asking, I never saw you. This room is in the middle, so you should have good sight lines. I live directly above this room on the upper level."

"Appreciate it." Jon handed him an American one-hundred-dollar bill. "I'll have a package coming hopefully by the latest tomorrow morning."

"I'll keep an eye out for it. If you need anything, text me. My business card is in the rooms by the phone."

"Mind if I park behind the dumpsters in that alley behind the motel?"

Chapter Ten

After they settled into their surprisingly clean room, Jessica tried reading, napping, and repacking their stuff, but nothing distracted her for any length of time. She leaned against the headboard on one of the two double beds, remote in hand, flipping through channels. Her gaze kept roaming to the flimsy door. She pictured it flying off the hinges in the middle of the night as men stormed through to kill them.

Footsteps crunched through the hard-packed snow on the sidewalk outside. She tensed as they moved closer and closer to their room. The shadow of a man moved through the curtains as he passed by the windows. His steps grew quieter until they couldn't be heard at all. Jessica sighed and rubbed her stomach.

Bryce set his tablet aside and padded across the worn carpet to the washroom.

Jon waited for Bryce to shut the door, then lifted the comforter on the adjacent bed revealing a black duffle bag under the bedframe. "The guns are here. Don't worry. I'll be awake tonight watching over you and Bryce while you sleep."

"Good. If I need them, I know where they are."

Bryce came out of the bathroom, picked up his tablet, then climbed into her bed. "Dad, can we play on the new gaming console? Will you play too, Mom?

Jon said, "Sure. We'll play together."

Jessica wrapped her arm around Bryce, nestled him into the crook of her shoulder, and kissed the top of his head. Despite the craziness of rushing out of the house in Cochrane, he seemed unfazed. *He must get his bravery from his father.* "I'm looking forward to playing. I haven't played video games in at least twenty years."

Bryce said, "Twenty years?"

"Yes, and nothing as fancy as this."

After connecting all the cables from the television to the game console, Jon squeezed in beside her and Bryce. "Think we're ready to go. Game's in."

Bryce set his tablet aside in favor of a controller. "Oh, boy. This is gonna be awesome."

They'd splurged on extra controllers at the drugstore across the street, so every member of the family would have their own, including the baby Jessica carried. Gaming proved to be an excellent distraction. Jessica couldn't help but laugh when she nailed Jon's cart with a blue shell.

Bryce caught on fast, giggling as he steered around the racetrack. Normally, they limited his screen time to a few hours per day, but under the circumstances, their routines were out of whack. Once they got settled in their new temporary home, she'd have to reimplement the usual rules. Her son needed as much stability as she could give him with them, not only being on the run but expecting a new baby.

Jessica set her remote aside. "We should probably order dinner."

"Sure. I'm getting hungry," Jon said. "We passed a chicken chain restaurant a few blocks away from here. I'm sure they deliver."

"Okay. Sounds good. I'll look up the number and

call."

Jon stood and groaned, holding his lower back. "I'm hopping in the shower while we wait for the food. You okay to play alone, buddy?"

Bryce, intent on the game, answered without taking his eyes off the screen. "Yes."

Jessica found the phone number for the restaurant and ordered enough food to carry them through the night. The next step stirred butterflies in her stomach—the anticipated arrival of the delivery person. Hours had passed, and besides that one man, no one had come near their room. Maybe, just maybe, they'd escaped their followers.

Jessica eyed the strap of the bag sticking out from underneath the bed, grateful she'd made Jon teach her how to shoot. She kneeled on the floor, then glanced at Bryce. His forehead was creased in concentration as he stared at the television. She grabbed the strap and pulled the heavy bag closer. She unzipped the main compartment, pushed the opening aside, and stared at the collection of guns within. Jon made sure they were well-equipped.

A small handgun she'd practiced with sat on the top. She checked the chamber for bullets. *Loaded.* After putting the safety back on, she stuck it in the back of the waistband of her maternity jeans, and covered it with her baggy, woven blue sweater. *Better safe than sorry.* The side pockets of the duffle bulged. Inside one pocket, she found a canister of pepper spray which she placed on a nearby table, then shoved the bag under the bed.

Jon had left the bathroom door ajar, and she couldn't help peeking inside. Her handsome husband's silhouette showed through the glass shower door. He stood a whole head taller than her, and his shoulders were broad and strong. Corded, sinewy, hard-labor-earned muscles traveled from his neck down to his calves. She longed for the first time in ages to run her hands along those muscles and through the downy, sandy-blond hair spattered across his chest.

With the exhaustion and nausea from pregnancy weighing her down, making love had been pushed to the back burner, and Jon being a loving husband, hadn't complained. Of course, now that the mood had arisen, they were sleeping in the same room as their son.

She sighed and perched on the edge of the bed closest to the door to wait for their delivery. Her tummy rumbled. She took her mind off Jon in the shower by focusing on food. Her mouth watered, thinking of roasted chicken and fries with a good coating of gravy. The cherry cheesecake for dessert would also be a real treat.

The water turned off. Jon came out of the shower with a towel wrapped around his waist and his hair wet and slicked back. Jessica bit her lip and met his eyes.

His signature mischievous lopsided grin lit his face. "Of all times, sweetheart." He laughed as he strutted across the room, flexing his muscles. "I better get dressed before the food gets here."

Tease. "Definitely." Clothes wouldn't help her state much, knowing what he looked like underneath them.

****

Jon sat in a chair by a window in their motel room with a shotgun equipped with a silencer across his lap. A blustery, cold winter wind whistled through the tiny crack under the door and shook the windows in their frames, potentially muffling other sounds, like approaching footsteps.

Being alone while awake at night gave him far too much time to think. He glanced over his shoulder at the bed in the far corner. Bryce had fallen asleep a few hours earlier. He slept in his usual pose on his stomach with his mouth open catching flies, as his mother Sally would say. *Mom, I'm so sorry.*

The weight of the world rested on his shoulders. Everyone he loved was a target thanks to his past. He never imagined joining the FBI would place his whole family in danger and Jessica's family by extension. But dwelling on the past wouldn't help with his current dilemma.

Jessica's chest rose and fell in sleep, her long, blonde, silky hair draped across both pillows. For the time being, she needed him close for protection, but once she and Bryce were settled in the safe house, he would go on the offensive. Playing the waiting game and hiding while the FBI collected enough evidence to get Jones wasn't the only option.

Active members of the bureau couldn't justify eliminating Jones without an immediate threat to safety, but Jon wasn't active, not anymore. He'd retired two years earlier after a hostage situation took a preventable deadly turn and a suspect ate his own gun. After all the murders he'd witnessed while undercover, and the justified kills he'd been forced to make, that last suicide was one dead body too many. He could never harden his heart and grow accustomed to loss of life the way some agents did. Every death haunted him.

Jon seesawed his head to alleviate tension in his neck. The seconds ticking by on the wall clock moved in slow motion. He stood, stretched, and paced the room to get his blood flowing. *Can't get fatigued. Must stay alert.*

Light shone through the curtains in the window, and the rumbling of an engine penetrated the howling wind. Jon shifted the edge of the curtain enough to peek outside with one eye. A dark blue truck circled the few vehicles parked in the lot. Snow covered the license plate, but a crack across the windshield in combination with a large dent on the front bumper made it distinctive.

Two men in black parkas and black balaclavas, one around six feet tall and the other half a foot shorter, with guns, exited the truck, leaving it running. They jogged to the room on the far left. Each man pressed their face to the windows on either side of the door. Jon dropped the curtain. *What are the odds they aren't looking for us?*

With only four rooms between the men and their room, they'd be at his windows in no time. Jon unplugged the television, eradicating all sources of light in the room. With the drapes pulled all the way shut, the men shouldn't be able to see anything. By the grace of God, they didn't have night-vision goggles.

Jon tiptoed across the old green carpet away from the windows, clutching his rifle, and crouched between the two double beds by the duffle full of weapons. With their rental parked behind the dumpster instead of in front of their room, maybe the men would move on.

He grabbed the burner phone sitting on the side table between the beds, yanked Sean's business card out of his back pocket and texted him. With his history as a military man, odds were good he'd be awake that night to keep an eye on his property.

—*It's Jon Kent. Two men with guns are looking in the room windows.*—

Sean replied, —*I know. Already phoned the*

police.—

Jon shoved the phone in his pocket and picked up his gun. Best-case scenario, Jessica and Bryce would sleep through the whole episode unaware of how close they came to being discovered.

Shadows crept across the drapes, stopping in front of the windows. *They're here. Shoot. Keep going.* The looming figures remained. Jon held still, not daring to move a muscle in case his movements created shadows in the curtains. The two dark figures moved right, likely headed to the next room. Jon released the breath he'd been holding and gulped air into his lungs. *That was too close for comfort.*

The faint whirl of sirens penetrated the howling of the wind. Jon rolled his eyes. Why did police always have to blare their sirens and give suspects a heads-up to flee? How many cars could there be to swerve around at two o'clock in the morning? The men would get away and return when the heat died down.

Chapter Eleven

Jessica opened her eyes to lumpy shadows in the darkness. At first, the unfamiliar surroundings disoriented her, then she remembered the motel room far from home. She sat up in bed. As her eyes adjusted, a shadowy shape shifted in the chair by the window. "Jon, is that you?"

The television switched on. She blinked, adjusting to the sudden light. Jon stood from the chair and perched on the edge of the bed beside her hip. He whispered, "Shhh. I'm here, sweetheart. Bryce is still sleeping. It's 4:30 in the morning."

"Why did you have the TV off?"

"We had visitors."

The lingering cobwebs in her mind evaporated. "Visitors?"

"Two men showed up a few hours ago in a dark blue truck. They stared in all the motel windows, including ours. Sean called 911 from upstairs. Police sirens spooked them, and they took off."

"Think they were looking for us?"

"Probably. Unless they were looking for one of their girls. Just because this place is kept clean, and Sean seems to be a decent guy doesn't mean it isn't shady."

Jessica shivered and yanked the blankets up to her chin. "They must've been here for us."

Jon yawned. "Maybe, but they haven't been back.

We should be able to slip out of here unnoticed."

"You're pale. Why don't you sleep for a few hours? I'll keep watch."

"No. Sam's package should be here sometime this morning. I'll sleep on the plane."

Jessica's brow furrowed. "Aren't you going to be on edge during the flight, too?"

"We'll be disguised and have new names by then."

"Disguised?"

"Yes. We're getting the same treatment as someone would in the witness protection program. We'll be given new identities, wigs, a vehicle, and an address."

Her heart thumped. Losing her identity on top of losing control of her life? "But we aren't starting over, are we? Giving up everything?"

He wrapped an arm around her and kissed her forehead. "No. We're not giving up our home." He rested his hand on her stomach. "Once you three are safe, I'll end things."

Oh, no, you're not, Jon Kent! Her voice raised to a heated whisper. "You aren't leaving me and Bryce alone in a strange place while you risk your life. Let Sam and the FBI do their job."

"Jess, I'm sorry. But I need to kill Jones. If I don't, he's just going to keep coming after us. He bought his way out of going to prison once already. Want to go through this again?"

I can't believe this is happening! Jessica shoved Jon's arm away, padded across the scratchy, worn carpet to the washroom, and locked the door, putting as much distance between them as she could. She was usually level-headed and slow to anger, but with hormones raging, her temper flared red hot. It took every ounce of control not to smash everything in sight.

She plunked down on the toilet seat for lack of a better place to sit. Jon's logic was sound, but what if he got himself killed? Besides, she'd be alone, pregnant, and stuck looking over her shoulder until he returned.

Jon's voice carried through the door. "I have an idea. What if my mom and your aunt were relocated to our safe house? Sheriff Hank can't watch over them all day."

"Give me space. I'll think about it while I shower."

"All right."

Thanks for dropping that bomb, Jon. Better than lying about it or taking off, I guess.

She set the water on warm and stepped into the small, glass shower stall. In the heat of the moment, she hadn't stopped to consider toiletries. But, of course, Jon had unpacked hers and placed them in the stall with his own. She huffed. *Why does he have to do something considerate and make it so hard for me to stay angry at him?*

Sighing, she massaged strawberry-scented shampoo into her scalp. Having her aunt and mother-in-law around would be a huge help. Especially if their situation dragged on. But could she handle being holed up with them in close quarters? They'd gotten along fine when Aunt Debbie had ended up stuck at the ranch with them during David's rampage, and Sally was a sweetheart. And they'd be safer too. *Why does Jon have to be right? So frustrating!*

Jessica finished her shower and wrapped herself in a towel. *Ah, cleanliness.* A loud rapping came from outside the bathroom. Her fingers trembled. She lost her grip on the towel, and it pooled on the floor by her feet. *Must be the door to our room.*

Pressing her ear to the door, she strained to listen. She could make out Jon's and another man's voice, both calm and jovial. *Must be the owner or a delivery person.* Her racing heart calmed. She bent, retrieved her towel, and wrapped it around her goose-pimpled skin. With only her nightgown and undergarments as clothing options, she'd have to wait until their visitor left to exit the bathroom.

A few minutes later, the front door shut. She cracked the bathroom door open. "Jon? Is it safe to come out?"

"Yes. It was the owner, Sean. He dropped off a box of donuts, breakfast sandwiches, and coffee."

"That was nice of him." She took her dirty clothes off the bathroom counter and went in search of a pair of leggings and a sweater, her go-to pregnancy outfit. She unzipped her suitcase slowly, hoping not to wake Bryce who somehow slept through just about anything.

"I've got water heating for your tea."

She tugged a black, knit, cotton sweater over her head. "Thanks."

After pulling on grey leggings and a pair of thick blue and grey striped socks, she sat across from Jon at the small round table and unwrapped a sandwich. "Would you ask Sally to talk to my aunt. Have them decide if they're willing to relocate? It's a big ask. Debbie hardly leaves the farm at all. She won't last at Hank's house for any length of time before she's back home."

"It's a huge ask. I texted my mom a little while ago."

Of course, you did. Why wait for me to make up my mind? "But I'm not okay with you leaving to hunt Jones on your own. It's a last resort. Not to mention I don't feel like visiting you in prison."

"That wouldn't happen."

"How can you be so sure?"

"It would be self-defense. Jones would try to kill me on sight."

"Great. That's not comforting at all, Jon."

"I promised I wouldn't lie. So I'm not."

"I appreciate it. But you better include me in the decision-making. Which you *aren't* now."

"My intention wasn't to exclude you. I knew you'd say yes when you calmed down. You're just as worried about them as I am."

"We're in a horrible situation, and I feel completely out of control. The last thing I need on top of that is you making decisions for me."

He reached across the table and clasped her hand. "Sorry, sweetheart. The stress and lack of control is getting to me too. I won't do anything without your consent, okay?"

"You've been putting on a good front, but I see through it. You're shaken by this. More so than you were when David was on the loose. You don't have to hide it. Lean on me."

"I'll try, if you promise to do the same." His phone pinged. "Our package was delivered to the office. Sean's on his way here with it."

"That's a relief. We need to get out of here."

Jon stood by the window beside the door and peeked around the edge of the curtain. Upon Sean's arrival, he opened the door and accepted the medium-sized cardboard box.

He set it on the table. "Ready to find out where our new home will be?"

"As ready as I'll ever be. Open the box."

Jon sliced the tape across the top with his pocketknife. He reached inside and pulled out a plastic bag containing three passports and two wallets full of new identification, including driver's licenses, credit cards, and social security numbers. "How original. We're the Smith family now."

"Makes sense. It's a very common name."

"I'm Bryan Smith, you're Sarah Smith, and Bryce is Max Smith."

Jessica reached in the box and pulled out wigs, caps, and sunglasses. One headpiece was skin-colored without hair. "What is this supposed to be?"

"Ah, that would be my new bald look. You tuck your hair underneath it. It's the best way to drastically change a man's image."

"I like my dark brown wig with the bob hairstyle, but they didn't send a wig for Bryce."

"Little boys usually fly under the radar. In this case, your wig matches his hair, so it makes you blend in."

She nodded. "That's clever."

Jon reached inside the box and pulled out an envelope. "Our plane tickets must be in here." He peeled open the envelope and pulled out three boarding passes. "It'll be somewhat like home."

She read the ticket in his hand. "Bountiful, Utah. Never heard of it. Have you ever been?"

"No."

Jessica flipped open her laptop and searched online for information. "It'll be a little like home. Bountiful is on a mountain range. 40,000 people. Little bit bigger than Cochrane. And they have a hospital with a maternity ward. It's only twenty minutes from Salt Lake City."

"Our flight leaves at ten this morning. We have three

hours to get there and through security. Better wake Bryce, put on our disguises, and hit the road."

****

Jon ran big gobs of gel through his hair, slicking it back and flattening it to the top of his head. He applied the skin wig and pulled his cap down. While undercover he'd become accustomed to wearing disguises daily. *Perfect.*

He gazed at Jessica in the mirror as she pinned up her hair, then secured her wig. "I love your blonde hair, but brunette's a sexy look for you."

She smiled one of the wide, warm smiles he loved. "Thanks. You look so different bald. I could walk by and not recognize you, and I'm your wife." She ran her hand along his shoulder. "It accentuates your muscle tone."

"Thanks." He kissed her. "Remembering our new names is key. We need to practice in the car on the way to the airport."

"Yes, Bryan." She frowned. "That sounds so wrong."

"You'll get used to it." Jon moved the curtain aside and scanned the parking lot. The last thing he needed was an audience. *No one. For now.* Pulling the hood of his parka over his bald disguise, he jogged to the car, then parked in the space in front of their room.

The door swung open. Jessica emerged with Bryce, or he should say Sarah emerged with Max. That would take getting used to. Jon cranked the heat and ran inside the room for the suitcases. Time wasn't on their side. Missing that flight wasn't an option with gangsters on their tails. *Damn you to hell, Hugh Jones.*

He shoved the suitcases in the hatch, then jumped in the driver's seat and floored the accelerator. After studying maps online, Jon had planned to take a longer, more deserted route to the airport. But with their package coming so close to their flight time, he'd be forced to take the most direct route.

Jessica peered over her shoulder at Bryce in the backseat. "Buddy, we're taking an airplane to Utah. That's where we'll be living for now."

He perked up with a mouth full of donut. "We get to fly in an airplane. Cool."

"Pretty exciting, eh? We even got new names. My name is Sarah, and Dad's name is Bryan."

"What's mine?"

"Max."

"I don't like it. Why can't my name be Chase?"

Jon shrugged. "Sorry. Sam picked the names. There's nothing we can do about it now."

"Okay. Can we name the baby Chase at least?"

"It isn't a bad name for a boy. What do you think, Bryan?"

"It's a nice name, Sarah."

Bryce laughed.

Jon glanced in the rear-view mirror. "What's so funny, Max?"

"You and Mom playing pretend like kindergarteners."

"It might seem funny, but it's serious. You can't laugh and draw attention to us at the airport or on the plane, okay?"

"Are we being followed by bad guys again?"

"Maybe. But that's why we're wearing our disguises. To hide so we stay safe. Keep the cap pulled down, okay?"

Bryce's lips trembled as he tugged on his hat.

"Okay."

"Hey, don't be afraid. I'll never let anything happen to you."

"Promise?"

"Yes, buddy. Scout's honor."

Glancing in the mirrors, Jon kept an eye on all six lanes of the highway as they moved through the area of Red Deer called Gasoline Alley. Morning traffic was moderate with people commuting to work but moving at a good pace. A dark blue truck with a cracked windshield traveled in the lane to the left of them three cars back. Cracked windshields in Alberta were commonplace. Road maintenance crews regularly dropped a rock and sand mixture on the roads during the winter.

With all the vehicles between them, Jon couldn't see the front end to determine if it had the same large dent on the bumper as the truck from the previous night. He pounded the accelerator, signaled, and moved into the far-right lane, creating distance. A few hundred meters up the road, the truck made a move. Jon glimpsed the dent as it shifted into the lane next to them.

"We have company. A dark blue truck in the lane over a few cars back. I'm taking the next exit. Brace yourselves, I'm punching the accelerator and slamming on the brakes. We have to lose them, fast."

Chapter Twelve

Jessica glanced in the driver's side mirror and fought to hold panic at bay. "They're only one car back. I recognize the man in the passenger seat. I saw him at the gas station in Chestermere."

"How did they track us? I would swear they passed us by at the motel." Jon kept one hand on the wheel and shoved the other in his pockets. "Unless—check your coat pockets and your purse."

"Why?"

"Tracker."

Jessica grabbed her purse off the floor. "When I was filling Bryce's cup, a man bumped into me and knocked my purse off my shoulder." She dug to the bottom. *Tissue, lipstick, something foreign.* She pulled a plastic oval-shaped device out of her purse and showed it to Jon. "Is this it?"

"Yes. Throw it out the window."

How could I have been so careless? Jessica cracked her window. Frigid air blasted her face. She stuck the tracker through the opening and shut her window. "Now what?"

"We're taking that exit."

"But we're already on top of it! Bryce, plant your feet against your father's seat and push backward." She grabbed the bar hanging above the passenger door and pushed her feet against the floorboards.

"Hold on." Jon slammed on the brakes and forced his way into an impossibly small space between two cars taking the exit ramp.

Jessica's heart thumped faster. *Oh no! We're going to crash!* The car behind them braked hard, stopping an inch from their bumper, and blasted the horn. *Phew. We made it.* "Bryce, are you okay?"

Bryce said, "That was so awesome. Do that again, Dad. I'm Max, remember?"

Jessica cringed. *Why does he have to be such a dare devil?* "Good job remembering, buddy." She turned toward Jon. "You almost got us rear-ended. One patch of ice could've been disastrous. What were you thinking?"

"I'm keeping us alive. The truck couldn't get over. They had to keep going straight. Put the car rental place in the navigation, please."

She searched and found an address. "Turn left at the lights. It's only a few blocks away."

"Good. We need to get rid of this SUV." He signaled left, moved into the turning lane, and stopped at the red light.

"What do we do now? We only have another two hours and forty minutes before our flight, an hour and a half drive, bags to check, and security to get through. Plus, followers."

"Yes, but we have identification now. Including credit cards. We're returning this car and getting another rental. Worst case scenario, we buy tickets on the next flight out of the airport to an American destination."

She inhaled a few deep breaths. "Right. I forgot about the cards in the new wallets. What if they're watching the airport? They must have guessed that's where were headed."

"We can't keep running in different directions. The first flight lands in Los Angeles, the second busiest airport in North America."

"What if they get on our plane?"

"On the off chance they can manage to get on our flight, we'll lose them before we catch our connecting flight to Salt Lake City." He parked in front of the car rental office and turned in his seat to face Jessica. "Go ahead inside. I can't return and rent under different names. Rent anything but a black SUV. Okay?"

"Got it."

Adrenaline sped her footsteps on the way inside. Time was of the essence. The last thing they needed was for those men to track them down again. She stood at the front of the line waiting for a rental agent to become available, tapping her foot on the floor to let out some of the excess energy. Within five minutes, she had the good fortune of being able to rent a silver luxury sedan.

Jon threw the luggage from the SUV into the trunk, then sprinted inside to return the SUV.

Jessica locked the car while they waited. She glanced into the side mirror to check on Bryce in the backseat. He pursed his lips and his tablet sat abandoned on the seat beside him.

Jessica turned in her seat to face him. "It's okay. We'll never let anything happen to you."

Bryce nodded.

Jon emerged from the rental office, then jogged over to the car and jumped behind the wheel. "Caps off everyone. They'll be watching for them now. Max, can you reach behind you into the front pocket of my suitcase and grab my toque?" He slammed his foot on the accelerator.

"Got it."

"Give it to Mom to wear. Then we'll really look different."

Jessica secured the hat over her wig. "Think this will do the trick?"

"It should. With me bald and your hair covered, we look different. The back windows are tinted, so Max should be hidden."

"Think we'll make our flight?"

"If we don't stop or get pulled over for speeding. Keep an eye out for cops."

"Sure, I'll keep watch." *For the bad guys, too.*

****

Jon kept his eyes glued to the mirrors as he weaved his way through traffic, landing them in the far-left lane, usually the fastest. The blue truck didn't appear during the hour-long drive to the Edmonton International Airport, but that didn't mean anything. The chance of them not encountering trouble in the airport was slim to none.

Although he'd promised to tell Jessica everything, his suspicions weren't something she needed to know. To make matters even dicier, he'd been forced to leave all their weapons with Sean in the motel office. FBI identification or not, he'd never be allowed to check a duffle bag full of guns on a plane. If need be, he'd kill those thugs with his bare hands.

Better she doesn't know that either.

He pulled into the car rental parking area outside the airport and piled their luggage on a trolley while Jessica signed the tablet the rental agent handed her to return the vehicle.

Bryce tugged on his sleeve.

Jon faced him. "What's wrong, buddy?"

Bryce pointed to the terminal. "There's a man staring at us through that window."

Jon spun around. One of the men from the blue truck moved away from the window. *Knew we'd have company.* "He's gone now, see. We'll be okay."

Jessica reached for Bryce's hand. "Walk with me, please."

Instead of pulling away as he had the past few months, Bryce took his mother's hand and held on tight. It tugged at Jon's heart strings. *Enough is enough.* He formulated a plan as they walked across the parking lot into the terminal. As he suspected they would be, the men's and women's washrooms were beside each other near the entrance to the airport.

He stopped beside an airport security guard. "Can you watch this trolley so we can use the facilities? It was a long drive."

"No problem, sir."

"Sarah, I need to use the restroom. Take Max with you into the women's restroom. Don't come out for ten minutes."

"But we need to get through security. Max is a boy. Take him with you."

"I can't wait, sorry."

He hurried away before she had a chance to argue the point further. Looking over his shoulder, he waited until Jessica and Bryce went into the ladies' washroom to make his move. He whistled on his way into the men's room, acting nonchalant, to draw attention from his followers. They wanted him more than Jessica and Bryce.

As he passed the mirror by the sink, he detected

movement behind him out of the corner of his eye. The three stalls in the men's room were unoccupied and the only other man in the washroom stood at the hand dryer for a few seconds before leaving. The stalls would offer the most privacy. As Jon swung the door of the furthest one open, a fast set of footsteps approached from behind.

Jon closed the stall but didn't lock it. Through the crack in the door, he could make out the man from the gas station. He stood about five and a half feet, a head shorter than Jon, the smaller of the two men, and he carried at least thirty pounds less on his frame. *Come closer. That's it. Now.* Jon leaned his shoulder into the door, slamming the metal into the man's face.

The man stumbled backward. Blood trickled out of his nose. He sneered. "You're gonna pay for that."

Jon exited the stall and closed the gap between them. "I'd like to see you try." He gritted his teeth and cleared his mind, forcing back the rage wanting to blind him.

"Yeah, I'll wipe the floor with you." The man threw a fast, obvious right uppercut.

Fighting with anger instead of reason was the best way to lose a fistfight. Clearly, his opponent had forgotten that basic rule. Jon grabbed his wrist, twisted his arm behind his back, and propelled him into the second stall.

Can't have witnesses. This has to end fast.

He pressed his attacker's face against the back wall, leaning him awkwardly over the toilet, and frisked his pockets. In the man's right coat pocket his hand closed around something long, skinny, and cylindrical. *A syringe.*

The man tried to twist out of Jon's grip. "Let me go. I'll leave you alone."

Jon pulled the needle out of the man's pocket and held it in front of his face. "What's in here?"

"A strong sedative. We were supposed to knock you out and drive you across the border."

"How long does this stuff last?"

"Twelve hours, at least. Last guy I used it on was out for sixteen."

Jon stuck the end of the syringe in his mouth, pulled the cap off with his teeth, and spat it out on the floor. *Perfect. At least I don't have to break his neck.* "Hold still."

"What?"

Jon stuck the needle into the carotid artery of the man's neck, hoping the major artery would spread the drug into his system faster, and pressed the plunger halfway. The man's body went limp in Jon's grasp. Grunting under the dead weight, Jon spun him around and positioned him in an awkward sitting slouch on the toilet, locked the stall, pulled himself over the metal wall into the adjacent stall, then left the washroom.

Where's the second man?

****

Jessica guided Bryce past a few women chatting as they washed their hands, into the large, handicapped stall, the one furthest from the door, and locked it.

"Mom, I don't have to pee."

"We're safer in here for the time being. Your father said to give him ten minutes."

Bryce sighed. "Okay."

The women's voices moved further away. Silence settled over the washroom.

Bryce asked. "Has it been ten minutes yet?"

"No, buddy. Just a little while longer."

Thudding, heavy, yet swift footfalls echoed across the tile floor, moving toward their stall. They belonged to either a large woman or a man.

Jessica leaned toward Bryce and whispered in his ear. "Don't move. Stay quiet."

He nodded with wide eyes.

She positioned her body in front of Bryce and peered through the cracks along the door. *Almost sounds like Jon.* Except Jon would call them by name rather than waste time searching the bathroom. She saw the back of a dark-haired man's head as he pushed open the stall doors on the opposite wall.

How dare he come after me and my son! Lowlife scum!

Jessica slipped her hand inside her purse and felt her way into the back zippered pocket where she kept pepper spray. Her hand caressed the familiar, round, metal canister.

She pulled it out slowly, not wanting to accidentally squeeze the trigger and pepper them instead of their enemy. Her pulse thudded in her eardrums, one wrong move or missed attempt could be disastrous. She slipped the canister in her pocket. A door on their side of the room creaked open. *No time to lose.*

Jessica yanked the scarf off her neck and tied it around Bryce's face. She whispered in his ear under the cover of creaking hinges. "I'm protecting your eyes. I'll uncover them after I spray the bad guy."

She kissed the top of his head and held him close barely keeping tears in check. What if she never got to hold him again? She let him go and climbed on the toilet seat, grateful she'd worn sneakers. Peeking over the wall into the cubicle next to them, she waited.

An attractive, slim woman with dirty-blonde hair crept into the washroom with something black in her hand. She unraveled it and pulled it over her head. *A balaclava. The woman from my house!*

The woman came up behind the large man, jumped, swung her arm back, then landed a karate chop on his neck. "Hiya!"

The man crumpled onto the floor.

The woman raised her head and met Jessica's eyes. "Hurry. Take Bryce and go. He won't be out for long."

Jessica pulled the scarf off his eyes. "Come on, Bryce." She took his hand and led him out of the stall.

Their rescuer blocked their path. "Don't tell anyone about me, or this, including your husband. Nothing happened in here. Got it?"

Jessica said, "I won't. I can't thank you enough for this and for the men in Cochrane. Who are you?"

"There's no time for chit-chat. You never saw me. Get out of here. Now."

****

Jon jogged out of the men's bathroom and around the corner to the ladies. He glanced around making sure no one paid him any attention. Everyone seemed to be moving with a purpose toward their destinations. He ran inside the women's washroom and came face to face with Jessica and Bryce. A man lay on the floor behind them.

"You guys, okay?"

"Yes."

"How'd you knock that guy out?"

Jessica looked over her shoulder and shrugged. "It wasn't us. We were in the handicap stall and another woman got offended by his presence in the ladies', I guess. She chopped him in the neck and left."

Bryce glanced between his mother and Jon but said nothing.

Something sounded off about her story, but there was no time to press the issue. He took the syringe with the rest of the drugs out of his pocket and jabbed it in the man's neck.

Jessica asked, "What's in the syringe? Where did you get that?"

"The other guy followed me into the men's room. I found this in his pocket and used it on him before he could jab me." Jon grabbed the man by the armpits and dragged him into a stall.

"Do you need help, Jon?"

"No, sweetheart. He's too heavy for you in your current condition."

Jon's back screamed as he lifted the man into a sitting position on the toilet. He locked the stall, then slid out into the one beside it. "Let's go. Hopefully no one finds these guys before our flight takes off."

If the police carted me off to jail, leaving Jess and Bryce alone—best not to think that way.

They exited the bathroom, checked their luggage at the baggage counter, and went through security. In the lounge by their gate, they settled into chairs in a corner away from everyone else to wait for their boarding call.

Jon tucked the bald skin wig in the pocket of his carry-on suitcase, then ran his hands through his hair to dislodge as much gel as he could. "Take the wig off and unpin your hair. Put the toque on Bryce."

Jessica followed his instructions. "Why?"

"We'll look different in case anyone finds those guys and reviews the camera footage. The disguises are useless since those guys saw them. When they wake, they'll tell their boss about them."

"How long do we have?"

"The smaller guy told me it was a potent drug. Twelve to sixteen hours. They both got a half dose so we should have about six hours which is plenty." She shook out her hair, which caused her bigger pregnancy bosoms to shake, temporarily muddling his brain. "Um—we're more likely to get stopped by security or police."

She leaned into him and breathed in his ear. "What did you do with that duffle?"

His body warmed a few degrees. *Shoot, she made the connection.* "It's safe. Sam will retrieve it from the motel office and send it to us."

"So, we have no weapons?"

He held up his hands. "Sweetheart, these are deadly weapons with my training. Plus, Sam will have someone stash something at the safe house for me." He paused. *Damn.* "Don't look behind you. Three security guards are searching the lounge across from ours."

The flight attendant made an announcement. "Now boarding first class, flight 760, to Los Angeles."

Jon stood. "Come on, guys. That's us. Take the passports and boarding passes, Sarah. I got the luggage."

Bryce touched Jon's arm. "We won. We got away from those bad guys chasing us. We're safe now, right?"

Jon patted his shoulder. "Yes, we are." *I hope we are. What else could possibly go wrong?*

Chapter Thirteen

After two uneventful flights, Jessica gazed out the passenger window of the black SUV assigned to them at the airport, along with house keys, an address, a revolver, and a map.

They'd just driven past a two-tiered, green metal, "Welcome to Bountiful" sign. The rolling hills and snow-capped mountains surrounding the city reminded her of home. A sense of calm washed over her. They could make a good life here for however long it took for their nightmare to end.

She peered into the back seat at Bryce who stared out his windows. "What do you think of our new city, Max?"

"Do they have Happy Clowns restaurants here?"

Jon chuckled. "There must be one somewhere. Hungry, Sarah?"

"Yes, actually. I could go for a nugget meal. I'll search the navigation." She typed Happy Clowns into the point of interest tab and hit search. "There's one in West Bountiful."

Bryce cheered. "Yeah! I like it here."

Jon glanced at him in the rear-view mirror and smiled. "A man after my own heart."

"Dad, are there bad guys here?"

"Haven't seen any since the airport in Canada. We're safe now, buddy."

After the drive-through, Jessica set the navigation for their new home. She braced for a dirty hole-in-the-wall. *Hope for the best but prepare for the worst.*

Jon turned onto what would be their new street. Massive trees lined either side in front of mature, well-maintained, ranch-style houses spread out on large lots. A typical, snow-covered, suburban American neighborhood in the winter. The navigation system announced their arrival in front of a large, red-bricked rambler with a long driveway leading to a two-car garage.

Jessica studied the house. "Is this the right place? There's smoke coming out of the chimney."

Jon fished inside his pocket and retrieved the slip of paper he'd been handed at the airport. "Yep. This is it. You stay here. I'll go check it out."

He left the engine running and strode up the concrete walkway leading to the front door with his holster open and his hand on a revolver.

Jessica's heart raced.

The front door flew open. Sally raced outside and wrapped her arms around Jon's shoulders.

Any reservations Jessica had about sharing a home with her mother-in-law vanished without a trace. After what they'd been through the past few days, the face of a familiar loved one was a blessing.

Bryce pulled on the door handle, but the child lock kept him inside. "It's Grandma."

Jessica chuckled. "It sure is. Pretty exciting having her here, eh?"

"Mom, let me out."

"Hold your horses." Jessica climbed out of the SUV. The wind stung her cheeks. She pulled her hood over her hair and opened Bryce's door. She tugged his toque over his ears and zipped his coat. "Go ahead, buddy."

Instead of pushing her away like he normally would when she straightened his clothes, he kissed her cheek. "Thanks, Mom."

She touched her face and smiled. He'd gotten to the age where girls had cooties, and kisses were fleeting in nature. Bryce ran up to Sally and wrapped his arms around her legs. He'd warmed up to Jon's soft-hearted mother quickly.

Debbie came out in her coat and boots with Sally's coat draped across her arm. After Debbie handed Sally the coat and accepted a hello embrace from Bryce, she wrapped her arms around Jessica and held her close. "Oh, thank God, you made it in one piece. We were worried sick."

"It's good to see you. I'm so happy you're here. I thought you'd stay at the farm with your rifle."

"Trent promised to take care of the farm. Come on in where it's warm. I'll put the kettle on. We have a fire blazing."

Jon patted his mother's shoulder. "Go on in with Max and warm up, ladies. I'll bring in the bags."

Debbie looped her arm around Jessica's and led the way. "Wait till you see this place. Six bedrooms, three baths, and a renovated kitchen."

The front door led her into a large living room with maple hardwood flooring. The focal point was the wood-burning fireplace. Jessica inhaled the homey scent of wood, reminding her of the living room at the ranch in Lewistown. They hung their coats on the wall pegs in the mud room and lined their wet boots by the door to dry.

Bryce sat on the rug in front of the television with

his bag of toys and flipped through channels while Jessica, Jon, and Sally settled onto the cozy, broken in, black leather sectional beside the fire.

Debbie walked through the adjoining dining room into the spacious kitchen. "Did you three eat? I could reheat some of the stew we made earlier."

"It's okay," Jessica said. "We stopped at Happy Clowns on the way. Tea is perfect."

Jon pulled Jessica's legs into his lap and rubbed circles into the balls of her feet. "How are you handling all this?"

"Now that we're safe, I'm exhausted. The adrenaline is totally gone."

"Good. Means you and the baby are relaxed."

"As long as you're here, I'll be calm."

Sally perked up. "Where else would he be?"

Jessica pursed her lips and stared at Jon.

Jon sighed. "I'm here for the time being. If the feds don't make good progress in the next few months, I'm taking matters into my own hands."

Sally unleashed the mom look, complete with narrowed eyes and crossed arms. "What exactly does that mean?"

"I'll take out the man who's after us so we can go home and live in peace."

"Jon, you're retired. It isn't your place. Let the FBI take care of it."

"That's the thing, Mom. They haven't done a good job of that so far."

Sally said, "They got us all here safely, didn't they?"

"Trent didn't do a good job," Jon said. "Debbie protected you when those thugs broke into her house. And we didn't have an easy time getting here either. Two thugs followed us the whole way and tried to kidnap us at the airport."

"What? How would they have gotten you out of there without being noticed?"

"Luggage. They make big suitcases, Mom."

Sally paled. "My goodness. How'd you get away?"

Debbie set a tea set on the table and distributed mugs and spoons. "I'd sure like to hear about that, too."

After everyone fixed their tea, and Debbie settled in next to Jessica, Jon told them about their adventures in Red Deer and Edmonton.

Jessica bit her lip. Whoever their female rescuer was, she'd specifically asked to keep her existence a secret. But after her appearance on the nanny cam in Cochrane, the mystery woman was already on Jon's radar. With them miles away from Edmonton, she had to come clean if she expected Jon to be honest with her.

Jessica cleared her throat. "There's more to the story."

Jon said, "I thought so. What happened?"

"It wasn't just any woman in the airport washroom," Jessica said. "It was the same one who shot those men in Cochrane. She had the same balaclava."

Jon asked, "Why didn't you say so in the first place?"

Jessica said, "She asked us not to tell anyone about her. Given she was still in the washroom hiding, I decided to wait to tell you."

"Who could she be? And how would she know where to find us? The only explanation I can come up with is that she's connected to either Jones or the FBI." Jon sighed. "Either way, she helped us, so I guess it doesn't matter."

Jessica wiggled her foot to give Jon the hint to keep rubbing. "How worried should we be about being found?'

"Jones is a multi-millionaire with tons of contacts. From what I read in the FBI file from Sam, they've traced Jones' operation to various locations on both sides of the border. They have no stakes in Utah, which is why this location was chosen for us. Given enough time though, you can find anyone anywhere. We need to have our guard up."

Jessica sipped her tea, studied the faces of the loved ones surrounding her, and counted her blessings. They'd all been dragged into this mess with Hugh Jones by association, and they accepted it with grace. No one flung blame or uttered a single complaint. Instead, they surrounded them with love and understanding. And by some miracle, they'd all made it to Utah. She prayed to whoever might be listening their luck would hold, and Jones wouldn't find them.

****

Hugh sat across from Angel in an upscale Italian restaurant in downtown Kansas City. Candles in sconces lit their small, private dining room away from prying eyes. Total privacy was well worth the added expense of the reservation, especially for Angel.

Her perfect, curvy, long-legged figure commanded attention from everyone around her. When they'd entered the restaurant, people stopped eating to gawk. Nothing aggravated him more than stares from simple-minded, nosey, jealous bystanders who were beneath him. How he longed to unleash bullets on them all.

But he had her all to himself now. He swirled the expensive Cabernet in his glass, inhaling its earthy tones, before swishing a large mouthful inside his cheeks.

Angel smiled. "I love the wine you picked. It's delicious."

"Nothing like fine wine in the company of a fine woman."

"I've enjoyed spending time with you, too. Will you tell me more about yourself?"

Isn't that sweet. She's interested in me. "Depends on what you want to know."

"Anything. You're a foodie. What else do you enjoy?"

"You."

Her cheeks turned an adorable shade of pink as she chuckled. Something about the rich, warm tone of her voice and her dainty, graceful movements stirred emotions in him he'd never felt before. *Must be getting soft in middle age.*

She fingered the stem of her glass. "Besides me. Do you like movies, ballet, art, opera, music?"

"I used to enjoy the theater. It takes extra talent to perform live without outtakes and all the computer-animated, garbage effects. It's been—my goodness—at least five years since I've been."

"That's a real shame."

"It is. We'll get Chuck to find us tickets. Thank you for jogging my memory. You're good for me."

"I'm glad. You're my hero. My Richard Gere. Handsome like him, too." She reached across the table and took his hand. "I feel like Julia Roberts in *Pretty Woman* with the new clothes and the wining and dining."

The ringing of Hugh's phone interrupted their tender moment. He scowled and glanced at the screen.

Recognizing a Canadian area code, he answered.

"Yes."

"Mr. Jones, this is Carl Franz. My men missed their check in, and I can't reach them. They last reported tracking the targets to a motel in Red Deer outside of Edmonton."

More incompetence. Hugh paused to rein in anger simmering at the surface and threatening to boil over. "How many men did you send?"

"Two."

His voice inadvertently rose an octave. "Just two? Your incompetence irritates me. You don't cheap out on a job for me. The cost of my transportation services just quadrupled."

"What? That's outrageous. I won't—"

"Cross me again, and you'll regret it." Hugh pushed the end button on his phone, longing for the old days when he could slam a phone receiver onto its base after that sort of aggravation.

Candlelight reflected concern in Angel's bright, evergreen-colored eyes. "Everything okay?"

"Some unpleasant business. Nothing to concern yourself with."

"I'm here if you need me."

How touching. "I'm fine."

There was a lot more to Angel Saunders than met the eye. A warm, tender heart lay beneath those luscious breasts. With his domineering persona, he saw terror, respect, and loathing in the eyes of those around him, never concern, warmth, or tenderness. Funny how it never bothered him until now.

He enjoyed being the man in charge, the one everyone feared, but maybe there could be more to life. After all, he'd done a lot of awful things and he wasn't getting any younger. Maybe in private he could be a good, doting caregiver to a woman he'd saved from a dim, unpromising profession and redeem himself.

Angel stood. "Please excuse me while I visit the ladies' room."

"Of course."

The minute the door to their lounge shut behind her, his blood pressure climbed. He hated letting her out of his sight in public where anyone could steal her away. Having Angel under his roof wasn't enough. He needed to stake his claim and make his intentions known to the world. But first, he needed to get the ball rolling on Jon Kent.

His nemesis would be even harder to capture after all the failed kidnapping attempts.

Hugh grabbed his phone off the table and scrolled through his contacts for an important phone number. He called this number sparingly because Ed Henson, the single best investigator/assassin in the United States, charged exorbitant rates.

Hugh hesitated before sending a message. The promise he'd made to David Hayes to kill Jon's pregnant wife weighed on him. A twinge of guilt had burdened him for years since he'd had Henson kill Jon's first wife, and she hadn't been pregnant. Most women and children were gentle creatures by nature and didn't deserve a violent death. Thinking of his own Angel, he made his decision. *The hell with David. Helping him across the border was enough.*

Hugh typed a text message and hit send.

—*Find Jon Kent. Bring him to me yesterday.*—

Bubbles appeared on his screen then a reply.

—*Busy. Want me to drop what I'm doing? Pay*

double on delivery.—

Hugh rolled his eyes. A lot of money, but well worth it to get the pleasure of witnessing Kent hogtied, beaten black and blue in front of him. He texted his reply.

—Done.—

Chapter Fourteen

Jon added another thick log to the fire burning in the living room hearth. The blustery winter winds and the frigid temperature outside created an uncomfortable draft throughout the house. Being stuck inside day after day, instead of having a ranch to care for, meant having tons of energy and few ways to burn it.

For a month and a half, they'd all been holed up together inside the house ordering everything online, including groceries. The women had taken over the kitchen to keep busy. Poor Debbie, also a farmer used to nonstop work, baked cookies daily and dusted clean surfaces for something to do. Bryce played in the fenced backyard and did the work the homeschooling network provided without complaining, but he had to be feeling trapped.

Jon had taken Jessica out once to meet an obstetrician at the nearby hospital. The others hadn't been out of the house at all. Something had to give. The latest update from the Kansas City FBI field office mentioned an operative being almost established within Jones' inner circle. Almost wasn't close enough. Jon set a mental timeline for the end of the month in just over two weeks. If the FBI couldn't produce concrete results by then, he'd go after Jones on his own, despite Jessica's reservations.

Sally kneeled beside him and placed a hand on his

shoulder. "Son, this isn't easy on you, but you're doing a great job staying here protecting us."

"Thanks, Mom."

"I was thinking maybe Debbie and I could take Bryce to a matinee. The movies are dark and usually deserted on a Tuesday afternoon. He needs a break."

"He does. Make sure Debbie takes the revolver."

"I will. Do something special with your wife. She needs it."

Jon stood and brushed wood dust off his hands. He found Jessica sitting at the table in the kitchen nook with a mug of tea, scribbling in a notebook.

He gave her shoulder a gentle squeeze. "Hey, sweetheart. Did my mom mention taking Bryce to a movie?"

"Yes. I'm a bit nervous about it, but I'm sure it'll be okay."

"They'll be fine. We've been careful, and every delivery person has been legitimate."

She twisted in her chair to face him. "You've been patrolling at night, haven't you? Walking around the block?"

"You noticed? Thought you were sleeping. I didn't mention it because I haven't found anything, and I didn't want to make you uneasy."

"I figured if you saw anything, you'd let us know."

Debbie, Sally, and Bryce came into the kitchen bundled in their winter gear to bid them farewell. As Debbie was about to shut the back door behind them, Jon asked, "Do you have *everything* you need?"

Debbie patted her handbag and winked. "Yes, we do. We have the keys and lots of money for snacks." She trudged out the back door and headed toward the garage.

****

Snakes coiled in Jessica's stomach as she watched them enter the garage from the kitchen window. "Aunt Debbie will keep them safe. Right?"

Jon wrapped his arms around her middle and snuggled her against his body. "They'll be fine. Besides, if Jones had any clue where we were, his people would have surfaced by now."

"You're right."

The SUV backed out of the garage. Bryce waved at her from the passenger seat. Jessica waved back and blew him a kiss. As they drove out of sight, alarm bells rang in her head, but she chalked them up to paranoia after all they'd been through.

Instead, she focused on the heat radiating off Jon's hard muscles and sending tingles across her skin. She spun to face him, pressed her body against his, and ran her hand along the stubbly, short beard he'd grown since they arrived. "We're finally alone."

"That we are. Took long enough." He lifted her tunic sweater over her head and tossed it on the kitchen table.

The cold draft from the window raised goosebumps on her warm, sensitive skin. A delicious blend of hot and cold. She popped open the buttons of Jon's plaid shirt and pushed it off his broad shoulders. Wrapping her arms around his back, she pressed her bare skin to his, and kneaded his lower back. He trailed kisses from her ear to her collarbone, and lower to her pregnancy-swollen breasts.

She moaned. Tension built low in her stomach. "We better take this to the bedroom in case they forgot something."

He lifted her off the ground. She wrapped her legs

around his waist, giggling as he jogged around the corner and down the hallway to the master bedroom. Using her foot, she pushed the door shut.

Jon eased her onto the bed the way he always did, as if she was made of porcelain, and leaned over her, propped on his elbow.

Gazing into his loving eyes, she reconnected with his soul. "I missed this so much." She trailed her fingertips over the stubble on his cheeks, relishing the scratchy sensation. "I missed you."

He smiled and kissed the tip of her nose. "Me too, sweetheart. There aren't words strong enough for how much you mean to me." His lips caressed hers in a soft embrace.

She parted his lips with her tongue and explored his mouth slowly and thoroughly. Boy, could he kiss. Jon's kisses still made her dizzy. They had at least two hours to themselves, and she intended to savor every moment.

****

Debbie scoured the parking lot as Sally drove them into the large outdoor mall. "Park as close as you can get."

Sally asked, "Where's the theater?"

Debbie said, "It's in the corner on the left. Across from the department store."

"Okay. Now I see it." Sally parked near the front of the lot. "Let's try not to use our names at all for anything, okay? If you want to tell us something, Max, call us Grandma and Auntie. And make sure you hang onto one of our hands."

Bryce replied, "Okay, Grandma."

"Stay here." Debbie put her hand on the passenger door handle. "Let me check things out first."

Debbie circled the SUV. Nothing could happen to her great-nephew while they watched over him. A dark-haired man Jon's age and size, a few rows over, glanced in her direction before crossing the lot and entering the department store. No one else gave Debbie a second look.

She opened Bryce's door. "Come on, you two. I reckon the coast is clear."

He climbed out and took Debbie's hand. "Let's hurry. I don't want to miss the previews."

Sally chuckled and took his other hand.

Bryce tugged on their arms, increasing their pace. Debbie didn't mind in the slightest. The sooner they were inside a dark room, the better. She held the heavy glass door for Bryce and Sally. After the two went inside, Debbie turned and took another look over her shoulder.

The man who'd crossed the lot minutes earlier stood beside his black sedan talking into his phone without a plastic bag in his hand from the department store. She took her phone out of her coat pocket, zoomed in on the man, and snapped a picture of him and his car. Unfortunately, she couldn't see the license plate. Maybe he needed privacy for his call. *I'll keep an eye out for him.*

****

Jon sprawled in bed with Jessica's head on his shoulder. She'd drifted off with an arm across his stomach and her leg draped across his shins. Pent-up tension had vacated his muscles for the first time in weeks, but sleep evaded him. Ever since Adam had invaded his dreams, insomnia plagued him. He couldn't let his guard down to sleep.

The only one aware of his sleep issues was Debbie;

they'd agreed Jessica didn't need to know. Debbie had noticed the bags under his eyes a week and a half ago and volunteered to stay up every third night and keep watch. Those were the only nights he got any sleep.

His mind drifted back to their safety, as it always did. His two-week timeline for the FBI to make progress had to be firm. Any longer left them too vulnerable to attack. If he needed to leave for Kansas City to take care of Jones, Debbie would need help guarding the rest of them. Jessica needed her sleep, and he doubted his mother would be able to shoot a fellow human being if the need arose without hesitation. He couldn't ask Sam for help because the FBI wouldn't want Jon interfering with their operation.

The only person he could think of who would help without alerting the FBI was Thomas Gaines, a freelance surveillance expert and computer genius. Thomas wasn't the brawny combat type, but he could set up cameras, motion detectors, hack into anything imaginable, and shoot any type of gun. He'd been a huge help during David's rampage the previous summer.

Guilt raised its ugly head as Jon studied Jessica's serene, beautiful face in sleep. She wanted him to stay. Should he trust his old colleagues to get the job done? If only there was a way to reach the undercover agent in Kansas City for more information.

His phone buzzed in the pocket of his jeans on the floor, pulling him out of his thoughts. He nudged out from underneath Jessica, kneeled on the carpet, and dug out his phone.

Debbie's text churned his gut.

—*I think we're being followed by this man.*—

An image popped up on the screen of an assassin he

recognized, Ed Henson. *Shoot. This is bad. Really bad.* He closed the bedroom door behind him and called Debbie.

She picked up after the first ring. "Jon. Thank God."

"Debbie, where are you?"

"In the theater. I went outside after the movie to check things out and spotted him for the third time. What do we do?"

A month and a half. It only took six weeks for Hugh Jones to find us. "Make sure there are a lot of people in the parking lot when you head to the SUV. Don't let on you know he's watching. Come straight home. Park by the back door. I'll be waiting there for you."

"But won't that lead him straight to us?"

"He already knows where we're staying. No way it's coincidence he appeared at the mall near you."

"Okay then. I'll get them home safe."

"Don't worry. I'm hanging up now to contact the feds for help." *You got some explaining to do, Sam.*

He stared at his phone after ending the call. With the connection to Debbie gone, the adrenaline kicked in at full blast. Not wanting to go into the bedroom and risk waking Jessica, he took the basement stairs, two at a time, to the laundry room in the basement. He opened the dryer and dug through a load of laundry for a clean set of clothes.

Once dressed, he texted Sam.

—Ed Henson is here. If the undercover is so close to Jones, how did you not know?—

Bubbles appeared on his screen followed by a message. At least Sam was being prompt in his reply.

—We've cloned Jones' phone. He hired Henson a few weeks back. I assumed Henson would contact Jones

if he was on your trail. At that point I would've warned you. The good news is Henson hasn't told Jones where you are.—

Jon shook his head, mind blown, as his fingers danced across his screen.

—If the shoe was on the other foot, I would've warned you. Thanks a lot.—

Sam replied.

—Sorry. Didn't want to worry you for nothing. Agents from the field office in Salt Lake City will be dispatched to track and neutralize Henson. We'll clean up the mess.—

Jon replied.

—Send someone to the house to guard my family.—

Jon entered the combination into the lock of the weapons safe tucked in the basement corner. Avoiding his past and keeping his hands clean of blood was no longer an option. He couldn't trust anyone else with his family's safety. Henson had evaded capture for too many years.

Chapter Fifteen

Jessica stood at a lookout near Bow Summit off the Icefields Parkway in Banff National Park. She stared into the crystal-clear, turquoise waters of Peyto Lake fed by the majestic, snow-capped Rocky Mountains towering above.

For a dream, the vividness of the scene, and her awareness of it, struck her as unusual.

An icy hand gripped hers. She turned her head. "Adam. How?"

"I brought you here. You're dreaming."

"A beautiful choice. Thank you. You proposed here."

His eyes crinkled, and the corners of his mouth lifted. "Thought you'd appreciate it." An instant later, his smile fell, and worry lines marred his handsome face.

Her heart tumbled into the pit of her stomach. He'd chosen a beautiful spot to soften the blow. "What's wrong?"

"When you wake up, Jon's going to tell you about a professional assassin in town. I know your instinct is to keep Jon close to protect the family, but you must let him go. He has to kill this man."

"Will he be, okay? Who'll keep us safe?"

"Jon's strong. Bryce, Debbie, and Sally will make it back to the house safe." His image flickered. "I've said too much. I'm losing the connection."

She could see through him. Tears filled her eyes as all traces of him disappeared including his icy grip. "I love you."

Four words hovered in the air by her ear. "I'll always love you." A cold kiss brushed her cheek.

****

Jessica sat up in bed finding it empty. She swiped tears from under her eyes, then yanked leggings and a sweatshirt from a dresser drawer. Instinct pulled her to the kitchen. Jon stood by the window, wearing his coat and boots holding an assault rifle.

"What happened?"

He glanced her way before returning his gaze to the window. "Debbie spotted an assassin in the parking lot at the theater. They should be back any minute. I wish they'd hurry. Field agents from Salt Lake City shouldn't be far behind."

"Bryce, Debbie, and Sally will be fine. You want to leave us under the watch of the FBI and hunt Henson when they get here."

His jaw dropped. "How?"

"Adam. He told me to let you go and that the others would make it back safe." *Be strong for Jon.* "I don't like you leaving us, but I have to trust you and him."

"Truth be told, I don't like it either, sweetheart. The last thing I want to do is leave you. But I'll be back, fast. I promise."

"I'm holding you to that."

The SUV pulled up to the back door. Jon went outside with the gun positioned over his shoulder, covering the vehicle while Bryce and the women came inside.

Bryce ran to her and wrapped his arms around her

waist, shivering from head to toe. "I love you, Mom."

She clung to him, needing the hug as much as he did. Pulling off his hat, she ran her hand through his silky, dark hair. "I love you, too, buddy. Don't be scared. You're safe. Remember Sam?"

"Yeah."

"He's sending agents to help protect us while they find the bad guy from the theater." Bryce didn't need to know Jon would be doing the finding. "Want some hot chocolate?"

Bryce nodded his approval.

She put the kettle on to boil and brought Bryce to the La-Z-Boy chair by the fire. Debbie and Sally settled onto the couch across from him. Jessica did her best to focus on the task at hand while removing his coat and boots. Letting her fear and worries show wouldn't be good for any of them. Bryce's tremors stopped as he gazed into the flames.

She grabbed a blanket off the couch and wrapped it around his shoulders. "We'll have you warm in no time."

"I feel better already. You're the best mom ever."

"Thanks. I try. The hot water should be ready in a minute. Extra marshmallows?"

"Uh huh."

Debbie stood. "I'll get it."

Jessica shook her head. "That's okay. I know how he likes it. Keep an eye on him?"

Debbie said, "Of course."

Her hands shook as she pulled mugs out of the cabinet beside the fridge and set them on the counter. She gripped the edge of the counter and squeezed.

Jon poured hot water into the mugs. "I know it's hard, sweetheart. But you need to relax as best you can for the baby." He rested a hand on her growing stomach. "I will *not* let anything happen to you or our kids."

Taking a deep breath, Jessica willed her pulse to calm. She needed to put up a confident front for Jon. The last thing she wanted was to distract him from the hunt.

She covered his hand with her own. "I know you'll take care of us, and I know you'll make it home safe."

Jon kissed the top of her head. "I'll dig out the marshmallows. Then I'm calling Thomas. No one's better at securing and monitoring a scene. He can stay inside with you while the FBI agents secure the outside."

"Good. I'd rather have him to rely on instead of strangers. But how long will you be gone?"

"However long it takes, sweetheart. Henson is a professional. I may have to circle him for a bit. Once he's taken care of, I'll be home."

"I have one condition. You contact me from that burner regularly. If you go more than four hours without checking in, I'll call Sam."

Jon nodded. "That's reasonable."

"When will you be leaving? After dinner?"

He wrapped his arms around her and leaned his forehead against hers. "The minute I catch sight of the first fed arriving. If Henson notices the feds, he'll retreat to regroup, then be much harder to find."

"Is this goodbye, already?"

"Yes, sweetheart. It is. Don't tell the others until they notice I'm gone. My mother might try to stop me."

Her voice hitched. "I love you so much. Be careful."

"You know I will. Don't cry. I need you to keep it together, and so does Bryce. He's already shaken."

She kissed Jon and breathed him in, committing his scent to memory. "I better get back to him."

Jessica carried the mugs to the living room and passed them around, stopping in front of Bryce. "Got room for me in that chair, buddy?"

He scooted over to one side.

She squeezed in beside him and draped an arm over his shoulders. The flames in the fireplace danced and swayed, carrying the sweet aroma of the cherrywood through the house. If it wasn't for the troubled expressions on her aunt and mother-in-law's faces, Jessica might be able to fool herself into believing this was all just a dream. A terrible nightmare they would awake from any minute.

****

Jon hung up his phone. Thomas, being the best and most reliable friend Jon ever had, agreed to drop everything to come to their aid once again. His flight would have him to their house sometime in the late evening. Jon planned to be gone long before then.

He opened the hall closet and pulled out a gym bag full of weapons he'd brought up from the basement earlier. He retrieved four boxes of protein bars from a cabinet and emptied them into the front pocket. Luckily, he'd found an insulated skin meant to hold water in the sub-zero temperatures. He filled the skin and capped it.

Resuming his watch, he waited for the feds. Five minutes later, a dark sedan parked on the curb across the street a few blocks down from their house. His phone pinged with a text from Sam informing him the house was under FBI surveillance.

Jon put on his winter boots, coat, and hunting gloves. After slinging the water skin over his shoulder, he picked up the gym bag. He lingered in the entrance to the living room and took in the view of his wife, the love of his life, snuggled in with their son. Wanting nothing more than to join them, he turned and slipped out the kitchen door.

Chapter Sixteen

Hugh inspected his formal dining room. Everything needed to be perfect for the special dinner he'd arranged for Angel. Killing the lights, Hugh took in the ambience. Elegant candles with gold bases sat on the cherrywood sideboard and table, reflecting a warm, yellow light on the sparkling clean, perfectly spaced, white chinaware. A fresh gardenia bouquet cut low enough as not to obstruct their view was displayed in a crystal vase on the center of the table. To the side of it, a bottle of pink champagne, her favorite, sat in a bucket of ice.

She'll love it. It's perfect.

Chuck approached from the adjoining kitchen. "Sir, you've a call on the main line."

Hugh's eyebrow raised. No one ever called the house to speak to him. The landline was reserved for the staff to conduct regular business pertaining to the household. Despite his best attempts at security, a landline would never be safe from eavesdroppers.

"Take a message, Chuck."

"I tried. Apparently, it's an urgent matter needing your attention."

"I'll take the call in my study."

Hugh strode toward the north wing, eager to get rid of his caller ahead of what could be one of the most important nights of his life. He sat behind his desk and flipped a switch to activate a scrambler to interfere with any bugging devices.

He picked up the old-fashioned receiver. "This had better be good."

"Hello, Mr. Jones. Can we speak freely?"

Hugh's temper spiked. A brazen move on the part of David Hayes to call him at home. But a deal was a deal. David had provided credible information about Jon's whereabouts; therefore, he was entitled to an update. There could be an added benefit. If Ed failed, David would be the next best candidate. "Yes. I have a scrambler on the line. What do you want?"

"I want to know why Jon and Jessica Kent are still alive, and I'd like to negotiate a new request."

"I sent an assassin after them." David didn't need to know killing the woman was off the table. David was a man without connections, and Hugh knew what his new face looked like. If David became troublesome, he'd be disposed of after he fulfilled his purpose. "A new request will cost you."

"I figured as much. What do you want in exchange, Mr. Jones? Another favor?"

"Maybe. Depending on what it is you want."

"I want the boy, Bryce Miller."

Jones raised his voice to make his response firm. "No, I won't let you harm a child. I draw the line there."

"I don't want to harm him. I want to raise him. He won't recognize me. I can be his long-lost uncle."

No way I'm subjecting a child to a sicko like you. "No. If you want him, you'll have to do that on your own." Hugh slammed the receiver on the cradle with satisfaction.

With that settled, he could get on with much more pleasant business. He sought out Angel in her wing of the house adjacent to his. He entered her empty sitting room. The fragrance of her lavender perfume contrasted with the charred wood from the fire blazing in the hearth.

"Angel?"

"In here. This necklace is giving me grief. Would you give me a hand?"

He followed her voice into the adjoining bedroom. His breath hitched. She stood in front of a floor length mirror in a black, sparkling, long-sleeved gown with a V-shaped back, ending just above her firm, round bottom. The dress brought out the green of her eyes. She met his gaze in the mirror and smiled.

He moved to stand behind her. "You look absolutely gorgeous, my angel." He took both ends of the necklace and fastened the tiny clasp.

"Thank you." She spun and ran her hands down the front of his jacket. "You're looking dashing in that tux. So, where are we going all dressed up like this?"

"First, dinner in the formal dining room, then a charity ball for the children's hospital."

"Wow. I've never been to a ball. Even better that it's for charity."

Hugh took Angel's arm and escorted her to the dining room. As he believed any gentleman should, he pulled out a chair for her before seating himself. Women, being more delicate and refined, deserved to be treated with greater respect than their vulgar male counterparts.

The past few months with Angel had resulted in a change of pace he hadn't expected. He'd maintained a hands-off approach to his business, allowing those beneath him to do his dirty work. Why immerse himself in the daily grind and frustrations for the sake of higher profits when his business already generated plenty?

Being a middle-aged man, it was high time he settled down.

Their gourmet, Italian menu included antipasto ahead of chicken parmigiana, and a dessert course he'd yet to decide on. During their dinner course, Hugh shuffled pieces of chicken around his plate in anticipation of dessert. He'd have to decide which one would be served.

Throughout their time together, they'd had many conversations as they got to know each other. The one thing he'd never asked about was her work since he didn't want to answer questions about his own. She seemed like a wholesome, decent human being in sharp contrast with her chosen profession. But with such a large decision looming over his head, he needed to know.

"Angel, there's something I've been wondering about. You said you had a proper traditional upbringing in Indiana."

"Yes."

"How could your parents have allowed you to work as an escort?"

"They don't know."

"Why did you do it?"

"Money for veterinary school. I applied for scholarships, but I didn't get any. After how hard I had to work to scrape by during my undergraduate studies, I decided faster money was the better way to go."

Hugh set his fork aside and took her hand. "Why not take out student loans?"

"It would have meant a lot of debt. The escort service paid well. After a year and a half, I would have had enough to support myself through school. But you saved me."

"What do you mean?"

A smile lit her face revealing her perfect white teeth. "You were my first client."

"And your last. You're too good a person to subject yourself to that line of work. Whether or not things work out between us, you'll never want for anything again."

"That's so sweet. How could I ever repay your kindness?"

"Being here is enough." He gestured for Chuck to remove their plates. "Bring us dessert. The chocolate torte, please."

Chuck collected their plates without disturbing the ambience of their meal, then ambled out of the dining room with a slight limp.

Hugh shifted his gaze to meet Angel's.

She asked. "You okay? You didn't eat much of your chicken. It was delicious by the way."

"I'm fine. Glad you enjoyed it."

Chuck slipped into the room and deposited their chocolate torte in front of them before making a hasty retreat.

Hugh studied Angel's face, waiting for her to break eye contact with him to look down at her dessert. But she didn't. "What do you think of the dessert?

Her eyes grew to the size of saucers. She picked up the pink three-carat diamond ring centered on the mound of dark chocolate deliciousness and laughed. "Is this what I think it is?"

Her joy was contagious. The nervous butterflies that haunted him throughout their meal flittered away. Her smile erased all doubts in his mind about how she'd respond.

He pushed back his chair and dropped to one knee

in front of her. "My angel, you've brought so much happiness to my life. I can't remember a time where I've ever felt this content and fulfilled. I never knew true love until these past months with you. Would you do me the honor of being my wife?"

"Yes! Yes! Of course, I will." She placed the ring on her finger and angled it under a pool of candlelight. "Such a beautiful ring. Thank you."

Hugh kissed her before returning to his seat. "I'm glad you like it. We'll begin planning immediately." He dug into his dessert with flourish, his appetite returning.

"Immediately? When do you want to get married?"

"I'm not as young as I once was. I was thinking in two weeks' time we could have our ceremony in the ball room."

She chuckled. "Okay. How many guests? I don't want a big wedding."

"I was thinking just family and close friends if that suits you. No need to include my business associates and casual acquaintances. The quieter we keep it, the better. The media would have a circus if word got out about our wedding date."

"I'd rather that short stint in my former profession stayed quiet, so I completely agree."

"We'll hire a discreet wedding planner to ensure our big day is everything you ever dreamed of."

"This is so exciting. I can't wait. Thank you." Her lips pursed as she stared at her ring.

"What is it? Is something wrong with the ring?"

"Oh, nothing like that. I was just wondering if I should wear it to the charity ball or leave it here, so no one notices. A ring this eye-catching would attract attention."

Hugh set his fork on his empty plate and mulled it over. The ring marked her as his trophy, and off limits, but at the same time they didn't need to attract unwanted attention. "I see the dilemma. Perhaps we should leave the ring at home for the time being. People tend to stick their noses where they don't belong, don't they?"

"Oh, they do. If anyone asks, can we say we met at a coffee shop?"

He threw his head back and laughed. "Yes, an easy cover story to remember since people will ask. The only one who knows the truth is Chuck, and he'd never tell. He's been the household butler since I was a mischievous teenager."

Chapter Seventeen

As dusk descended, Jon searched the backyard of
the safe house with his rifle at the ready. Hard snow
crunched under his boots, making his presence known,
but it couldn't be avoided. Odds were slim that Henson
would be lurking close by without the cover of full
darkness to mask his presence. No, he'd return in the
deep of night to catch them unawares. But he had to be
sure before he left.

Jon swung open the shed door. The strobe flashlight
on his gun revealed dry, thick, undisturbed dust on the
floor. No one had been in there in a long time. He shone
his light inside the garage window in every nook and
cranny including the SUV. *Empty.*

Confident Henson wasn't nearby, Jon trampled
down the path he took, to conceal his distinctive boot
prints. To avoid being spotted by the feds watching the
house, he hoisted himself over the back fence landing
behind the neighbor's garage. His destination lay a few
houses to the left.

For emergency purposes, he'd used cash to purchase
a car from a neighbor, promising to retrieve it later. He
scaled the fences in between houses, then knocked on the
back door of the brown brick rambler.

Allan, the elderly gentleman who sold him the car,
opened the door and waved Jon inside. He peered at Jon
over the rims of his round glasses. "What did you come

to the back door for? You here for the car?"

"Yes, please, Al."

"What took so long?"

Jon told a white lie. "It's a surprise for my wife's birthday. Thought I mentioned that when I paid you. Sorry."

"I don't remember that." Allan lifted a key off the hook hanging on the wall inside the door. "Well. You're here now."

"Thanks. Appreciate you hanging onto it for me."

After bidding Allan farewell, Jon drove off with a beige, five-year-old Chevy Impala. Its nondescript color and tinted windows would allow him to blend in with the other cars parked in the street.

Without Henson's cell phone number to trace his location, all Jon had to go on was Debbie's picture of the black sedan. A new Hyundai Sonata, likely a rental car. One that could easily be swapped for another.

Large snowflakes descended lazily from the clouds as Jon took a right turn. He turned on the wipers and kept just under the twenty-five mile per hour speed limit. He drove past each house in the neighborhood three times and searched every driveway, alley, and street for Henson or his car. He found no sign of either.

Undeterred, Jon parked a few blocks away from his house on the opposite side of the road from the FBI watcher, then killed the engine. Searching outside the neighborhood would be like looking for a needle in a haystack, taking him away from his family. As much as he hated sitting in a car for hours on end, staking out the house and letting Henson come to him made a lot more sense.

****

Jessica set her empty mug aside and debated fixing dinner. Worry for Jon churned her gut, but the others would be hungry, including the baby she carried. Sighing, she shifted out of the massive armchair carefully, not wanting to disturb Bryce who'd fallen asleep beside her after drinking his hot chocolate.

Debbie mouthed, "Dinner?"

Jessica nodded and headed for the kitchen. She stood with the refrigerator door open and took inventory of the contents and what should get eaten first before it spoiled.

Debbie came up beside her. "Fancy anything in particular? We still have chicken casseroles in the freezer. We've all had a trying day."

"Sure. Chicken sounds good for my queasy tummy."

"You, okay?" Debbie's brows furrowed. "The baby making you feel off?"

Sally came into the kitchen and glanced toward the back door. "Where's Jon? I can't find him anywhere."

Tears sprang into Jessica's eyes. She tried to suppress them, but one slipped out and trickled down her cheek. "He left earlier. He's gone to track down Ed Henson."

Debbie wrapped an arm around her shoulder. "Without warning or saying goodbye?"

Jessica looked down at her feet. "He told me not to say anything until you noticed he was gone. He thought you'd try to stop him."

Sally shook her head and clenched her hands together. "He's right. I would have."

Debbie met Sally's gaze. "Be strong for Jon. He's trained for this. You watch. He'll be home in no time."

Sally nodded. "You're right."

"Who'll be home soon?"

Jessica spun around to find Bryce standing behind her, rubbing his eyes. "Dad. He had to go out for a while to take care of something."

"When's he coming back?"

"As soon as he can, buddy." *Unless it's two minutes from now, it won't be soon enough.*

****

Around nine p.m., after Bryce and Sally had gone to bed, Jessica sat curled up in the armchair by the fire across from Debbie. Even with the chaos of their hiding place being discovered, she could barely keep her eyes open. But she was determined to stay awake until Thomas arrived. If anyone could help Jon, it was Thomas.

A knock reverberated in the stillness of the house. Jessica gazed toward the front door. Jon had been the only one answering the door for months. *Must be safe with the feds watching the outside.* She shifted her feet from underneath her legs and stood.

"No. Stay there." Debbie picked up the rifle leaning against the wall by the front door and put her eye to the peephole. "It's okay, Jess."

Jessica let out a breath she'd inadvertently held and made her way to the door, caressing her stomach. All this nervous energy and tension couldn't be good for the baby.

Debbie opened the door. "Thomas, come on in. Hungry? There's leftover chicken casserole in the kitchen."

He smiled. "Sounds delicious."

Jessica took Thomas' coat and hung it on one of the wooden pegs by the door. "Good to see you. Thanks for dropping everything and coming to our rescue again."

"You're very welcome. Hopefully one of these days trouble will stop finding you. Where should I set up?"

"The dining room maybe? There's no office in this house."

"The dining room works. Besides, anywhere near the kitchen is a good place to be with you and Debbie around."

Jessica chuckled. Thomas, although short and thin, ate nonstop.

Thomas opened his laptop and set it on the table. "Any idea where Jon is?"

"No, we haven't heard from him since he left this afternoon."

"Does he have that burner phone he called me from?"

"Yes, he promised to check in with me every four hours."

Thomas opened a browser and punched in Jon's number. "Good. I'll track his phone and keep an eye on his movements."

"That'd be wonderful. Where is he now?"

"Close by. Looks like he's right across the street."

Jessica leaned over Thomas' shoulder to peer at the dot on his computer screen. "I'm glad he's close."

Debbie set a plate and a mug of coffee beside Thomas' computer. "Here we are."

He gestured to the chair next to him. "Sit, Debbie. First, tell me exactly where you spotted Ed Henson."

"I saw him in the parking lot at the mall on south 625th West."

Thomas brought up a map of the area. "Where was he parked? Close to any stores?"

"We parked in the closest spot we could get across from the theater." Debbie pointed to the screen. "About here. He was four rows away from us. Closer to the department store."

Thomas said, "A lot of malls have cameras around their parking lots. If this one does, I'll get the footage. A license plate would be a good start."

"I knew we could count on you." Jessica stifled a yawn. "I need to sleep. Wake us if you need anything."

"I'll be fine. Sleep well." His hands flew across the keyboard.

She'd lost him. Once Thomas started working, he tuned out everything around him. Jessica admired his ability to dial in and tune out the world. Her thoughts swirled in a constant rhythm, planning, and trying to anticipate Bryce and Jon's future needs.

Once in her room, she dropped her clothes on the chair beside the bed. She slipped on an oversized nightgown, then climbed under the covers and cradled her stomach. As tired as she was, sleep wouldn't come. Bryce tiptoed into her room.

"I'm awake, buddy. Why are you out of bed?"

"Bad dream. Can I sleep with you?"

She pulled the comforter down and patted the spot beside her. "Climb in."

Bryce snored lightly almost as soon as his head hit the pillow. Having him in her bed wasn't a habit she wanted to get into, but after a trying day for them, why not? They both missed Jon, and they needed each other. She remembered Adam's words in the dream. *Jon's strong.* Comfort washed over her. Surely fate couldn't be so cruel as to rob her of the father of her child twice.

Chapter Eighteen

As he staked out the safe house from inside the Chevy Impala, Jon's phone buzzed just after two in the morning. He jumped at the unexpected vibration. He fished the phone from his pocket beneath the woolen blanket he'd bundled up in. He'd received a welcome message from Thomas who'd obviously been hard at work since his arrival three hours earlier.

—*I hacked into the mall's surveillance. Got a plate W30 8HR. Black 2018 Hyundai Sonata. Rented under alias Austin Gerard.*—

Jon typed.

—*Thanks. That's a big help. Any chance you could check motels and hotels?*—

Bubbles appeared on his screen ahead of a reply.

—*Already on it. I've started calling.*—

Jon replied.

—*I'll check the closest ones in person. I've got wheels. If you see anything suspicious around the house, call me.*—

Jon turned the key in the ignition and cranked the defroster. He tossed the blanket into the passenger seat and shifted the car into drive. As he was about to lift his foot off the brake, a dark car without headlights rounded the corner at the opposite end of the street two hundred yards away.

Jon shifted the car into park and killed the engine,

grateful his headlights were off. He hoped the exhaust smoke from his tailpipe wouldn't be illuminated by the faint hue of the snowy streetlights on the otherwise black street. All the houses had gone dark hours ago except for his own where Thomas burned the midnight oil.

Jon lifted infrared binoculars to his eyes as the car approached. At a distance, he couldn't make out the facial details of the driver, but they appeared to be a man gauging by the width of the shoulders. *Darn, no front plates in Utah.*

The car slowed in front of his house and stopped in the middle of the street. Jon reached beside the console and pulled out an assault rifle. *Something isn't right. Henson wouldn't be that careless.*

Jon grabbed the door handle and pulled. As he was about to swing the door open, the car drove toward him. Jon ducked in his seat and watched the driver pass in his side mirror. *Not Henson.* The eyes were spaced out further, and the nose bigger, but he drove a Hyundai Sonata and the plate matched.

Henson might not be the driver, but he'd paid someone to drive by. That didn't fit with the Henson from years earlier who always worked alone. But what were the odds of Henson returning the vehicle, someone else renting it the same day, then randomly driving by in the dead of night? *Too many coincidences.*

Jon sat up in his seat, curious to see if the feds had fallen for the distraction. The black sedan watching his house made a U-turn in the middle of the street and pursued the car. *I never would've fallen for that.* He got out of the car with the assault rifle to go along with the knife and handgun in his weapons belt. *Henson is going to show any minute*

Jon put on a burst of speed and sprinted down the sidewalk, then ducked behind his neighbors' garbage cans along the side of their house. From there he could see both his front and back yards through the fence slats. Minutes ticked by with no sign of Henson. *Where are you, you bastard?*

Despite his neck warmer, the hair on the back of Jon's neck prickled. He debated his next course of action. Although he was next door, the distance between him and his family seemed too great. But if he left his position and Henson was near, he'd give himself away.

Jon reflected on his encounter with the first set of thugs in the airport washrooms. They had sedatives. Their mission had been to take *him* alive. Not necessarily Jessica and Bryce, although they would have to be considered a bonus in the eyes of Hugh Jones. That complicated the situation for whoever pursued. A lot easier to kill from a distance than to subdue in close proximity. What would he do if he were in Henson's shoes?

I'm going about this the wrong way. I need to make my location known. Draw him away from the others. Hope he takes the bait.

This plan went against his instincts and all his training, but given the circumstances with Henson nearby, it offered the greatest likelihood of success. Jon tugged his neck warmer over his mouth and nose to fend off a chloroform attack. His clothing layers wouldn't protect from a bullet or a syringe, but he'd have to risk it.

He took long, slow strides through the snow toward the fence separating the neighbor's back yard from the safe house. The snow crunching under his feet echoed in the quiet, stillness of the frigid winter night. Climbing the fence would make him vulnerable. His adversary potentially waited to pounce on the other side.

Jon slung the rifle over his shoulder. His blood pumped faster. He took a few steps back and sized up the fence, steeling himself for what could be the most significant jump he'd ever take. No one in their right mind scaled a fence believing an assassin could be waiting on the other side.

After one last deep breath, Jon took a running leap. His hands reached the top of the fence. Using his upper body strength, he propelled himself over it. As his body dropped, he detected movement to his right. He angled his body in that direction and prepared to meet whoever waited.

His feet hit the ground. Footsteps crunched behind him. He turned, stepping on ice, then slipped. As he righted himself, a figure wearing a black balaclava and parka bent and charged, pressing his shoulder into him. Before they hit the ground, Jon grabbed his assailant by the neck, squeezed, and twisted his body to avoid getting pinned.

The assailant grabbed his forearms, loosening Jon's grip on the man's throat as they landed side by side. The ground jarred Jon's right arm, and he lost his grip. He rolled to get his arm free and reached for his knife. In that split second, something sharp pricked Jon's left arm.

I have minutes. One chance to save my family. Instead of swatting the man's arm away as he pressed the plunger, Jon arced his knife from his belt upward into the man's neck and sliced his throat. The man went still beside him with the empty syringe in his hand, blood sprayed out of his neck, soiling the clean white snow.

Jon's consciousness slipped. He fought to stay awake and focus through the fog in his brain. *Now to make it inside. I pass out, I could freeze to death.* His head spun like the first time he'd gotten into his father's scotch as a teenager. Standing would take too much effort. He dropped on his hands and knees and crawled toward the back door. He made it to the wooden deck and glanced up the five stairs with stars swimming in front of him. He fought to keep his eyes open and reached for the railing. His hand swiped past the railing and landed on the wood.

Crawl up them. Stay awake. Fight. You're almost there.

His hands and knees slipped, motor function failing, but somehow, he clambered up the stairs. A foot away from the door, he reached for the knob, then everything went black.

****

Jessica stood over her sleeping body beside her bed. Bryce snored lightly beside her. *This is one strange dream.* A cold breeze hit the side of her face. She turned and found Adam beside her. Even in her subconscious dream state, she was aware of reality. *Two visits in one day.*

"What's wrong, Adam?"

He glided over to her bedroom window and pulled the curtain. "Come see."

She hustled over and peered outside. A man wearing a black mask lay facing away from her with a massive pool of red spreading in the snow underneath his body. "No, that can't be Jon."

Adam touched her shoulder. "It's not. Look by the back door. See him?"

"Oh my God! No! He's lying face down. What happened?"

"Relax, he got injected with a sedative. He'll be fine." Adam spun her around and put both hands on either side of her face. "You have to wake up to save him. He's freezing to death. He needs a hospital, but you can't go with him. You must stay here."

"No, I …"

"Don't argue. Do it. Wake up, now!"

Jessica pinched her arm hard. The dream scattered, and her eyes flew open. She scrambled out of bed and sprinted down the hallway to the dining room. "Thomas! Come quick! I need your help."

Thomas stood from his chair; eyebrow raised. "Okay. What's the problem?"

"It's Jon. He's on the deck frozen, unconscious, and drugged. Come."

"How do you know?"

"I don't have time to explain, and you'll never believe me."

Jessica flung open the back door. Jon's face lay an inch away, frosty, and unmoving. "No. God, no." She reached under his scarf and put her fingers to his neck. "He's got a pulse."

She shook his shoulder. "Jon! Wake up!"

Thomas scrambled outside beside her. "We need to get him inside. Get his feet."

Jessica picked up Jon's legs. "Hurry!"

Thomas lifted Jon's shoulders. "On three. One, two, three."

With their combined efforts, they carried Jon through the kitchen door and laid him on the floor.

Jessica shut the door, grabbed her phone off the

kitchen counter, and dialed 911.

A male dispatcher answered on the first ring.

She kneeled beside Jon. *Thank heavens.* "We need an ambulance."

The dispatcher asked, "What happened, ma'am?"

"My husband seems to have fallen on his way in from the garage. We just found him outside. He's frosty and might have hypothermia." She proceeded to give them the address.

"Okay, ma'am. Ambulance it is. Sit tight. Won't be long."

She hung up the phone. "Thomas, what do we do about the dead body?"

"I'll turn off the lights and shut the curtains. The neighbors won't notice a body in the middle of the night in the pitch-black dark. Then I'll go outside and direct the paramedics through the front door. They'll be preoccupied with Jon."

"What should I do?"

"Get dressed, then call Sam to clean up the mess. I'm assuming you want to go to the hospital with Jon?"

Adam's warning raised goosebumps on her skin, but she needed to be there. *I'm sure I can get Sam to send an agent to watch over me and Jon at the hospital.* "Yes. But what about the others? The agents watching the house obviously weren't doing their job."

"Go get ready, fast." Thomas yanked the curtains shut. "Don't worry about Bryce or Debbie and Sally. I'll put up cameras around the house and keep watch. Also, I would bet the feds will take watching this place a lot more seriously now."

She kissed Jon's forehead, then scrambled down the hallway. Not wanting to open drawers and wake Bryce, she grabbed her clothes from the chair and flung off her nightgown. Once dressed, she sprinted back to the kitchen, grabbed her phone, and kneeled beside Jon. His steady pulse kept hysteria at bay as she phoned Sam to tell him about the body in the backyard.

Chapter Nineteen

Jessica sat beside Jon's hospital bed for the second time in the past year, waiting for him to wake. Far too often for her liking. Tonight, thanks to Adam, she'd found Jon in time. He had a mild case of hypothermia but would be fine once the sedative wore off.

Two feds, one male and one female, were stationed outside the door. They'd quieted the doctor who'd wanted to contact the local police after seeing the illegal sedative in Jon's lab results. Jessica agreed as Jon had killed someone in their backyard. The fewer the people that knew that tidbit, the better.

After Adam's warning to stay away from the hospital, the FBI presence comforted. But why did Sam send two agents instead of one? When she asked, they said they were still investigating. But investigating what was the question. Henson had to be the dead guy in the yard. Who else could it have been? Maybe the feds feared Henson had shared their location with Hugh Jones?

A short female nurse with her hair pulled back in a severe bun came into the room. "Hello. I'm checking his vitals. They're fantastic. You doing okay? All this must be stressful for you and the baby."

Jessica instinctively wrapped her arms around her stomach. "We're fine."

"Are you sure? I have a friend who's a nurse in the

maternity ward. She could give you a quick exam. Listen to the baby's heart with a Doppler."

Jessica shrugged. *Better safe than sorry.* "It couldn't hurt, I guess. We can take one of the guards with us."

"Are you in some kind of danger?"

"We could still be, yes."

"Oh, dear. Well, let's make sure you and that baby are healthy. Follow me."

The nurse led her out of the room. Jessica had her bearings from her last appointment with her obstetrician. The maternity ward was a few floors up. The female federal agent followed them down the corridor, making sure the elevator was empty before she'd allow them on. They rode to the third floor in awkward silence. The door opened, then the nurse led them around the corner to a hallway filled with exam rooms.

She stopped at the last one and ushered Jessica inside. "Go on in. I'll find my friend." She disappeared around the corner.

The agent held her arm out. "Wait. I need to clear the room first before you go in there. Walk in behind me."

Jessica swallowed around a lump in her throat. *What does she know that she isn't telling me?*

The agent pulled the privacy curtain shut. "It's clear. You'll be fine in here."

Jessica sat on the edge of the exam table. "You'll be outside the door, right?"

"Of course. I won't let you out of my sight."

"Can you please tell me what's going on? It wasn't hard to figure out you were assigned to protect me, and your colleague's been assigned to Jon. Something must be wrong."

"I'm not supposed to say anything. Sorry."

Jessica bit her lip to keep in what she really wanted to say— It's my life, I have a right to know what's going on—and instead tried a gentler tactic. "Okay, I understand. I don't want you to get in trouble."

"I'll tell you this much. You deserve to know. We're in the process of determining if it's safe for you in Bountiful, or if we need to relocate your family."

"Relocate again?" Her shoulders slumped. "I guess that would make sense."

"Sorry, I know it's a lot to handle. I'll be outside. Yell if you need me."

Once alone, Jessica pondered another move to a new unknown and unfamiliar town. The one she worried for most was Bryce. Instability and movement weren't good for children. But if it meant being safe, they'd have to move. *Is this nightmare ever going to end?*

The door opened, and a man in scrubs wearing a surgical mask entered the room. "Hello, Mrs. Kent. Let's see how you and that baby are doing. How far along are you?"

Jessica's pulse accelerated. She'd been expecting a female. Male nurses in maternity wards weren't common. Maybe he was a doctor? The agent would've checked his credentials before allowing him to enter.

"I'm in my eighteenth week."

He sat on a stool beside the exam table. "You're due for a WinRho shot." He pulled a syringe out of his pocket and uncapped it.

"No, that isn't right. My doctor would've mentioned it. Besides, my husband and I are RH positive, not negative."

He yanked the fabric of her sweater off her shoulder.

"Just hold still. Better safe than sorry."

Wait, he used my real name! Jessica shifted away from him and scrambled off the examining table. *I should've known something wasn't right!* She screamed, "Help!"

The man came up behind her and wrapped an arm around her neck and jabbed the needle in her arm. "I already took care of your guard. No help is coming."

She stomped on his instep, kicked him in the shin, and wiggled in his grasp, trying to get free. "Let me go! Help!"

He wrapped his massive hand around her throat. "Stop fighting. I don't want to have to do anything that will hurt you and your baby."

She held still. "It's too late. You already gave me that shot. Who attacks a pregnant woman?" She wormed her elbow lose and buried it in his stomach. "You sick bastard."

"Oof. Relax, lady. It's a sedative. Safe for pregnant women. You're only a hostage."

Hostage! Jessica screamed. "Help!" Someone else on the floor had to hear her screaming. *I should've listened to you, Adam.*

He squeezed her throat, limiting her oxygen. "Shut your mouth, or I might be tempted to shut it for you." He released the pressure on her throat.

The room spun. She gasped for air. *I'm running out of time. But I can't fight. My baby can't die. I can't die.*

His voice echoed as if they were in a tunnel. "That's right. Good girl."

****

Jon opened his eyes. *Where am I?* He bolted upright. The room tilted, and his brain was foggy. *Damn sedative.*

The beeping, equipment, and the awful antiseptic smell said a hospital room. Someone must have found him on the back step. *Where's Jessica? She would've come here with me.*

He unhooked his hand from the IV line. Jon checked the tiny washroom inside his room and found no sign of her. He opened the door to his room and peeked into the hallway. Two men, he presumed feds, stood outside.

The larger one on the right spoke, "I'm Agent Rook." He gestured to the other man. "And this is Agent Francis. How are you feeling? Can we come in and talk?"

"Sure. But first, where's my wife?"

"We need to have this conversation away from prying ears, Agent Kent. Shouldn't you be in bed?"

"Don't worry about me. I'm fine." Jon stepped back and held up an arm. "Get in here." He closed the door and flipped the lock. "I'll ask once more, gentleman. Where's my wife?"

They exchanged a look as if deciding who would speak first.

Jon's heart raced. *Something's wrong.* His voice rose a few decibels. "Goddamn it, speak."

Agent Rook said, "We believe Henson kidnapped her from this hospital approximately nine and a half hours ago."

Jon ran his hands through his hair fisting them at the back of his head. "But I killed him. Why weren't you watching her?"

"You killed a different man. One we haven't identified yet. We had a guard on your wife. We think Henson disguised as a doctor, sedated her, put her in a wheelchair, and wheeled her out the delivery bay."

"What about the rest of my family?"

"They're at the safe house. We're moving you and them to a new location tonight."

Jon paced, exercising the rest of the cobwebs out of his system. "Where are my clothes? I need to get the hell out of here and catch the first plane to Kansas City. That's where he's taken Jessica. To Hugh Jones."

"But sir. You're retired. Let the FBI handle it."

Jon stopped an inch from Agent Rook's face. "I'm going. It's not up for debate. You move the rest of my family along with Thomas Gaines and give me the location. And they had better be under tight guard. I won't tolerate any more failures on your part. Do you understand me?"

Agent Rook took a step back. "Yes, sir."

****

Jessica's limbs weighed a ton. She forced her heavy eyelids open. After a split second, they shut on her again. She lay on something soft, and an engine droned around her. *Where am I? What happened?*

Then she remembered her fruitless struggle in the hospital room. Willing her head to the side, she forced her eyes open again. Her kidnapper sat in a chair across from her reading a newspaper.

He looked over the top of his paper and smiled. "You'll be groggy for a while longer. Go back to sleep."

Too tired to fight, she gave into the void sucking her down.

Chapter Twenty

Hugh sat across from Angel at the dining room table amid selections of fabrics, color swatches, and catalogues. Their designer had made suggestions, but Angel requested she leave the samples so they could explore and make selections together. Not Hugh's idea of entertainment, but the pure delight in Angel's eyes had him acquiescing.

He chuckled, thinking of the saying about a happy wife leading to a happy life. Soon she'd be his wife, making him the luckiest, mostly cold-hearted son of a bitch around.

Angel held up a swatch of a deep emerald green. "What's so funny?"

"Nothing. Your joy is contagious. That green is perfect, my angel. It matches your beautiful eyes."

"I agree. That designer was going on and on about pastels being the rage, but they aren't for me." She held it beside Hugh's face. "I think it'll compliment your light skin tone, too."

"Good, we'll use it for all the linens and decorations, along with crisp white dishes."

"Perfect. White roses for my bouquet and the table settings would be lovely."

"It's settled then. That was easy."

Chuck bent beside Hugh's ear and whispered, "Sir, you're going to want to come with me immediately. A matter requires your attention."

Hugh stood without hesitation. Chuck wouldn't disrupt them unless it was important. "I have business to take care of, my angel. Why don't you inform the designer of our choices?"

"Sure. You go take care of whatever that is."

Hugh kissed her cheek, then followed Chuck through the kitchen and down the hallway past a wing of unused guest rooms to the old library. *What in the hell?*

Chuck tipped a first edition of Harper Lee's *To Kill a Mockingbird*. An old lever spun the bookcase to the side, revealing a set of rooms. A sitting room filled with antique furniture and an old wood-burning fireplace led to a large bedroom and adjoining bath. When his great-grandfather had built the house, he'd included these secret rooms to be used as a sanctuary for members of their criminal organization hiding out from the law.

Hugh was only mildly surprised to see Henson sitting in an antique glider. "Where's Jon Kent?"

"He'll be along shortly."

"On his own or is someone else escorting him here?"

"He'll come of his own volition. His wife is your prisoner. She's asleep in the bedroom."

Hugh peeked around the corner. Sure enough, a woman with long blonde hair slept in the bed. "What the hell? You were supposed to bring Kent, not his wife. I don't want her death on my conscience. Get her out of here, now. Then bring me *Jon* Kent."

"I thought you'd be pleased. You had no qualms about me killing his first wife."

"Jon Kent, now!"

"A man in my line of work doesn't stay alive and escape capture by making mistakes. I weighed the options. With Kent already having his guard up from the first sets of morons you sent after him, I had no choice. I couldn't take him down alive like you wanted. My associate tried and got his throat cut. The only way to guarantee you the chance of meeting him face to face was leverage."

"What am I supposed to do with her?"

Henson stood. "We should move this conversation out of here before the meds wear off and she wakes."

Hugh exited the secret passage with Henson and Chuck into the old library and restored the book to its proper position. He ran his right hand through his hair to signal a silent order to Chuck, then pushed a button under the third shelf of the bookcase to lock his captive in. "I can't believe you did this."

"Relax. It'll work out. Keep her tucked away from everyone here, and don't let her see anyone's face. After Kent's dead, blindfold her and drop her off somewhere."

Hugh's skin heated as he fought to maintain his composure. "Get the hell out of my house."

"What about my money?"

"You didn't hold up your end of the bargain. Leave. Now."

Henson stood his ground. "I'll be watching. When Jon Kent shows, you better pay up."

"No one goes against me and lives." Hugh met Chuck's gaze and blinked twice. Their established set of signals served them well. "You'd best remember that."

Henson's voice oozed menace. "You know what I do for living, Mr. Jones. Unless you want to spend your whole life looking over your shoulder, I suggest you fork over the cash."

Chuck pressed a revolver to the back of Henson's

head.

Hugh moved to within an inch of Henson's face. "I'm giving you one more chance to leave. Just one."

Henson ducked. Chuck pulled the trigger. The bullet split wood as it embedded into the wainscoting an inch from Hugh's head.

Henson twisted around Chuck, wrapped his arm around his neck, and pressed his revolver into the butler's temple. "Don't even think of contacting me again. No amount of money in the world will be enough. You step aside and let me pass, or your butler is dead."

Hugh stepped aside. "Fine."

Henson moved down the hall, keeping the gun trained on them until he disappeared around the corner.

"Mr. Jones, sir."

Hugh turned to face his loyal servant. "Yes, Chuck."

"With all due respect, you should've had me pull the trigger instead of giving him another chance to leave. Henson is a snake in the grass."

"I didn't want that kind of mess inside my home. Besides, you heard the man. He weighs risk before making any moves. He wouldn't dare cross me."

"I hope you're right, sir. Shall I prepare a meal and arrange necessities for our unwanted guest?"

"Please do. Who on staff knows she's here?"

"Just me and the guard on duty at the gate. We took her in the secret passage under the statue in the garden."

"Good. Tell the guard to keep his mouth shut. She will make good bait."

****

A mechanical churning roused Jessica. Her eyes opened this time. Whatever she'd been drugged with seemed to have worn off. Her gaze darted around her strange surroundings. She was alone in a bed still fully clothed. That was a relief. She jumped out of bed and padded around the room on the plush, dark-green carpet. A thick layer of dust coated every surface of the old Victorian-era bedroom furniture, including the four-poster bed she'd woken in.

The only source of light came from bright lamps on either side of the bed. Not a single window provided light, giving any sense of what time of day it was, or any means of escape.

Finding a door, she twisted the knob, and it opened. *A proper bathroom. Thank goodness.* After relieving herself she wandered back through the bedroom, finding an elegant sitting room furnished in a similar Victorian manner with an old crystal chandelier hanging from the ceiling. Again, no windows.

An elderly, non-threatening gentleman in a butler's uniform moved an old-fashioned feather duster across the shelves of the bookcases lining the wall. She froze. A cloud of dust drifted by, and she sneezed.

He turned to face her and smiled. "Hello, my name is Chuck. I'm the butler and head of staff." He pointed to a silver serving dish on the coffee table. "I brought you homemade chicken soup and rolls. I wasn't sure what you'd be able to handle after that loathsome man, Henson, drugged you."

She hadn't been expecting smiles, sophistication, and manners in a captor. "Thank you."

Unsure of what else to do, she sat on the sofa staring at the old-fashioned, silver serving set.

Chuck said, "I assure you it's safe."

Not wanting to starve her baby, she lifted the silver dome, revealing a steaming bowl. The aromas of chicken and root vegetables permeated the stale air. Her tummy rumbled. She brought a large spoonful to her mouth. The broth tantalized her tongue with various herbs and spices, a fancy restaurant version of chicken soup rather than something from a can.

Chuck put his duster down and perched on an uncomfortable looking chair across from her. "You won't be harmed. My boss was most upset about your kidnapping. He doesn't want you here."

"Okay, so when can I leave?"

"You can't."

Jessica stopped to consider the situation. Something didn't add up. Hugh Jones was responsible for her kidnapping. Of that she had no doubt. But why wouldn't her kidnapper have killed Jon while he was sedated? And whose throat did Jon cut?

She set her spoon aside. "What will he do to Jon? It's him your boss, Hugh Jones, wants, isn't it?"

"I must go. I'll be back in the morning with your breakfast." He pulled a small bottle out of his pocket and set it in front of her. "Your nausea pills."

"Wait."

"Yes, Mrs. Kent?"

"Please, would you let me call my son? I know you hate Jon, and I won't ask to talk to him, but my poor son is probably beside himself with worry."

"I'll ask my superior."

Chuck tipped a book on the upper shelf of the bookcase. The bookcase swung open, revealing a hallway. Chuck stepped through and the opening slammed shut behind him. She scrambled over to the bookcase and lifted the same book. Nothing happened.

Shoot. There must be a way to lock people in here. Fantastic. Why didn't I listen to you, Adam?

Chapter Twenty-One

Jon climbed out of Agent Rook's car and sprinted up the lane to the front door of the safe house. He let himself in with his key.

"Dad, you're home." Bryce wrapped his arms around his waist. "Where's Mom?"

What do I tell him? Poor kid. I'm barely holding it together. "Don't worry. She's okay. I'm leaving soon to pick her up in Kansas City and bring her home."

"I want to come with you."

"You can't. I'm sorry. You need to go with Grandma, Aunt Debbie, and Thomas. Mom and I will come join you as soon as we can."

"Promise?"

Jon gazed into his son's innocent eyes. "Yes, I promise." *Please let me be telling him the truth.* "We all have to pack. You included. Make sure you don't forget anything because we can't come back here."

Bryce hung his head and walked away, taking a piece of Jon's heart with him.

His son was in pain, and his wife was being held by one of the most despicable men alive. All because of him and serious negligence on the part of the FBI. But dwelling on those negative thoughts wouldn't put his family back together.

Jon hurried into the dining room to find Thomas. Not only did he find him, but also Debbie and Sally, along with another unexpected guest, Sam. Jon wasn't sure whether to be grateful or crucify him.

Sam stood. "Jon, there aren't words for these situations. Nothing I can say will make things better, but I'm here to help."

"Help. Well, that's fantastic. The field office here sure did a stand-up job of that, didn't they?"

"Listen to me. I've been in touch with Dawn Chamberlain, the special agent in charge of the Kansas City field office. Her undercover operative notified her Jessica is being held at Jones' estate, but she's fine. Jones has no intentions of harming her."

"Bull. Hugh won't let her leave alive."

"Hugh is very distracted right now. He's planning his wedding, which is taking place on his estate this coming weekend."

Jon's brow raised. "That doesn't sound like the Hugh Jones I know. Besides, I'm not leaving Jessica there for four days. I told Bryce I'm leaving tonight."

Sam said, "Look if you'd like, we'll fly to Kansas City tonight and visit the field office."

"Okay, that's a good starting point. I'll agree to that—for now."

"I'll involve you in the whole process. I promise. But please, let us do it our way. Then we can move you both to the new safe house in Oahu with the rest of your family."

Jon's voice rose. "Hawaii?" He forced the volume of his voice down so Bryce wouldn't hear him yelling from his bedroom. "How do you not have enough on Jones for an arrest warrant? He kidnapped my wife."

"He didn't ask for Jessica to be kidnapped. Henson did that on his own because he was too much of a coward to take you on directly."

"That may be true, but he's keeping Jessica at that estate against her will. It's enough."

Sam sighed and placed his hands on his hips. "Look, if that's what you want, fine. We'll storm in, find Jessica, and arrest him. But remember, Jones can afford the best attorneys. If we don't have enough, he'll weasel his way out of trouble. We need to get him on something serious enough to warrant a long sentence."

"I'll provoke him. He'll try to kill me. Then you'll have him." *More like help me get to him and I'll kill him myself.*

Sally dabbed her eyes with a tissue. "Jon, no. Do it Sam's way."

"Mom, it's not up for debate. We need to make sure Hugh Jones isn't a threat once and for all. What's the point in rescuing Jess only for her and the kids to be in danger again?"

Debbie wrapped an arm around Sally's shoulder. "Jon's right. If we had let him go after Jones when he wanted to weeks ago, we'd be safe at home in Lewistown. This has to end."

"Well, we better go pack, then." Sally shoved her chair in and wrapped her arms around Jon. "You be careful. You hear?"

"Don't worry, Mom. Jess and I will be in Hawaii with you by the end of the week."

Sam said, "All right, Jon. I'll make some calls. Not sure how your wife will feel about you risking your life. But if you're determined to be bait, who am I to stop you?"

Thomas cleared his throat. "I don't mean to butt in, but how did Henson track you here? If you can't pinpoint the leak, then there's no point moving the rest of us. Jones will find us again."

"I think I know what went wrong," Jon said. "After the altercation in the airport washrooms with the thugs in Edmonton, we had to ditch our disguises so security wouldn't recognize us from their surveillance footage. But that only made it easier for someone like Henson to find us instead."

Thomas said, "That would do it. Security systems aren't safeguarded well. Very easy to hack into."

Sam said, "That only happened because they were on Canadian soil out of our jurisdiction. This time around, federal agents will be moving everyone into protective custody. Hawaii will be safe. We only acquired our first properties there recently, and it isn't common knowledge yet even at the bureau."

"I hope not because someone blew the whistle about Lewistown which started this whole thing. First things first, we get my wife back." Jon stood. "I'm packing a bag. Be ready to leave within the hour."

****

In the wee hours of the morning, after the longest four-hour flight of his life, Jon disembarked the plane with Sam in tow, at the Kansas City International Airport. They couldn't exactly discuss things surrounded by other people, and any common ground they had related to other cases, which were also confidential. After a few failed attempts at small talk, Jon had tried reading and watching movies, but he couldn't focus on anything other than getting Jessica back.

Sam said, "Want to get a hotel for the night and go at this from a fresh set of eyes in the morning?"

Heat flamed in Jon's cheeks as he struggled to

control the rage bubbling to the surface. "How the hell do you expect me to sleep?"

"You have to get a handle on your emotions. I can't even imagine how hard this is, but you've got to detach somehow and get your head in the game. Jess needs you at your best."

"Are you forgetting I took a sixteen-hour nap? Sure, you're right. I need to calm down and maintain a level head. But the only way that'll happen is if we get to work."

"Okay. We'll catch a cab to the field office. The team working Jones' case can fill us in on the details over takeout. Then I'm getting a room. I've been awake for over thirty-six hours."

"Fine. I can read through files while you sleep."

****

With escape being impossible, Jessica dragged the uncomfortable chair Chuck had occupied, to the large bedroom, locked the door, then leaned the chair against the bottom of the knob to stop it from opening. If someone came into her fancy prison, she wouldn't be at their mercy.

Jessica settled onto the bed and leaned back against the plush cushions to consider her situation. She was being kept in a secret area of what had to be a huge mansion, judging by the size of this bedroom, and adjoining bath, plus the sitting room. The house would have to be large to conceal the space they'd locked her in.

The high-end finishings didn't lend to a prison cell. More of a luxury hiding space for Hugh Jones or maybe some of his high-level staff to lie low from the authorities. What bothered her most was not knowing what she'd find on the other side of the bookcase if she managed to escape.

Jessica pondered two options. The first, stay put and try to be a good guest to not annoy her captor while she waited for Jon to rescue her. Jon would come. She had absolutely no doubt. But would he know about this secret area of the house?

The second option, escape. Chuck was a feeble old man. Tons of heavy knick-knacks and decorative pieces cluttered the shelves in the sitting room. After the first day passed, she'd have a sense of how things would be. If Chuck came alone to deliver every meal, she could wait beside the bookcase and bludgeon him in the head to knock him out and run. But then what?

Without knowing the layout of the house, or how many goons to watch out for, she'd have no idea where to hide or which way to go. Hugh Jones might not have as many reservations about killing her if he discovered she'd attacked his old butler.

Jessica held her stomach and the baby growing within. She couldn't risk the life of her unborn child by angering her captor, and Jon wouldn't want her to. Playing nice and trying to get information wouldn't hurt, but she couldn't risk trying to escape without help.

The mechanical clang of the bookcase opening pierced the silence of her bedroom. She leaped out of bed and pressed her ear to the door.

Chuck said, "Mrs. Kent, I brought you some clothing and toiletry items as well as a pitcher of water, a carafe of tea, and a tray of snacks. Help yourself."

After the bookcase clicked shut, she moved the chair and opened the door a sliver. Chuck had left her alone again. She padded into the sitting room. A tray of fruits and veggies and another of meats and cheeses rested on the table in the center of the room. On the sofa, Chuck had left three big shopping bags.

She popped a grape in her mouth and rifled through the bags. He'd brought her five bulky sweaters and five pairs of leggings similar to what she wore, but in much higher quality fabric. The tags were left on everything. Those clothes would've cost her a whole month's pay as a preschool teacher. Another bag held undergarments, and the last one makeup and toiletries. Gauging by the fancy packaging, they also hadn't come cheap.

Healthy food and expensive clothes? When they'd run from Jones' thugs; this hadn't been the kind of treatment she'd anticipated if caught. More like tied to a chair with nothing to eat and drink. If they were trying to soften her anger at being kidnapped and baited to get Jon, it wasn't working. But she'd wear the clothes, use the toiletries, and pretend to be grateful. For now.

Jessica poured tea into a China cup, then lifted it to her mouth. She blew on the hot liquid, then sipped. A square of paper rested on the saucer. She set her tea aside and unfolded the paper. Tiny handwriting covered every square inch of the small scrap of paper. She held it closer to her face.

The FBI knows where you are. Flush this down the toilet. I'll send more info if I can.

Jessica flushed the note. The sender hadn't signed their name, and the message was vague. It didn't say if or when she'd be rescued. She drank her tea and did her best to relax.

At least someone in this house is on my side and knows I'm here.

Chapter Twenty-Two

Jon sipped his sixth cup of coffee in an office at the FBI building in Kansas City. Sam had gone to his hotel for the night leaving him alone to dig through the current files on Hugh Jones. They only went back a few years, and after reading through the last box, Jon hadn't found anything useful. He'd asked for the old paperwork to be brought out of storage from when the FBI conducted the raid on the mansion after Jon's investigation.

After a decade, he still couldn't fathom how Hugh Jones had managed to escape charges with all the damning evidence he'd collected over a year-long investigation. Jon's blood boiled. A judge had excluded the audio tapes he'd risked his life to amass. If anyone had noticed his wire, he would've endured a more painful death than Frank Hennessy did.

A brief knock sounded before the door swung open, and Trent walked in. "Hi, Jon."

"Good to see you, Trent."

"I'm so sorry about Jessica. What can I do to help?"

"Did Sam send for you?"

"Yes. He wants me to keep tabs on you, but I think I have a lot more to offer."

"I can use help. Sam ditched me for sleep."

Trent closed the door and swept his eyes over the desk and ceiling tiles. "That coffee looks like gut rot. Let's find a drive through at a real coffee shop. My treat.

Then we'll come back and dive in."

Jon caught the drift. Trent suspected there may be listening devices, and he had information to pass along. "The coffee is atrocious, and I could use the fresh air to clear my head."

Once they were outside the building, Trent led the way to his rental car. They drove in silence until they were out of sight of the FBI building.

Jon said, "What do you need to tell me?"

"I think you suspect this as well. If I'm open about my suspicions, I need you to promise it stays between us."

"Of course."

"Someone is crooked. I checked out the folks in Lewistown while taking care of Debbie's farm. No one there sold you out to Jones. If the info didn't come from one of us, then where?"

Jon sighed. "I suspected a dirty agent, but I didn't give it a whole lot of thought. I'm more focused on getting my wife back. If you want to keep searching for that leak, I'd be grateful."

"I'll do my best to search discreetly. The minute I log into the server, I'm leaving a trail. If the person responsible gets wind of what we're looking for, things could get dangerous. This isn't our territory."

"If there's a leak in this field office, we'll know by the weekend."

Trent braked at a red light. "How?"

"Local agents briefed Sam and I on a plan to infiltrate Jones' mansion this coming Saturday at his wedding. The catering company has agreed to let agents impersonate their wait staff. Sounds like a solid plan, right? But it falls apart if someone tips Jones off, and he fires the caterers."

Trent signaled right and pulled into a twenty-four-hour drive through. "That would put a wrench in things. But then we would know."

"Apparently, there's an undercover in Jones' inner circle. The special agent in charge here, Dawn Chamberlain, is keeping the identity of this person under wraps and they report only to her. That makes me think she already suspects a leak."

"Sam doesn't know who this agent is either?"

Jon shook his head. "No. Which is probably for the best. The leak could be anywhere. That's why I'm pretending to go along with Saturday's plan but coming up with my own."

"Whatever you need, or decide, I'm with *you*, Jon. I was sent to help your family, and I intend to. You served your country and risked your life. You deserve better than this."

Jon glanced at Trent. *Why is he so determined to help? Is he pumping me for info to take back to Sam?* No, that didn't feel right. But there was something else going on. He'd keep Trent close until he figured out what it was. "Thank you. It's nice having someone on my side. First things first, we search that office for bugs, then we get to work."

They returned to the office and discovered a mountain of file boxes stacked against the wall from floor to ceiling. After sweeping for bugs to ensure their privacy, they unstacked the boxes and divvied them up.

Jon downed the rest of his Americano and dropped the empty cup in the wastebasket. "Well, at least there are years written on the boxes."

"Do the years correspond to when you were

undercover?"

"Looks like it."

Trent sucked Frappuccino through a straw, then set his drink aside. "There's so much. How did Jones escape all this?"

"Jones never gets his own hands dirty. He gives orders. I had him on tape ordering hits and being present for them as they were carried out by his enforcer, but a dirty judge threw the tapes out of evidence. None of his associates would dare testify against him."

Trent whistled and shook his head. "So, he's a dirty mobster and basically untouchable."

"Legally. But with the internet and social media, if those tapes got out, they'd do him some damage. They might be a bargaining chip to get me through his door without having to kill his security team. We look for them first."

After three hours of searching without success, Jon lifted the lid on his final box and stared inside. He emptied the file folders and stacks of reports onto the floor, finding nothing but the bottom of the box. Even though his tapes were thrown out of evidence, they wouldn't have been destroyed, and transcripts would've been made as he'd turned them in.

Jon stood and ran his hands through his hair. With all this stress, he wouldn't have any hair left if things continued to drag on and go sideways. He went over to Trent's side of the office as he lifted the lid on the last box in front of him. "Find anything?"

"No tapes or transcripts so far." Trent handed him more files before coming to the bottom of his box. "Someone beat us to it and took them."

"Yes. But when? And who? They're a decade old.

There's nothing in the logs of anything being taken from these boxes." Jon kicked the nearest box across the room. "I won't be getting leverage on Jones without them."

****

Hugh leaned against the bathroom door and smiled. His future wife lounged in the tub, up to her neck with bubble bath, wearing only cucumber slices on her eyes. A welcome distraction from the stressful situation inflicted on him by Henson.

His source at the FBI tipped him off to a plan to infiltrate his home using the catering company to get the woman back. The whole situation annoyed him to no end. They'd already done a tasting and chosen their menu. To avoid more complications leading up to the wedding, he'd use subterfuge. He'd retain the catering company and fire them ten minutes before they were meant to arrive.

If the feds had definitive proof he had the woman, they'd be banging down the door instead of sending undercovers to sniff around. Should he dump Jessica Kent somewhere and rid himself of the grief? Jon Kent was on Hugh's territory at the FBI field office downtown. He could send a crew of men after Jon, but with cameras on every building downtown and in every smartphone something could go wrong.

No, he'd hang onto the woman and let Jon come to him. Knowing Jon, it wouldn't be long until he made an appearance.

"My angel."

She took the cucumber slices off her eyes. "Yes, baby?"

"May I join you?"

She sat up and scooted over to one side. "Of course.

Come on in."

He unbuttoned his shirt and let it fall to the floor. "I had to let the caterers go. I heard they had a rat problem."

"Oh no! What are we going to do for food? The wedding is in five days. I thought we had everything planned."

He climbed in the bath. "Don't worry. I've taken care of everything. The head chef from that Italian place you love is preparing the same menu for us." Reaching for Angel's foot, he pulled it into his lap and massaged her instep.

"That's a relief." She moaned and bit her lip. "Umm. That feels good."

Sweet Jesus. His body hardened. He could never tire of arousing this perfect specimen. He sucked on her big toe. "Should we move this to bed? Maybe come back to the tub after?"

She smiled at him with flushed cheeks. "You read my mind."

Who says money can't buy happiness? If he hadn't paid three grand to rent Angel for the night, he never would've met the most amazing and beautiful woman in the world.

She stood and bubbles dripped down her milky, flawless skin revealing hard nipples and luscious curves. No other woman could ever compare. His pulse raced, and his head swam. He clutched the sides of the bathtub as he came to a stunning realization. She wasn't a mere trophy to him anymore, or a demonstration of his status in society. He'd become dependent on this woman. She held his heart in her hands with the ability to crush him, and it was too late to do anything about it.

Chapter Twenty-Three

Meredith tucked her hair under a plain, dark blue ballcap and put on thick eyeglasses before boarding a flight to Washington, D.C. No one would be looking for a woman presumed dead, but she'd lived in the area for too many years not to take precautions. Returning to the site of her old life risked exposure, but she had to do it.

Jon's missing tapes represented almost a full year spent undercover away from her. A year of Jon's life he'd never get back, living amongst the worst types of criminals imaginable. They represented her lonely tears and lost dreams, and they led to her kidnapping which destroyed their marriage. But more than that, those tapes were leverage, and she banked on that value ensuring their survival.

She retrieved a list from her backpack, then for the hundredth time, scanned the names of active and inactive agents who'd logged out the evidence boxes. Given that the tapes had been around for a decade, and the investigation had been ongoing the whole time, the list wasn't short. And the names on it were also scattered all over the country.

The majority lived in Kansas City, but something, call it instinct, pulled her to Washington. A few higher-level agents resided there. Some people moved up the ranks through nefarious or political means having nothing to do with performance. The type of person who might smuggle evidence out of FBI custody for their own purposes.

The seatbelt light blinked on, then the pilot announced their upcoming landing. She tucked her list away and buckled her seatbelt as the plane descended toward Washington. *I'm finally home.* Her heart squeezed. She missed being Cynthia, the happy teacher and wife with a loving family and home. If Hugh Jones hadn't interfered, she'd still be living in her townhouse with Jon, and they'd have one or more kids.

She shoved those unproductive thoughts aside. Wallowing in what could've been wouldn't help. She'd learned that lesson the hard way after not being able to teach because she was too consumed with the past and revenge. Her heart was crushed when Jon moved on with Jessica, but it wasn't nearly as painful as seeing Jon miserable, alone, and unhappy. Since Jessica had come into his life again, he'd transformed into his old self. The man he'd been before Hugh Jones ripped their lives apart.

Meredith had no intentions of interfering in their lives no matter how things played out. The decision of whether to leave the letter for Jessica on her wedding day had weighed on her for months, but she had to warn Jessica of the consequences of marrying Jon after suffering the pain of losing him and everyone she loved.

Jon had what he'd always wanted, a family. All she wanted was to be Cynthia again so she could finally see her family in Maryland. The only thing from Meredith Green's life worth hanging onto was Agent Trent Cooper. The best friend she'd ever had. Without him, she'd still be a shadow of herself, afraid to take control of her life and push back against the evil pinning her down.

But could she leave everything about Meredith behind? She reached in her empty pocket for the comfort of cold metal, feeling naked without her gun. Cynthia never would've followed those men inside Jessica's house. She wouldn't have been able to raise the Smith & Wesson she'd smuggled across the border, and her hands wouldn't have been steady enough to shoot two men in the back of the head without missing.

After killing two people, she'd expected to feel guilt and remorse, but she didn't. She'd rid the world of two horrible men who would no longer victimize and traffic innocent women. With her hand still in her empty pocket, Meredith came to a frightening realization. She'd enjoyed killing those men and wanted to do it again.

What kind of person am I?

The screeching of the plane's brakes on the runway snapped her into the present. She needed to stay focused on her mission and lock her emotions away until things calmed down enough for her to process.

She slung her backpack over her shoulder and blended into the crowd moving through the tunnel into the terminal. With her head down, she strode out the nearest exit where a line of taxis waited. As she placed her hand on the back door of the nearest car, someone grabbed her shoulder.

"Cynthia, is that you? It's been years," said a bubbly female voice behind her.

Crap! At least it's only an acquaintance from teacher's college. I hope the British accent works. "No, darling. You must have mistaken me for someone else."

"Oh, sorry. You're a dead ringer for an old college friend of mine."

Cynthia opened the car door. "No worries. I must be going. Important meeting." She shut the door in the woman's face and touched the driver's shoulder. "Drive, please. Head east to the suburbs."

That was close!

She got out of the cab a few streets over from the house of the first suspect on her list. Assistant Director Georgia Pruitt lived alone and was out of state. Meredith had searched the area on *Google Maps*, but she wanted to see the house in person and get a sense of the neighborhood before returning after nightfall.

Meredith stuffed her hands in her pockets to keep them warm as she strolled along the sidewalk. The sun shone on a rather pleasant winter day, warming her face. She'd missed the more temperate winters of home while freezing her butt off in Northern Colorado.

This was a nice, established neighborhood. Birds chirped in tall trees and pecked at seed in bird feeders, her only company. Driveways sat empty, and no cars passed. With it being the middle of the day, people were at work in the city. She hadn't factored that in during her planning.

As she approached the assistant director's house, a woman carrying cleaning supplies came out the front door. *A cleaning lady.* Meredith slowed her steps. The woman lifted the welcome mat, pulled out a key, locked the door, then replaced the key in its hiding spot.

Meredith strolled past the house, turned the corner, then doubled back. *Now's the time to do this.* She jogged up to the house, retrieved the key, and let herself in. Meredith braced for a deafening alarm system to go off that she'd need to disarm, or a dog to charge and start barking, but neither happened. Perhaps the agent felt capable of protecting herself without any assistance. *Not smart.*

Meredith shrugged. *Oh well.* It made her life easier. She slipped out of her boots on the entrance rug, taking care not to leave tracks on the clean hardwood floor, as she wandered into the main living area.

The house was sparsely, yet tastefully, furnished in creams with blue accents. Meredith tugged open the cabinets and drawers in the kitchen. Everything had its place, not a speck of dirt or dust on any of the dishes or shelves. The assistant director either liked things clean and organized or ate out a lot. The one coat closet had four coats and four pairs of shoes in it. No bags or bins stuffed full of junk to sort through. *This should be fast. In and out.*

Meredith jogged up the stairs to the second floor. She searched in the master bedroom, under the bed, the walk-in closet, and in the dressers. No tapes and no keys to a safe deposit box or storage locker. She moved onto the guest bedroom and did the same, then the home office. Nothing. After searching the basement, Meredith came up empty.

She locked the front door, placed the key under the welcome mat, and ambled down the driveway as if she belonged. Although she'd come up empty, she could cross Georgia's name off her list. She'd have the whole night to focus on searching one more house, and she didn't need to case it out because she'd been there before.

From a few streets away, Meredith called a different cab company than the one she'd taken from the airport. She had put everything back the way she'd found it at the assistant director's house, but as Trent always said, better to cover your tracks.

Chapter Twenty-Four

In the wee hours of the morning, at her target's home cloaked in darkness, Meredith swung open the back gate, cringing as the metal hinges squeaked. Her steps were muted by the thick, dormant, unmown grass as she hustled inside, shut the gate, then hid in the black shadows behind the garden shed.

Her chest heaved, and adrenaline surged through her veins. This wasn't a quiet spot in the suburbs. To the contrary, this target lived in a busy neighborhood in the city. He wasn't home, but the neighbors were, and the houses were on top of each other. She took one deep breath, then another, before making her move.

She crept toward the house. About halfway there, light from the neighbor's house shone through the fence posts leaving a pattern of lines on the lawn. *Shoot!* Meredith scurried to the side of the house and crouched by a small basement window.

Door chimes jingled. Someone next door, no way of knowing who with the fence in the way, whistled *The Four Seasons* by Vivaldi. A lighter flicked, and the whistling stopped. A plume of smoke drifted into the sky, then the whistling resumed.

Meredith rolled her eyes. *Of all the rotten luck.* Someone outside smoking on a Thursday night at three in the morning. Her plan was to look for a spare key, but a window would do. She popped the screen off. *Hope it's unlocked.*

She pressed her hands on the glass, took a deep breath, then pushed. The window slid open. She studied the opening. Maybe her luck wasn't so bad after all. If she turned sideways, she'd be able to squeeze through.

She shone a flashlight inside the house. The window led into a room with a low ceiling. The drop to the floor wouldn't be far. A twin bed was shoved in the corner, and directly below the window stood a metal cabinet, likely storage for weapons.

At least thirty cardboard filing boxes were stacked on the floor against the walls. Meredith groaned. She'd have to look in every single box and restack them in their exact order unless the tapes turned up elsewhere. This search would be a lot more tedious than the last. *Best get started.*

She held her backpack in the opening, aimed for a stack of boxes, and let go. The backpack landed on the top box of the nearest pile, then tumbled forward onto the concrete with a loud thud. Meredith cringed and switched off the flashlight.

The whistling next door stopped.

A male voice said, "Who's there?"

Darn. If he comes too close to the fence, I'm busted. If she ran back the way she came, he'd be able to see her. Her only escape was to continue forward.

Meredith threw herself on the ground, twisted her body sideways, clasped the window frame, and wedged her shoulders through the opening. She grabbed the cabinet as she wiggled through and crawled on top of it. Fortunately, the metal held her weight. She reached through the window for the screen she'd propped against the house, then snapped it into place. After shutting the window, she lowered herself onto the concrete floor.

She opened a box from the nearest stack. A cloud of dust greeted her, and she sneezed. *Only old papers. This will do.* She stood on tiptoe and lifted the box onto the top of the cabinet to cover the window in case the neighbor got nosey and decided to have a closer look.

The last thing she needed after making the risky trip was to get caught, and she was on a tight timeline. The wedding and Jessica's attempted rescue would happen in two days. With a potential leak in the Kansas City field office, the rescue attempt would never go off without a hitch. If her search came up empty, she'd have to rethink the situation and find another way to intervene. Hugh Jones would have eyes on Jon and the feds, but he wouldn't see her coming.

She pulled on the cord hanging from the ceiling and a lightbulb flickered to life. The metal cabinet caught her attention. A locked weapons cabinet would be the perfect place to hide something important. She tugged on the doors, as expected they didn't budge. *The extra key must be around here somewhere.*

Trent had a similar cabinet for his guns and always kept one key on his person. The extra key was taped in a nook beneath his kitchen sink. Jon used to keep his extra key taped to the bottom of the utensil drawer. A logical choice. Kitchens tended to have the most hiding spots.

Meredith bounded up the stairs to the kitchen. She yanked out the top drawer and rifled through it. Nothing. She peered underneath the drawer and shone her flashlight in the opening. Again nothing. She repeated the process for the next three drawers and came up empty. As she pulled out the largest bottom drawer, something clanged on the linoleum. She pushed the drawer in. On the floor were three keys on a ring, stuck to a piece of packing tape.

Three? What are the other two for?

She ran down the staircase to the basement and tried the keys in the metal cabinet. The second key she tried clicked and turned in the lock. She swung the cabinet doors open. Inside, she found a wide array of guns, knives, grenades, a bulletproof vest, and a weapons belt. The type of gear you'd expect an active agent to have. But no tapes.

One of the keys was a regular one that would unlock a door. His office? No, why tape his office key to the bottom of a kitchen drawer. *This must unlock a door in this house.* She wandered through the rest of the basement in search of a door, possibly a hidden door. But other than the small room she'd landed in, and a two-piece bath, the rest of the space was undeveloped.

The main floor was open concept. The only doors led to the basement, the powder room, and a coat closet. She pushed the coats aside in the closet and knocked on the wall, finding no hollow areas.

Next, she headed upstairs and searched the master bedroom, the bathroom, then the guest room. No locked doors. She stood at the midway point of the staircase and studied the layout of the main floor and the upstairs.

What am I missing? Her gaze traveled to the ceiling in the upstairs hallway, landing on a door she'd missed. *The attic.* She grabbed a broom from the linen closet, hooked the broom head through the handle, and pulled. The door dropped, and a ladder came down from the ceiling.

As she climbed the wooden rungs of the ladder, the air grew colder and staler. Once she reached the top step, she shone her flashlight into the space. The attic was partially finished. A wooden floor had been installed over the rafters, and a square space had been framed and drywalled. Sure enough, there was a door.

Meredith tried the knob. Locked. But one of the remaining keys fit. She twisted the knob and pushed the door open. Inside, she found more filing boxes and another metal cabinet identical to the one in the basement. The remaining key on the ring opened it. She swung the doors opens, and her jaw dropped. *Oh my God!*

Sitting in the base of the cabinet amongst other boxes was one neatly labeled "Jon's tapes." *Son of a gun. You're the dirty agent. Why am I not surprised?*

Chapter Twenty-Five

Jon unrolled a set of blueprints for the Jones mansion across the coffee table in his shared hotel room. Sam wanted his babysitter, Trent, to have eyes on him twenty-four hours a day, so they were bunking together. It could've been worse. At least he didn't have to share a room with Sam.

Having already smashed the bugs on the phone and in the light fixture, they were free to plan around Jon's missing tapes. Jon wanted to find a way into the mansion the following night, ahead of the wedding the next day. During the wedding, the property would be crawling with security, and if things went well, a bunch of FBI agents posing as caterers. And to make the situation more complicated, Sam didn't want him anywhere near it.

Trent handed him a mug of coffee and sat on the couch beside him. "What are we looking for?"

"Dead space. There are hidden rooms in his mansion. I heard about them from his staff when I was undercover, but no one knew where they were or the way in. That's probably where he'd stash Jess."

"I bet he paid an architect to adjust the blueprints to hide the space. I don't think we'll find it this way. We need someone on the inside to help us."

Jon ran his hands through his hair. "You're probably right. At gunpoint if necessary. There are at least two people in that mansion who know where Jess is being kept. Hugh Jones and his butler, Chuck."

"He's got a butler? That's old-school rich." Trent's phone rang. He looked at the screen. "I got to take this." He walked into the bedroom, shutting the door behind him.

Jon crossed his arms and stared at the door. Trent wanting privacy for his call wasn't unusual, but Jon had a feeling the call was connected to him. *I'm sure there's something he isn't telling me.*

He debated using one of the drinking glasses resting on the table across the room to eavesdrop, but if he got caught, Trent would be less likely to trust him.

Trent swung the bedroom door open with gusto and came out smiling from ear to ear. "Your tapes are on their way here from Washington."

"Washington?" *What the heck were they doing there?* "How?"

"I'll be getting them via FedEx First Overnight."

"From whom? The crooked agent? Did you convince them to have an attack of conscience?"

"No. A private investigator found the tapes. I couldn't go searching with Sam watching me, so I enlisted help."

"And they're for sure my tapes?"

"She found them in a box labeled 'Jon's tapes.' "

"Wow. Okay. We listen to them when they get here. If they're legit, I'll call Hugh and try to exchange them for Jessica."

Trent sat beside him on the couch again. "Do you want to know who the dirty agent is? Or would you rather stay focused on Jessica until she's rescued?"

"Think it'll rattle me?"

"Maybe. He had a lot more than your tapes. She

found file boxes full of evidence locked up in an attic room."

Jon sipped his coffee and tried to focus through the haze of sleep clouding his consciousness. "A pile of evidence. That's bizarre."

"Why? It makes sense to hold onto incriminating stuff if you want to blackmail people long term."

"But did she find anything to support blackmail? If you're going to the trouble of smuggling evidence out of FBI custody, there's no way you're leaving a money trail. She should have also found cash. Maybe recordings of phone calls. Something more."

"So, what are you saying?"

"She needs to keep investigating. You two may be rushing to the wrong conclusion." Jon yawned. "Since I'm not convinced this agent is as dirty as you suspect, you may as well tell me who had my tapes, then we'll catch a few hours' sleep while we wait for them to arrive."

****

Jessica woke to metal gears grinding as the bookcase slid open on Friday morning; an instant reminder of her captivity from the second she opened her eyes. She grimaced, then stood and stretched. Her lower back ached like a toothache, and her limbs were heavy. Sleep hadn't come easily on an old, uncomfortable mattress likely from the same era as the shag carpeting and the antique furniture.

Chuck said, "It's me with your breakfast, Mrs. Kent. Enjoy. I'll be back at lunch time."

As she moved the chair she'd propped against the bedroom doorknob, the bookcase whirled shut. Her plan to pump Chuck for information had failed. Since the first time they met, Chuck had dropped stuff off, then fled immediately, as if he'd been told not to interact with her. Her request to call Bryce had also been denied.

She opened her bedroom door and inhaled the delicious aroma of bacon and eggs. A plate of fresh fruit also awaited her along with a new pot of tea. Her tummy rumbled. The baby was hungry. Getting dressed could wait.

Jessica annihilated the deliciously salty bacon and eggs, then lifted the empty cup and saucer into her lap. Since the first message after her arrival/kidnapping, she hadn't received anything else from the mysterious letter writer. She wanted to lift the cup to see if there was a slip of paper underneath it, but she also dreaded finding nothing.

Rip the bandage off, Jess. Get it over with. She took a deep breath and raised the cup. *Finally. Another note!* She hastily unfolded the scrap of paper and strained to read the small print.

Sit tight. You will be rescued tomorrow. Flush this.

Jessica crumpled the paper in her fist, stormed to the bathroom, and flushed it down the toilet. *If one more person is vague with me, I'm going to sock them in the mouth.* Why couldn't the note say, be ready at this specific time tomorrow, and look for this specific person? No, of course not.

She ran a bath in the antique claw foot tub and added lavender foam. Her back needed a good soaking, and she needed to clear her mind. She sank into the tub, disappearing under the lavender-scented bubbles, and shut her eyes, focusing on the calming aroma.

The note said to sit tight. Translation, do nothing and wait. But all she'd done for the past few days was wait.

If she waited, and the rescue attempt failed, then what? Jon's thoughts had to be similar, and chances were good he had a plan of his own that could get him killed.

I'm not helpless. Enough is enough. I'm taking matters into my own hands.

****

Hugh sat up in bed, wearing a black silk robe with his initials embroidered in gold stitching on the sleeve. Angel was beside him in her matching robe. Every morning they woke next to each other, and he had their breakfast brought to them in bed. Such a drastic change from how he'd lived before.

He used to pop out of bed the minute he opened his eyes, hurry to the shower, then race out the door to his first commitment of the day. Usually, a breakfast meeting with a rich jerk like him before walking the floor of his casino. Now he let his staff handle the day to day and ignored his pompous friends.

But his hands-off approach wasn't without issues. He pushed his scrambled eggs around his plate with his fork. Incompetence pushed his temper to its limits and killed his appetite. Kent was in his city, on his territory, and he should've been dead months ago. All because Henson was too much of a coward to do his job. Hugh longed to beat Jon black and blue and cut him to ribbons, before putting a gun to his head and pulling the trigger. Obliterating that pretty face of his.

Angel touched his arm. "Are you okay? You've barely touched your food."

The genuine concern in her furrowed brows chipped away at his thirst for vengeance but didn't sate it. Nothing could. But his focus should be on her. The love of his life he never believed existed. He pasted on his most charming smile. "I'm fine, my angel. Just going over all the details in my head for tomorrow. I want everything to be perfect for you."

"Ahhh. You're so sweet. Don't worry. If you show up and say, 'I do,' I'll be the happiest woman in the world."

He caressed her cheek and kissed her, tasting salty bacon on her lips. "Don't worry. I wouldn't miss it for the world."

His phone rang. The vein in his neck bulged. Why was it every time he was in the midst of a tender moment someone had to call and piss him off? He didn't recognize the number, but with the wedding happening the next day, he answered. "Hello?"

"You have my wife, and I want her back."

Jon Kent? Speak of the devil. Hugh scurried out of bed and into the hallway, shutting the bedroom door behind him. "Maybe I do. Maybe I don't."

"Don't play games with me. Either you let her go, or I'll plaster my tapes of you all over the internet."

"You're full of it. My contact at the FBI destroyed them years ago."

"You think so? I'll refresh your memory."

Jon's muffled voice came through static. *What should we do with him, Mr. Jones?*

Hugh leaned on the wall and put his hand on his forehead, his chest rising and falling rapidly as he listened to his own voice on the recording.

Cut off each one of his fingers. Pour gasoline on him. Burn him alive. Then chain him to a big rock and drop him in the Missouri River.

Those tapes meant nothing before the age of social media, but nowadays, if they got out, the consequences could be massive. And what if Angel heard them? "What do you want?"

Jon said, "I'll make sure these recordings never see the light of day in exchange for Jessica."

"I'm supposed to trust you?"

"Do an internet search. I haven't posted them. But I promise if you don't let Jessica go and stop targeting my family, they'll be uploaded. If you leave us alone, those tapes will never see the light of day."

Tightness squeezed Hugh's head. *Dammit! My blood pressure.* He struggled to keep his voice neutral. He wouldn't give Kent the satisfaction of knowing he'd gotten under his skin. "I'll consider your proposal."

He hung up, threw his phone on the floor, and stomped on it. The screen shattered. *Son of a bitch! He thinks he bested me again!*

Chuck shuffled around the corner. "Is everything okay, sir?"

"No. It's not. But it will be."

Chapter Twenty-Six

Jon shoved the burner phone in his pocket, cracked open two miniature bottles of scotch from the minibar in his hotel room, and poured them into a glass. What meant more to Hugh Jones? His reputation or revenge? Two qualities defined him: stubbornness and the meanest of mean streaks.

He glanced toward Trent sitting across the room. "Want a drink?"

"No, thanks. What did Jones say?"

"He said he'd consider my proposal."

"Think he'll make the exchange?"

Jon downed the scotch. The liquid burned his throat on the way down, but it also kept him from jumping out of his skin. "I don't know. Even if he agrees, we'll have to be prepared for whatever he might try to pull."

"True. But that tape you played for him was damning. I don't think he'd want the recording circulating."

"Maybe. But he can always get his PR team to claim the tapes are fabrications." Jon ran his hands through his hair. "Either way, I need to confront him. *Translation, kill him.* We stick to the original plan. I'll find a way into the mansion tonight while you run interference with Sam, so he doesn't try to stop me."

"What are you going to do with those tapes?"

"We'll see. When I confront Jones later, one of us

will die. Probably him. But if it ends up being me, upload those suckers all over the internet."

Trent nodded. "I will."

Hold on, Jess. I'm coming, sweetheart.

****

Jessica sat with her legs up on the antique sofa with Jane Austen's *Pride and Prejudice* open in her lap. The sweet smell of almonds and vanilla wafted off the fragile pages as she flipped them. The book was probably a rare and extremely valuable first edition, but if Hugh Jones didn't want people handling his books, then he shouldn't lock his prisoners in with them.

The gears in the bookcase clanged. Jessica glanced at the grandfather clock as the book slipped out of her hands and onto the sofa. *Ten fifteen in the morning?* She froze. Chuck wasn't supposed to return until lunch. So much for bludgeoning Chuck in the head when he came through carrying her dinner. She sprinted into the bedroom, shut the door, and wedged the chair under the doorknob.

Chuck spoke in his usual calm but firm tone. "Pack your things, Mrs. Kent. Time to go."

She yelled through the door. "What do you mean, go?"

"Mr. Jones is letting you leave. I'm driving you to the InterContinental Kansas City where your husband is staying."

I'm free? Can I trust him? If they wanted to hurt her, they would've done it by now. She put on her parka. Earlier that morning, she'd stashed a brass figurine of a swan in the inside pocket. The weight pulled her coat down on one side. She zipped the coat to even out the hem on the bottom, praying her baby bump would distract from the bulge of the swan.

She opened the door and met his eyes. "Just you and me? No other goons?"

He chuckled. "Just one feeble old man, Mrs. Kent."

"I doubt you're all that feeble." She thought about taking the fancy clothes they'd gotten her but decided against it and pulled her boots on. "I'm ready."

"Bag up the rest of your stuff. We've no use for it here."

"No offense, but I don't want any reminders of this place."

He shrugged. "Suit yourself. Let's go. Follow me." He turned and headed through the opening between the bookshelves.

She stayed close as he led her down a hallway with cherrywood wainscoting, lit by black cast-iron wall sconces. As he shuffled along, she spied the outline of something on his lower back, tucked in the waistband of his dress pants. *A gun?*

He turned a corner, opened a door, and stood aside. "After you."

She approached the doorway and paused. A set of stairs descended into the basement. She wrinkled her nose. Stale air tinged with mildew rose from below. This couldn't possibly be a way out.

Maybe they'd installed a camera in her prison. What if they saw the notes or caught her manhandling the first editions? "Please don't make me go down there."

"Don't be alarmed. There's a secret passageway in the cellar, leading to the back of the house."

She touched his arm. "Would you mind going first? I've always been frightened of basements."

"If it makes you feel better, I will." He descended

slowly, putting each foot on the same step before continuing to the next. He peered over his shoulder. "Coming?"

Jessica descended the first few steps with one hand on the railing. The other grasped the swan in her pocket. Chuck continued his slow pace with his attention fixed on his feet. No wonder he'd wanted her to go ahead. Probably to save himself the embarrassment of her scrutiny. Getting old must suck.

It's now or never, Jess. Her adrenaline surged as she crept up behind him with her hand wrapped around the neck of the swan and waited to make her move. He'd treated her well. She didn't want him to fall too far and break a hip, or worse, die.

Chuck placed his first foot on the second to last step. She swung the brass figurine over her head with both hands, then slammed it down on top of his head. His eyes rolled back, and he went limp.

She scurried around him and lunged for the ground, catching his head an inch before it hit the concrete. Tears rolled down her cheeks as she eased him down. Blood trickled out of a wound on the back of his head where she'd clocked him. She'd never before in her life intentionally hurt another living thing.

His chest rose and fell, and his pulse beat steadily under her fingers on his neck. *At least I didn't kill him.* She frisked his blazer pockets, finding a key with a Toyota symbol on it. Maybe he'd told her the truth about driving her to Jon, but she couldn't trust a man who'd played a part in keeping her captive.

The bulge in his waistband was indeed a revolver. Unfortunately, he wasn't carrying a cell phone. She shoved the gun, the swan, and the key in her pockets.

Now what? Had Chuck told the truth about the cellar being a way out?

She ran down the hallway to a massive but ordinary cellar with wine bottles on racks in straight rows from floor to ceiling. No doors. But then again, the secret rooms she'd been held in were hidden behind bookshelves. If a book opened the secret passage upstairs, then something in the cellar would have to trip an opening.

Instead of books, bottles lined the walls, but the setup was similar. In the library, the trip wire had been on the second shelf of the bookcase. She stood in front of the wine rack furthest to the right to gauge where the trip wire would be if set to the same height as the one upstairs.

The third or fourth row seemed about right. She took the bottles off the third shelf and set them on the floor. Nothing happened. She did the same with the bottles on the fourth shelf. Again, nothing happened. She pursed her lips and stood back to get a better view of the space between shelves, but the shadows obscured the opening. Standing on tiptoe, she groped along the back of the third row. Her hand brushed something thin, cylindrical, and metal. *A lever?*

She tugged and metal gears creaked and groaned to life. The shelf on the left split into two sections. One side shifted backward, making a loud grating noise as if something scraped pavement, creating an opening. Daylight and cold air streamed down a staircase leading outside.

She cringed and listened for approaching footsteps. If no one in the house had heard the passage opening, it would be a miracle. Her stomach churned. Chuck had told the truth, and she'd assaulted him.

Two males in animated conversation headed her way. She swallowed around a lump. She couldn't discern their words, but they were getting closer by the second.

"It's Chuck." A male voice said, "Oh shit! He's unconscious. Call an ambulance."

The other said, "What was he doing down here?"

"Probably getting wine."

Phew! They didn't know I was with him. But when Hugh finds out, he'll know.

Jessica tiptoed up the stairs leading to a huge backyard full of dormant grass with lumps of melting snow scattered throughout. She jammed her cold, wet hands in her pockets and ducked behind a bronze statue of an angel. The statue sat at an odd angle from shifting over to reveal the passage to the basement.

Her eyes widened. If anyone happened to look out a window and notice the statue facing sideways, she'd be caught. But if she pressed the button on the neck of the statue, which she guessed would seal the passage, the men in the basement might hear the concrete shifting.

Jessica peeked around the statue to get a sense of her surroundings. She needed a way out and fast. High, metal fencing surrounded the whole property with tall, fat evergreen trees lining the inside of the fence for privacy. The only way out seemed to be the front gate, and it was guarded by two men. *Shoot! Think, Jessica, think.*

Chuck intended to use this passage. If he really meant to drive her off the property, the Toyota couldn't be far away. Maybe in a garage? Mansions usually had separate massive garages.

The trees. They'd give her cover and allow her to move around the perimeter of the mansion until she found the garage. She sprinted for the nearest evergreen about fifty meters away and crouched behind the tree. Her chest burned as she inhaled fresh, cold air into her lungs. The guards hadn't moved from their post.

Behind her, the road on the other side of the fence curved, as if the mansion was on a huge crescent. The neighbors' houses appeared small in the distance. Too far away to risk making a run for it. Finding the Toyota seemed like the better option.

She scurried from tree to tree toward the back of the mansion. Branches rustled behind her. *Stay calm. Probably a squirrel or a bird.* She turned her head. *That's no squirrel.* She lunged forward, slipping in the snow, and landed on her knees.

A man dressed in winter camouflage wrapped his arms around her, snug, but not forceful or rough, and placed a white gloved hand over her mouth. "Shhh. I'll let you go if you promise not to scream. Nod, please."

She nodded. The man's aftershave jogged her memory, but she couldn't place the voice. Maybe he was a fed scouting out the property ahead of the wedding? If he worked for Jones, he wouldn't be hiding in a tree wearing camouflage.

He let her go. "Sorry. I had to stop you. How did you escape? You're supposed to be in the hidden rooms."

"First, who are you?" She jumped to her feet and took a few steps backward. "And who do you work for?"

"I work for whoever pays me." He took her by the arm. "Follow me. We need to get you out of here before Jones notices you're gone."

She yanked her arm away. "Hold on a second. Are you the ass, Henson, who kidnapped me at the hospital in Utah?"

"Guilty, sorry."

"You're sorry?" Jessica hissed. "Who the hell kidnaps a pregnant woman from a hospital?"

"I had my reasons." He took her hand and dragged her along the trees farther away from the front of the house. "But I stuck around to make sure you were safe. Didn't you get my notes?"

"You wrote the notes?"

"Yes, I bribed a servant to smuggle them to you."

Jessica asked, "Where are you dragging me?"

"To a hole I cut in the fence. Stop fighting. We're almost there."

"Why would you kidnap me and then help me escape?"

"I want Hugh Jones dead," Henson said. "I knew if I brought you here, Jon would follow, and he'd take care of Jones for me. Your escape screws up my plan. I'll have to improvise."

"Did you tell Jones where to find us in Lewistown?"

"No. I don't know who did. And before you ask, I found your family by hacking into surveillance videos at the airports." He handed her a car key and lifted a section of fence. "I have a rental parked up the road. There's a full tank of gas and navigation. I'll make sure no one follows you."

She pulled the Toyota key out of her pocket. "We'll swap. This was in Chuck's pocket."

The corner of his mouth lifted. "You disabled the old man. That's how you escaped. Good for you."

Nausea crept up her throat. What kind of person gets a kick out of someone hurting an old man? "Yeah, well, thanks, I guess."

She crawled through the opening in the fence and

ran up the road, looking over her shoulder the whole time. Henson was only one person. He wouldn't be able to stop a swarm of Jones' men, and he wasn't deserving of her trust.

Nearing a row of cars parked along the side of the road, she pressed the unlock button on the key fob. A vehicle beeped close by. Around the next bend, she found a black, four door sedan. As she climbed into the car, a black SUV passed by.

Hope they aren't looking for me! She pressed the ignition button and drove in the opposite direction of the SUV, having no idea where she was or where to go. *Wait a minute.* Chuck said Jon was at the InterContinental Kansas City. She searched it in the navigation and brought up a route. *Half an hour away?*

Something rang inside the car. Keeping her eyes on the road, she reached for the glove box, and pulled out a burner. *Oh, thank God! Finally, a phone!*

She declined the incoming call, pressed *0* on the keypad, and asked the operator to patch her through to InterContinental Kansas City. "May I speak to Jonathan Kent, please?"

"We don't have a guest by that name, sorry."

Did Chuck lie about where Jon was staying? Unless the reservation was under someone else. "What about Sam Gardner?"

"I'll connect you to his room."

Jessica waited as the phone rang on the other end. She glanced in the mirrors. *Crap!* A black SUV traveled a few cars behind her. They'd followed her. *Pick up, Sam.*

"Hello?"

"It's Jessica Kent."

"Jess? Are you okay? Where are you?"

"I'm driving to the InterContinental Kansas City. But I have a tail. What should I do?"

"Drive to the front doors. Don't worry about parking. I'll be there."

"Where's Jon?" The phone beeped. Sam had ended the call. *Surely, he'll tell Jon what's happening.*

Chapter Twenty-Seven

Jessica drove the speed limit, focused on the instructions coming from the navigation system. She glanced in the side mirror. The black SUV advanced, pulling directly behind her. One man drove and another rode in the passenger seat. Her heart thudded in her ears as she clutched the steering wheel, turning her knuckles white.

She debated taking a side trip to lose the SUV, but she didn't know the city. And the hotel was a few short miles away. Also, after being followed so many times, she might be overreacting. They might not be tailing her at all.

The SUV signaled right and turned into a gas station. She let out her breath and sighed. Now, she'd be able to focus on finding the hotel and Jon.

The navigation system announced the hotel would be a hundred yards ahead on the right. A tall, beige structure stood out from the adjacent shorter buildings in the distance. *That must be it.* As she got closer, the lettering above the top story became legible, *Intercontinental.*

She passed a courtyard featuring a large fountain. Centered within the water, three statues kneeled, reaching for the sky, imploring for help from above. Jessica could relate. She'd accept help from just about anywhere now.

She drove around the building and an awning came into view over what had to be the main doors. Sam ran toward her waving his arms over his head. *A familiar face, finally.* She parked at the curb, then jumped out of the car, not bothering to shut the door. She threw her keys to the approaching valet.

Sam took her arm while keeping a hand on his service weapon in its open holster. "Hurry." He led her through the lobby to the elevators. "We'll go to my room where it's safe, then call Jon."

"Where's Bryce?"

"He's with Debbie and Sally in Oahu at a safe house."

"Oh, okay." Her heart ached at the distance between her and Bryce. "When can I join them?"

"As soon as it can be arranged." Sam pushed the button for the third floor. "How are you? Did they hurt you?"

"No. Just the opposite. They fed me and bought me expensive clothes."

"How did you escape? Did the undercover agent inside the mansion help?"

The elevator opened, and she followed Sam down the hallway. "No. No one inside the mansion helped, but I had help from another unusual source." Jessica told him about her escape and Henson.

"Wow. That was brave of you." Sam slid his key card in the lock and held the door open. "Are you hungry or thirsty? I'll have something sent up."

"A glass of water would be wonderful." She took off her boots and coat, then sank into an armchair in the sitting area beside the bed. *Freedom at last.*

Sam's phone pinged. He stared at the screen for a

few minutes, then pocketed the phone. His hands shook as he used tongs to drop ice cubes in a glass, and water sloshed over the edge.

Strange. I've never seen him like this. "You, okay?"

"Oh, the shaking? Adrenaline. I've got to make a ton of phone calls. Let everyone know you don't need to be rescued during the big bust tomorrow morning."

"But you'll call Jon first, right?"

"Of course." He sat on the bed and picked up the receiver to the hotel landline. "I have Jessica here in my room. Yes, she's fine. Don't worry. A bit anxious to see you is all."

Jessica strained her ears, but she couldn't make out the other side of the conversation.

"Uh-huh. Yes, okay." Sam hung up and smiled.

"Where's Jon?"

"At the field office where plans were being finalized for your rescue tomorrow." His phone pinged, and his smile fell. His fingers flew across the screen, his brow furrowed. "I'll take you there now."

"Oh, okay. Makes sense. He would want to be sure Hugh Jones ends up behind bars." *More like dead, but Sam doesn't need to know that.*

She put on her coat and followed Sam out the door to the elevators. When they got to the ground floor, instead of heading through the lobby to the front doors, Sam headed in a different direction.

She asked. "Where are we going?"

"To the parking garage. My car is there."

The hairs prickled on the back of her neck. Awful things happened in dark, shadowy parking garages. "Aren't there any other agents that could accompany us in case we run into trouble?"

"Why all the questions?" He huffed. "Don't you trust me?"

"No. Actually I don't. I was kidnapped from a hospital under the watch of the FBI."

"Fair point. But it's me. Not some rookie agent."

She bit the retort on the tip of her tongue and followed him outside to a black sedan on the end of a row of cars in the middle of the garage. Jessica gripped the door handle and tugged it open.

A female voice yelled, "Stop, Jessica! Don't go with him."

Jessica spun, and her mouth dropped open.

The mysterious woman from the bathroom in the Edmonton Airport came around the silver compact car parked behind them with a handgun pointed in Sam's direction. "He's a dirty agent. You can't trust him."

Sam's eyes widened, and his face blanched. "Cynthia? Cynthia Kent? But you're supposed to be dead."

Cynthia positioned herself in front of Jessica with her gun trained on Sam. "Really? And how would you know that? Huh, Sam? I disappeared, remember? No body?"

Mind blown, Jessica froze and glanced between Sam and Cynthia. Suspecting the mystery woman could be Jon's first wife was one thing, but to have it confirmed—well, that was another thing altogether.

"I, ah, well. I just assumed." Sam sputtered. "We looked for you everywhere."

"And where are you taking Jessica?"

"To Jon."

Cynthia said, "You're lying. I found an attic room full of evidence at your house that belongs in FBI custody, including stuff on Hugh Jones. You're taking Jess back to Jones, aren't you?"

Sam shook his head. "It's not what you think. I was protecting that evidence. We knew Hugh Jones had someone inside the bureau, so I stashed those tapes because they were the most damning thing we had before the dirty judge threw them out. I figured there was a chance another judge would reverse the decision down the road when we uncovered new evidence."

Cynthia said, "I call bullshit. I bet you told Jones to look for Jon in Lewistown."

Sam shook his head vehemently. "No. I didn't. I swear. I would never do that."

Jessica's head spun. *Who do I believe? What do I do? First things first.*

Jessica faced Cynthia. "How could you do that to Jon? Take off like that and let him think you were dead?"

Cynthia kept her focus on Sam. "I didn't take off. The man who kidnapped you also kidnapped me. He was hired to kill me. Instead, he gave me a new identity. If I contacted Jon or my family, Hugh Jones would've known I was alive and sent someone else to kill me. So, I had to stay away. I came out of hiding to help put an end to this."

Jessica asked, "The letter on my wedding day. Was that you?"

Cynthia nodded. "After Jones targeted me, I suspected you might be next."

Two black SUVs approached, tires squealing, with guns hanging out the windows. Expecting Sam to take the lead and instruct them, Jessica looked his way. But then the reality of the situation smacked her in the face. Sam stood on the driver's side fully exposed because he'd parked in the first spot along the row. He had no time to react to save them. *This is not good. Oh my God! No, this is not good at all!*

"Take cover!" Sam jumped in the sedan and shut the driver's door behind him.

Jessica ran toward Cynthia and ducked into the small space between the sedan's back bumper and the front bumper of the compact car behind it.

She tugged on Cynthia's arm. "Get down. One of those SUVs followed me here less than an hour ago. I don't think they're the good guys."

Cynthia crouched beside her. "No. Feds don't roll up with AK 47s pointed out the windows."

Jessica crawled between the bumpers of four more cars, and Cynthia followed, putting distance between them and the shooters.

Jessica pulled Chuck's revolver out of her pocket and tried to calm her erratic breathing. If the cars didn't shield them, Jon might go from having one wife, to two wives, to none. Bile rose in her throat, and she swallowed it down.

Ping! Ping! Ping!

A volley of bullets slammed into the body of the car Sam was in. The back windshield of the car they hid behind shattered, and tiny pieces of glass rained down on them. Jessica covered her head with her arms. A scream from inside Sam's car pierced the air followed by moans.

Jessica glanced at Cynthia and raised her voice to be heard over the gunfire as bullets continued to impale the vehicles around them. "Are you okay?"

Cynthia yelled, "Yes, you?"

"Yes, but it sounds like Sam isn't."

Gunfire erupted from the opposite side of the men

firing at them. *The good guys returning fire?* Jessica sensed Jon was one of them, but she couldn't bring herself to look with the steady stream of bullets echoing through the parking garage and blowing holes in the vehicles surrounding him. Screams, wails, and moans came from the front of the sedan, and after what felt like an eternity, probably only a few minutes, the bullets stopped.

Cynthia peeked over the top of the car. "I think the guys who shot at us are all dead." She crouch-walked up to the back of Sam's sedan.

Jessica followed, needing to see with her own eyes that the threat had ended. She peered over the hood of Sam's car. A man stumbled out of the driver's door of the SUV, staggering as blood poured out of a wound in his thigh. He started to raise his gun in her direction.

Jon hollered from behind the SUV. "Jessica, get down!"

The man with the gun stumbled in a circle toward Jon.

No, you don't! Jessica aimed for his center mass and pulled the trigger again and again, until the chamber was empty. Blood pulsed out of four wounds in his back, and he collapsed in a puddle.

Jessica turned sideways as her stomach heaved, and she lost her breakfast on the pavement.

"Now they're all dead." Cynthia placed a hand on her shoulder. "Are you okay?"

"Yeah. That was...I've never killed anyone." Jessica's eyes filled with tears. "Well, I did hit Chuck over the head earlier. I hope I didn't kill him, too."

Cynthia's brows furrowed. "I understand. The men in your house in Cochrane were a first for me. I nearly upchucked, too. But, hey. Don't you dare feel bad about this. They tried to kill us. If it makes you feel any better, he would've bled out from the leg wound and died regardless."

"Oh my God, Sam."

"I think you've seen enough blood and gore." Cynthia opened the front passenger door, turned her head, then covered her mouth as Sam's hand fell out. "Gross. Don't look. He's definitely dead."

"His cell phone is in the breast pocket of his jacket. Could you grab it?'

"Good thinking." Cynthia frowned, reached into the car, and pocketed the phone.

Footsteps pounded the pavement. Jessica opened her arms as Jon embraced her and buried his head in her shoulder. "Please tell me you're okay, sweetheart."

Jessica clung to him never wanting to let go again. "I'm okay. Sam's dead. And I don't know how to tell you this, but..."

Jon glanced in Cynthia's direction. Her face was buried in Trent's shoulder. "Who's the other woman?"

Cynthia lifted her head and looked into Jon's eyes.

Jon's grip on Jessica slackened. "Cynthia?" His knees buckled.

Cynthia's eyes filled with tears. "Yes, Jon. It's me."

Jessica wrapped her arms around his waist to hold him up. "That's what I was about to tell you. You better sit down." She walked him over to a bench by the hotel door as sirens whirled in the distance.

Jon sat on the bench and gaped at Cynthia as she approached with Trent. "Someone better start talking. What the hell is going on?"

Trent's gaze traveled everywhere except to their

faces. Jessica cradled her baby bump. After this conversation happened, would Jon want to stay with her or go back to his first wife who looked cozy with Trent? *What's up with that?*

Since no one else spoke up, Jessica did. "She's the mystery woman from my house in Cochrane and the airport, but I didn't know who she was until Sam said her name. I had my suspicions, but it seemed like such a stretch. I kept them to myself with all the craziness happening around us."

Cynthia reached for Jon, then let her arm drop to her side instead. "You have to know I didn't leave because I wanted to. I didn't have a choice. Hugh Jones hired Ed Henson to kill me. Ed spared my life and gave me a new identity but forbade me from contacting you or my family."

Pain laced Jon's words. "Why did you listen to him? You should've called me. I could've protected you."

"Jones wanted me dead to punish you. If he was able to find out who you were, then I figured we'd never be safe again. And who's to say he wouldn't have gone after the rest of our family?"

Jon glared at Trent. "You knew the whole time, didn't you? She's the so-called investigator who found those tapes in Washington."

Trent nodded. "We met years ago by chance at a coffee shop in Colorado. She's a close friend. I couldn't betray her confidence after she asked me to keep quiet."

Jon asked, "Didn't you two think it was an awfully big coincidence that Sam sent Trent to help me?"

"Yes, we did think it was fishy." Cynthia's forehead creased. "But I don't think he knew I was alive. When he saw me, it looked like he'd seen a ghost."

Jessica said, "She's right. He looked like he was going to faint."

Cynthia said, "But I never trusted Sam, even when you were working with him years ago. And it turns out I was right not to. He told Jess he was taking her to you in this car."

Jon said, "We arrived as the bullets started to fly. When Sam called, I was at the field office. I had to keep up appearances that I was going along with tomorrow's plan."

Cynthia's brow raised. "Was he telling the truth? I thought for sure he was taking Jessica back to Hugh Jones. Sam had those tapes and a huge pile of FBI evidence locked in his attic."

"He was acting strange. Nervous to the point of shaking." Jessica's stomach churned. "Could he have been telling the truth about stashing the evidence to protect it?"

Trent held up a hand. "Hold up a minute. He's not innocent. Cynthia was right to stop him from leaving with you. Sam was supposed to stay in his hotel room and wait for us to get there."

The hotel door swung open. Four agents went to work unrolling police tape around the perimeter of the crime scene while three others dropped numbers by the bullet holes and casings.

A petite woman with a confident stride approached them.

Jon whispered in her ear. "That's Dawn Chamberlain."

Dawn said, "Jessica Kent, thank goodness you're okay. It was such a relief when Sam phoned in that you'd escaped. Where is he?"

Jessica pointed to the car. "In there. He's dead."

"Oh, no. That's awful. He was such an excellent and dedicated agent." Dawn tsked and shook her head. "Trent, take Jon and these ladies to your room. I trust you can collect yours and Jon's clothes and guns for evidence? I presume you two killed these men?"

Jessica said, "I shot one of them, too."

Dawn grinned. "Well, well. You're an interesting woman, Jessica Kent. I look forward to getting to know you. I'll send someone up to get your statements after the scene is secure. Once the press gets wind of this, they'll be storming the place."

Jessica stayed quiet. She had no desire to get to know Dawn Chamberlain at all. The woman's blasé reaction to Sam's death, and her inappropriate smile at learning Jessica had killed a man, gave off the same slimy air Ed Henson had about him. Dawn Chamberlain was not to be trusted.

Chapter Twenty-Eight

Jon sat in the sitting area of the hotel room with Cynthia and Trent, trying to digest all that had taken place while Jessica showered. An awkward silence had spread between them. Cynthia and Trent fidgeted in their chairs. Cynthia looked his way every few minutes, eyes full of pain. His heart was raw. Dammit, he was so angry with her for leaving, but he also loved her.

She looked so different then she had at their townhome in D.C. on the morning she'd been kidnapped. Her auburn hair was dyed dirty-blonde, the color of his hair, and a foot longer. She'd never been out of shape, but now she was a picture of fitness. Trim and muscular.

Cynthia met his gaze again. "Can we go somewhere and talk, please?"

"That's probably best. The balcony? It's cold, but the lobby is probably packed from all the commotion."

Trent took her coat off the hook by the door and draped it over her shoulders. As Jon pulled on his own coat, jealousy reared its ugly head. Cynthia was his wife, but so was Jessica.

He shivered as he stepped outside. The early afternoon sun wasn't enough to counteract the biting, early spring wind.

Cynthia jammed her hands into her coat pockets. "I'm so sorry. I hate that I hurt you, but it hurt me as much." Tears poured down her cheeks, and her body shook.

"Come here." He pulled her into his arms and inhaled the same raspberry perfume she'd always worn, but so much about her had changed. Because of him. "This is my fault. I should've protected you better and looked for you harder. My job caused all this."

She pulled away and wiped her eyes with Trent's sleeve. "What's done is done. I don't know where we go from here, but Jessica is good for you. She makes you happy and she's expecting your baby. And Bryce is adorable. You have what you've always wanted, a family. I won't get in the way of that."

She's as selfless as ever. "But what about you? That's what you've always wanted, too. Are you and Trent…?"

"No, he's a close friend. Don't be angry with him."

"You and Trent could've trusted me to keep your secret. I could've helped."

"I thought it would be easier on you not to know. I had no intention of telling you. But with the way things played out tonight, I didn't have a choice."

"I should thank you. You risked your life for us after losing everything because of me."

"You're welcome. But I was helping myself, too. If Jones lands behind bars for any length of time, I'll be able to see my family again in D.C."

"After all that's happened this past week, one way or another, I'm ending this tomorrow," Jon said. "I'm curious about something. How did you get to Jessica so fast?"

"Henson called, confessed to being my assassin, apologized, told me Jessica had escaped and would need help, and then he hung up on me. Talk about a crazy conversation. I was in my room on the fourth floor keeping tabs on Sam. Trent bugged his room for me a few days ago."

Jon laughed. "When did you become a super sleuth with a gun? What happened to the gentle special-needs teacher who wanted stricter gun control laws?"

She shrugged. "Honestly, I don't know who I am anymore, and if Hugh Jones buys his way out of trouble, I'm stuck being Meredith Green."

"Meredith Green? That's the identity Henson gave you?"

"Yes. I have no idea what Henson's end game is here or who he's working for. It's definitely not Hugh Jones."

"He probably has a hate on for Jones like we do. I know for a fact Henson normally kills his marks. You don't want to cross him. Did you hear anything interesting in Sam's room?"

She sniffled and crossed her arms. "No. He must've been communicating by text. I was listening for anything to explain all that evidence he had stashed. But I got nothing. I assumed he was paid to make that stuff disappear."

"The problem with that theory is cash. Trent said you didn't find any. Unless he had a safety deposit box and kept the key on him. But why go the trouble of building the space in his attic only to keep the profits elsewhere?"

"A gambling problem? I don't know. But the one thing as valuable as cash is information. Maybe he has skeletons in his closet. Now that he's dead, we'll probably never know."

"Sam wasn't perfect. He made mistakes, sometimes

big ones, but he was my friend. I don't believe he went dirty." Jon slid open the balcony door. "Why don't we continue this inside? It's cold out here, and I think we're good now. Friends?"

"I'd like that." She smiled. "Wait a minute." She reached into her pocket. "I forgot about this in all the commotion. It's Sam's phone."

Jon took it from her and pressed the home button. "This might give us some much-needed answers if we can get past his facial recognition or passcode."

Cynthia took the phone from him. "I'll get my stuff from upstairs and start working on it."

Trent handed them fresh mugs of coffee. "Are we okay?"

Jon patted his shoulder. "Yes, thanks for taking care of her."

Trent met Cynthia's gaze with puppy dog eyes and smiled. "It was my pleasure."

Pangs of jealousy clawed at Jon's insides, even though Jessica was the woman for him, but Cynthia couldn't have stumbled upon a more loyal and kinder admirer. Maybe she'd give him a chance. They both deserved the kind of happiness he shared with Jessica.

****

After her shower, Jessica sank into a chair in Jon and Trent's shared bedroom. She and Jon would need their own room. Sharing one with Trent and Jon's first wife could get more than a little awkward. That was if Jon still wanted to be married to her and not Cynthia.

Should I stay married to Jon? She loved him. Boy, did she love him. But she loved Bryce and their unborn baby, too. And this life wasn't safe for them. She caressed her growing baby bump. *At least we're safe*

216

again for now, little one. I can't wait to see your big brother and give him a huge hug.

Jon came in, shut the door, and sat on the edge of the bed. "Feel better, sweetheart?"

"A little. You?"

"Better now that you're safe. I was terrified something would happen to you and the baby because of me."

"So, what happens now? You have two wives."

He held out his hand. Jessica took it, and he settled her in his lap. "No, Cynthia was declared legally dead. Our marriage was dissolved. I only have one wife, and I wouldn't trade her for anything in the world."

"But don't you still love her?"

"Of course. I always will. But she's my past and you're my future. I loved her, but I'm in love with you."

An honest answer. Jessica smiled. If he continued to give her honesty, they'd have a chance at their happily ever after. "What happens to Cynthia now? And us? Hugh Jones will keep coming."

Jon caressed her stomach. "I'm not going to let that happen. And we're not relying on the FBI."

"I don't like the sounds of that, but I know there's no other choice. The FBI can't protect us from Hugh Jones." She stroked the scratchy stubble on his cheek. "Be careful, please. I can't lose you."

Chapter Twenty-Nine

Hugh sat behind his desk and waited for his men to return. Since he'd smashed his cell phone, he'd relegated himself to the landline in his office. The crew he'd sent to pick up Jessica should've been back ages ago. The nerve of her. Where did she get off attacking Chuck after being granted her freedom? Now, she needed to die, too.

Angel stuck her head around the corner. "You should watch the news. There's been a crazy shooting downtown at the InterContinental Kansas City. An FBI agent died."

Hugh bit his lip to keep from screaming. Things kept getting worse and worse. His men were supposed to grab her and take off. "I'll be there in a minute, my angel. I need to make a quick call."

"Okay." Angel shut the door to his study.

He dialed his FBI contact. "What the hell happened?"

"You tell me. I ordered Agent Gardner to bring her to the field office as you instructed, to get her outside the hotel. Your goons were supposed to grab her and run. Not kill an FBI agent and fire off a gazillion rounds in broad daylight."

"If it had been just the one agent and the woman, they wouldn't have opened fire. You screwed it up somehow. Can you get me the woman?"

"No. She's too well-guarded now. Agent Gardner's

218

superior from the DC office authorized a plane to move her and Jon to another safe house."

"Where?"

"They won't tell me. Since your goon tracked them in Utah, they suspect a leak in my office."

"If I find out you're lying, so help me God. And this little incident today, it better not lead back to me."

"Your family has been under surveillance for a century, and the men you sent to the hotel are known associates."

"Figure it out. Remember, if I go down, you'll be coming with me. Your colleagues won't think of you in a very pleasant light once they learn you've been taking bribes from criminals. And your time in prison will be made even more unpleasant with my connections."

"I'm one person. What am I supposed to do?"

"That's your problem, not mine. Figure it out." He slammed the receiver onto its cradle. "Dammit!"

Anger simmering at the surface boiled over. He hurled a glass vase at the wall. Shards of glass flew all over the room, and a dozen red roses slid to the floor. Hugh's blood pressure dropped, and he regained some perspective.

After years of practice, his hands always stayed clean. No one could prove he had anything to do with the shooting. The whole thing would blow over. But the incompetence. Nothing grated on his last nerve like incompetence. If his men hadn't been shot dead, he would've killed them himself.

He picked up the phone. Kansas City was *his* turf. He'd find out where that FBI plane went and contract out a crew nearby, and perhaps now would be a good time to unleash his hidden, and most potent weapon against them. While he and Angel lived happily ever after, the Kents would suffer their worst nightmare.

After finishing his calls, Hugh set out to find Angel. He checked the living room. The television blasted the news channel, but she wasn't there. As he approached her wing of the mansion, her adorable silvery voice echoed in the hallways. *I wonder who she's talking to.* He couldn't make out her words.

Her bedroom door was cracked open wide enough for him to peer in with one eye. Angel opened a dresser drawer, lifted her clothes, then stuck the phone beneath them. *Strange. Why would she hide her phone?* Come to think of it, she never used her phone in front of him. He'd believed it an act of courtesy, but now he wondered.

He retreated to the sitting room and summoned her. "My angel. Afternoon tea is ready."

"Coming." She came out of the bedroom. "Sorry to keep you waiting. Mom called. She and Dad ordered takeout last night and now they've both got food poisoning. They won't be able to fly in for the wedding."

"What a shame. Did you want to postpone?"

"Ahh. That's sweet of you to offer, but it's okay. I promised them we'd record the wedding and send them the video."

"Are you sure?"

She beamed and took his arm as they made their way to the lounge where coffee, tea, and finger foods would be waiting for them. "Yes. I can't wait to be Mrs. Jones."

He waited for her to sit. "I don't see crackers. I'll go fetch some."

Lies always rolled off his tongue without hesitation. Especially simple ones. He jogged back to Angel's room and pulled the phone out of the drawer. He touched the home button. The screen came to life and asked for a passcode. *Damn.* He'd have to keep her busy for a while and get his head of security, Ben, to get into her phone for the message and call logs.

****

After their snack, Hugh talked Angel into watching a movie in the home theater. They sat side by side in leather recliners and ate popcorn. Angel's adorable singsong laugh brought a smile to his lips despite his unease about her behavior. She was either the best actor he'd ever met, or the sweetest, most amazing woman in the world.

Considering he was far from a saint; did it really matter if her motives were pure or not? They both gained from their relationship. Maybe he should forget about the secrecy surrounding her phone. They were happy. What more could he ask for?

After the movie, he went to his study. He picked up the phone to dial Ben intending to call the whole thing off, then paused and hung up the receiver. There was a sealed envelope on his desk that hadn't been there before. Hugh picked it up and tore it open. Once he read whatever was inside, he couldn't unlearn it.

No. Not now. He stuck the envelope in the top drawer of his desk and walked away.

****

Jessica boarded an FBI Cessna bound for Oahu. She hated leaving Jon and Cynthia behind, but they'd insisted. After the assassination attempt outside the hotel, Jon didn't want her anywhere near Hugh Jones, and he didn't trust anyone but Trent to get her to the safe house.

Trent loaded their bags, then took the seat beside

her. "Ready?"

"Yes. I can't wait to see Bryce. Poor kid. He sounded okay on the phone, but he must've been worried. I doubt Jon's story about bringing me home fooled him."

"Probably not. Kids have strong instincts, and they don't question them the way we do."

"Can I ask you something?"

He nodded.

"Do you think our departure will go unnoticed? I can't help but worry we're leading Hugh Jones to the safe house."

"The risk is minimal. We weren't followed, and the only one that knows about our flight is Sam's boss." He chuckled.

"What's so funny about Sam's boss?"

"I chose to reach out to Assistant Director Georgia Pruitt for our flight because I know she's not dirty. Meredith searched her house before she searched Sam's place."

"I see the irony," she whispered in his ear. "What about the pilot?"

"The pilot is an FBI employee who isn't based here."

Jessica clutched the arms of her seat as the small plane lifted into the air. "Okay. We should be safe then."

He took her hand. "Don't worry. I've flown on this plane with this pilot before. And just think, Hawaii. I've never been. Have you?"

"No. But how much of it will we see? Won't we have to hole up inside?"

"The safe house is secluded on its own beach. The government bought it for special witnesses. We get palm trees, sand, and hot sun."

Jessica eased her grip on the seat and Trent's hand as the plane leveled off. "That does sound amazing. Lucky us. Maybe we can finally relax."

Chapter Thirty

Hugh pushed his dinner around his plate. No matter how hard he tried, he couldn't put the envelope out of his mind. He needed to read what was inside or burn the envelope and be done with the whole thing.

Angel took his hand. "Nervous about tomorrow?"

He plastered a smile on his face and lied. "Yes. I'm hoping everything goes off without a hitch."

"It'll be fine." She batted her long eyelashes. "How about I help you relax?"

"Isn't it customary for the bride and groom to sleep in separate beds the night before the wedding?"

She stood. "Silly superstitions. I think we're way past that, my love."

His body hardened and his pulse readied for the sensuous marathon to come. He laughed and took her hand. "I agree."

Giving his hand a playful tug, she led him to his bedroom.

She locked the door then held his hands and gazed into his eyes. "I'm the luckiest woman in the world. The past few months have been the happiest of my life. You're so caring, yet strong and commanding at the same time. I love you so much."

The sincerity in her eyes, and her kind words warmed him deep inside. The troubles of his day, and any doubts he had about her melted away. "I love you too, my angel. More than words can ever say."

****

At dusk, Jon strode away from the hotel with the hood of his coat up and his head down. Thanks to the plunging temperature, he blended into the crowd hurrying along the sidewalks of downtown with their shoulders hunched. The wind whistled between the buildings, stinging his cheeks. Traffic moved at a steady pace, and no one paid him any notice.

He caught a cab at the next intersection to the edge of the city, down the street from Jones' mansion. In case Jones had set extra guards ahead of the wedding, Jon set a brisk pace as he rounded the curve toward his property.

Things would get interesting if Henson still lingered in the trees. Jon wanted to kill the bastard for kidnapping Jessica while thanking him for sparing Cynthia. What a strange set of circumstances. Objectively, Henson's plan made sense and it worked. Jessica's kidnapping had drawn Jon out of hiding and pitted him against Jones.

Two valuable lessons had become clear from this experience. The first, once you entered the dark world of crime and crime fighting, there was no escaping. His vow to leave the darkness behind, and never take another life wasn't realistic. And second, the FBI couldn't be trusted. If something like this happened again, he'd hunt and remove the threat on his own no matter how much Jessica begged him not to.

Behind the cover of the trees, Jon slowed his pace along the side of Jones' property and searched for the hole in the fence.

"Pssst." Only Henson's head was visible in the evergreen directly in front of him. "Over there." Henson pointed to a section of the fence off to the right.

Jon bent the hole in the chain link back, crawled through, then jogged over to Henson. "Why are you hiding in the tree?"

"Like I told your wife. I work for whoever pays me."

"Can you be any more forthcoming? I'm not supposed to be here either. Maybe we can help each other. After kidnapping my wife, you owe me."

Henson said, "I don't owe you shit. I saved Cynthia's life and yours. I could've killed you when that sedative knocked you out in Utah."

"Why didn't you?"

"You know how killing someone haunts you. I won't kill decent people. Only scumbags. Besides, I do a lot of work for the FBI, so I didn't want to alienate them."

Jon asked, "What? Come again?"

"Where have you been? Under a rock? They use assassins to take people out, especially terrorists they don't have time to build cases against."

Jon's brow raised. Henson's story seemed too far-fetched and more like something the CIA or Homeland Security would do. "Jones is high profile, and he isn't a terrorist. Why are you here? It has nothing to do with Jessica or you would've split by now."

"He owes me money. Why don't you just go about your business and stop asking questions?"

"If it's only money, why haven't you made a move?"

"You're not giving up, are you?" Henson rolled his eyes. "I trust you'll keep your mouth zipped?"

"Yes."

"I didn't stick around for the money. The undercover working inside the mansion is an old friend.

I asked my friend to text me when Jones falls asleep. Then I'm going in to kill him. If things go down the way the FBI planned tomorrow, Jones gets taken alive. After last time, that isn't an option."

"I get what you're saying. If Jones was able to find me, then he'll be able to find your friend."

"Exactly."

Jon said, "I'm here to kill him, too. Two heads are better than one. Want to do this together?"

"Hmmm. I guess you're competent enough. Why not?"

Jon's phone vibrated in his pocket. He accepted the call. "Hello?"

Cynthia said, "I got into Sam's phone."

"Find anything helpful?"

"Nothing that incriminates Sam. But I did find an interesting text message exchange between him and Dawn Chamberlain."

Jon said, "Go on."

"She asked Sam to bring Jessica in for a statement. Sam refused. Dawn responded that Jessica would be safer at the field office than the hotel and promised to keep you and Trent there until he arrived."

"We told Dawn we were heading to the hotel, and she didn't stop us." Jon's thought spun into overdrive. "She must be the dirty agent. Unreal."

"I know. Pretty shameful for someone of her rank."

Jon clenched and unclenched his fist. "Thank God Trent requested the flight to Oahu through Washington. Do you have a number for Thomas Gaines?"

Cynthia said, "Yes."

Henson asked, "Dawn Chamberlain?"

Jon nodded.

"Christ. My friend might be compromised." Henson's fingers flew across the screen of his phone. "I never liked that woman."

Jon said, "Cynthia, call Thomas. Ask him to hack into Dawn's phone and banking records. He won't hit the red tape the feds will. We need to monitor her interactions with Jones."

Cynthia said, "Okay."

Jon said, "Then call Trent. He'll arrange for Sam's phone to be taken into FBI custody. Dawn needs to go down for what she did."

Poor Sam. I knew you were innocent, buddy.

Chapter Thirty-One

Hot sun, warm air, and palm trees greeted Jessica as she climbed off the plane in Honolulu. A welcome contrast to the late winter air in Utah and Missouri. Her long-sleeved tee and leggings clung to her skin as Trent ushered her into a waiting Jeep.

He started the ignition and cranked the air conditioning. "Want to stop for anything on the way? I could use shorts."

"I don't know. It's scary being out in public after holing up for months. The one time I went out, I got kidnapped."

"If it makes you feel better, we have a head start on whoever may be looking for us. Now would be the time to get what you need. The house is miles away from anything else."

A shiver ran up her spine. "Makes sense. Okay, let's get clothes."

They found a giftshop on the outskirts of Honolulu and stocked up on summer clothes, including straw hats and sunglasses to conceal their appearance. Jessica shed her sweaty clothes and boots in favor of a flowy blue and red summer dress with a floral print and a pair of white, flat sandals.

After some persuasion, Jessica agreed to lunch on the patio of a small café nearby. The breeze off the ocean left a salty taste in her mouth as she sipped her drink and ate her chicken long rice. Getting to sit and have lunch beneath the sun shining in a cloudless sky had become a luxury she'd never take for granted again.

She closed her eyes as she savored her last forkful of spicy rice and chicken. "Yum. This is delicious. I've never had traditional Hawaiian food."

Trent started in on his second fish taco. "I know, right? I feel like I've been deprived my whole life."

"If you don't mind me asking, what's going on with you and Cynthia? You both have that look in your eyes when you're together."

"Look?"

Jessica sipped her strawberry mocktail. "You know. Puppy dog eyes?"

He smiled. "I don't know about that."

"You can tell me. My lips are sealed."

"All right, all right. I would do anything for that woman. But I don't think she feels the same. I'm in the friend zone."

"I wouldn't be so sure. At first, I bet she was still hung up on Jon. They were ripped apart. But I see the way she looks at you, and it isn't the way you look at a friend."

"Maybe." He shrugged. "We should hit the road. Will you help with the directions?"

"Sure." Jessica stood and rubbed her bump. "Don't give up on Cynthia."

Trent pulled his phone out of his pocket. "This thing has been too quiet." He touched the home button. "No wonder, it's dead."

"We better plug that in."

They walked the few blocks to the car.

Trent dug his charger cord out of his travel bag and

plugged his phone into the USB port. "We'll go back the way we came and follow the directions from the airstrip."

"Makes sense."

Ten minutes into their journey, Trent's phone turned on and pinged ten times.

He picked it up. "Geez, Cynthia blew up my phone." His jaw dropped.

"What?"

"The dirty agent wasn't Sam. It's Dawn Chamberlain. She tried to separate you from me and Jon by ordering Sam to bring you into her office."

"Oh my God. You and Jon were bang on with avoiding the Kansas City office to get our flight. At least now we know who we can trust."

The directions led them north along the coastline to the more uninhabited parts of the island. Jessica marveled at the sight before her. Ocean as far as the eye could see, palm trees, and lush tropical plants dotted the landscape. Colorful birds she didn't recognize perched in the fruit trees. Paradise.

They rounded a bend and came upon a long, twisted driveway, leading to a small two-story house on the ocean with a wraparound lanai, perched on the top of a hill.

Jessica checked the instructions again to be sure they hadn't missed any turns. "This is it. Wow. What a hideaway."

Trent popped the trunk. "Go on ahead and see your family. I'll bring our stuff inside."

Jessica flew out of the car and dashed up the stairs. The door swung open, and Bryce bounded toward her.

She kneeled on the lanai and opened her arms in

time to catch him. Holding her firstborn nestled against her second, tears trickled down her cheeks and she laughed. "It's so good to see you. I missed you so much, buddy."

He held her tight. "Mom, don't leave me like that again."

"I didn't leave because I wanted to. I was taken, but I'm okay. And I'm here to stay."

Bryce pulled away and looked at the car. "Where's Dad?"

"He's making sure the bad guy who's been chasing us goes to jail."

Bryce frowned. "Okay. He promised he'd bring you to me."

"He did his best. Trent kept me safe on the way here. Dad should be here in two days tops."

"Okay." Bryce took her hand and tugged. "Want to see the beach and the fruit trees? Aunt Debbie and Grandma are on the back porch."

"All right."

He pulled her around the side of the house to the back porch. "Wait till you see. There's banana trees and mango trees and lemon trees."

"Really? Neat."

"Grandma's been making her special lemonade."

Sally and Aunt Debbie climbed out of their chairs and wrapped their arms around her in a group hug.

Aunt Debbie said, "Thank God, you made it. How's the baby?"

"The baby's fine. By some miracle, and thanks to Cynthia and the boys, I wasn't hurt at all."

Sally asked, "Cynthia who?"

Jessica said, "Jon's first wife. Didn't Thomas tell

you?"

Sally's knees wobbled and she collapsed in the nearest chair. "But she's…well, I guess she's not dead after all."

"Thomas would only say you and Jon were fine and not to worry." Aunt Debbie put her hands on her hips. "If he hadn't been so busy working on whatever he's doing for Jon, I would've made him give us answers. I did refuse to let him have cookies."

Jessica chuckled. "Denying his bottomless pit food was a good strategy. We better sit down. Apparently, I have a lot to tell you."

Chapter Thirty-Two

Jon crouched in the branches of an evergreen within sight of the angel statue. Henson did the same in the next tree over. Waiting until Hugh fell asleep had seemed like a good plan, but time ticked away. At one in the morning, they were still sitting ducks. The security guards' laziness in securing the perimeter had worked to their advantage—so far.

"Heard anything back yet?"

Henson said, "No. Either he's awake or something bad happened."

"Are you finally going to tell me who this friend is?"

"The bride. Also, my ex-girlfriend."

"Wow. My mind's blown. Talk about deep undercover and a massive betrayal. That's bad. Really bad. If Hugh finds out, he'll go off the deep end."

"Yes. Hence, why I froze my ass off hiding in this godforsaken tree for days. She's barely answering my messages, claiming to be busy with the wedding."

"Let's go in the passage. If it's guarded since Jess left that way, we'll deal with it."

"I'll disable the guards at the gate first." Henson came out of his tree with a small blowgun and a handful of tranquilizer darts.

"That'll come in handy."

Henson grinned. "Back in ten." The dormant grass cushioned his steps as he sprinted around the perimeter behind the cover of the evergreens.

Jon retrieved the Glock 19 Sam had given him earlier in the week. *Sam.* Things had remained strained between him and Sam since Jess' kidnapping, and now he would never get a chance to patch things up. The least he could do was make sure the man responsible never killed again and Dawn Chamberlain went down for her role in his death.

Henson appeared in front of Jon. "The guards are in dreamland. Let's go."

"You lead with the dart gun in case we come across anymore. Jessica said the mechanisms that open and close the secret door to the wine cellar are loud."

"Okay. So, we should expect company. On the count of three, we sprint for the statue."

Jon nodded.

"One, two, three."

Henson arrived a split second ahead of Jon, pushed the button on the statue, and stood back. The angel shifted across the ground, then turned sideways. The vague outline of a staircase greeted them in a dark hole in the ground.

Jon lay on his stomach, reached as far into the hole as he could, then shone a flashlight through the darkness. "Cellar's empty. Go ahead."

Henson scrambled down the stairs, and Jon followed. At the bottom, Jon pulled the lever to seal the passage, then extinguished his flashlight. They flanked the door, weapons poised, and stood still as the mechanisms ground, locking the concrete slab in place with a thud.

Footsteps raced down the hallway toward them. Henson angled the blowgun toward the hallway and waited for the men to get closer, then he blew one dart, loaded another in the gun, then blew a second dart in under a minute. The men didn't have time to react before collapsing in a heap on the floor.

Jon switched on the flashlight and shone it on two big and unmoving guards. "Holy. What kind of tranquilizer is in those darts?"

"Bear tranquilizer. A double dose."

"Sheesh. Remind me not to get on your bad side."

****

At his desk in the study, Hugh held up the offensive envelope and flicked a lighter to life. He held the flame to the edge, then dropped the envelope in the stainless-steel wastebasket beside his chair. *Let her have her secrets. Hell, I have more skeletons than any other man I know.*

A voice carried through the shut door. "Are you in there, Mr. Jones?" Ben rapped on the door. "Mr. Jones?"

Hugh rolled his eyes. "Yes, come in."

"What's that smoke?"

"I'm burning that envelope. What's it to you?"

"You didn't read the call logs, did you?"

"Not that it's any of your business, but I decided I don't want to know."

Ben turned sideways to fit through the door as he came into the room. He shut the door as the envelope turned to ashes. "Sir, there's something you *need* to know."

"No, I said."

"Your fiancée has been talking to Dawn Chamberlain every other day."

Hugh stood, fists clenched, and pointed at the door. "Get out!"

"Sir."

Heat bloomed in Hugh's brain. His office grew fuzzy. "Out!"

Ben fled into the hallway and shut the door behind him.

Hugh collapsed in the chair behind the desk and lowered his head between his knees. *No. No. No. It can't be true. Not my angel.*

****

Jon stepped over the guards and continued along the twisting basement hallway with the flashlight and his handgun poised in the air. "He used to keep a six-guard rotation. Two at the front door, two at the back door, and two in the house."

Henson followed. "These two didn't get a chance to radio for help. We should have time before any of the others come looking for them."

As they approached the staircase leading upstairs, Jon's flashlight illuminated a dark brown stain on the concrete. "This must be where Jess clocked Chuck. Then not even two hours later, she had to shoot one of Hugh's thugs. You know what taking a life does to you, right? There's no erasing that. Poor Jess."

"Beating yourself up won't change it. It's done. You can get philosophical later. We have a mob boss to kill." Henson pointed his blowgun at the stairs. "Go first. You probably know the house better than I do. I've never been in the bedroom wings."

"Sorry. It's been a long week." Jon climbed the stairs, turned the doorknob, pushed the door open, then peeked around the corner and whispered, "Clear."

Jon led Henson down a short hallway. The dimmed wall sconces cast their shadows upon the dark wooden wainscoting. But the lighting worked both ways. If anyone waited around a corner, their shadow would give them away.

Jon flattened his body against the wall at the end of the hallway. To get to the bedroom wings, they'd have to cross the massive lounge ahead of them, then turn left down another hallway. He met Henson's eyes and gestured ahead.

Henson whispered. "I'll cover you."

Jon continued into the lounge with Henson flanking him. The huge beige sectional couch was unoccupied, and the television screen black. The dark brown, shag rug absorbed their footsteps as they jogged across the room.

A metal door hinge creaked behind them. Jon turned. Before he could react, Henson blew a dart at the biggest security guard yet. The dart impaled the side of the man's neck. With an arm as thick as the average man's thigh, the guard yanked the dart out of his neck, then spun to face them scowling. He took two steps in their direction, then tumbled forward. The shag rug muffled the thud of the massive man landing face first on the ground.

Henson smiled, and Jon shook his head. No matter how despicable the enemy, Jon never got pleasure from inflicting pain. After this night, he'd never align himself with the assassin again. Another philosophical moment. Boy, he was full of them tonight. *Head in the game.*

Jon led them down the next section of hallway past the library and the laundry room, then the path forked. To the left was the guest wing, and on the right the master suite. Jon went left. It was customary for the bride to sleep separate from the groom the night before the wedding.

A puddle of light trailed beneath the double doors leading into the sitting room of the guest suite. Jon positioned himself by one door, and Henson did the same on the other.

Henson met his gaze and held up three fingers. He dropped one finger, then the second, and finally the third.

Jon grabbed one knob, twisted, and shoved the door open while Henson followed suit.

"Come in and lock the door." Angel sat in a blue velvet chair wearing a black silk negligee and robe. "What the hell, Eddie? I told you to mind your own business and stay away."

Henson said, "Why didn't you answer my texts? Dawn Chamberlain is under Jones' thumb. You could be compromised. We need to get you out of here."

"I no longer work for the FBI. I quit over a month ago. Aunt Dawn won't stop harassing me. It's getting old." Angel shifted a stray strand of hair behind her ear. "Hugh's blackmailing her. That's why she assigned me to the mansion. I'm supposed to search for the records he's holding over her head. But I decided not to. She deserves to rot for accepting those bribes."

"Wait. She's your aunt?" The part about the bribes didn't surprise Jon, but to send in her own family to save her butt—unconscionable. "Are you saying you're here by choice?"

"Yes, I want to be Mrs. Jones. Hugh's a wonderful man."

Henson's face turned red. "Are you insane? He's a murdering son of a bitch who traffics women and drugs."

Angel rolled her eyes. "And you were any better for me? That's in the past. Hugh's changed since we met. I think I can persuade him to go legit and ditch the life of crime."

Jon said, "Wishful thinking. Come with us and cut your losses while you still can. He just kidnapped my wife, then sent an SUV full of thugs after her when she escaped. His men murdered an FBI agent. What do you think he'll do to you when he finds out who you really are?"

"I've grown tired of this conversation." Angel reached inside her robe and pulled out a handgun. "You have two minutes to skulk back out the way you came, or I'll scream, and Hugh and the guards will come running."

"Don't even think of pointing a gun at me, sweetheart. Just because I used to love you, doesn't mean I won't blow your brains out." Henson's revolver appeared in his hand in the time it took Jon to blink. "Let's go, Jon. She's on her own."

Jon backed out of the room with his gun trained on Angel.

Henson followed him into the hallway and shut the doors. "She's lost her mind, and she'll tell Hugh we're here."

"That's fine. We'll wait around the corner for him."

Jon leaned against the wall with Henson at his side. Once again, silence stretched between them as they waited for their chance to make a move. Ten minutes later, fast footsteps approached the doors to Angel's rooms, followed by a knock, and Jones' voice calling her name.

Throughout the night, they never broached the topic of who would pull the trigger when the time came. Henson feigned indifference in Angel's room, but the hurt in his eyes said otherwise. With Henson being the scorned ex-lover, emotion may override reason which could spell disaster.

I'm ending this. Jon stepped around Henson with his gun at the ready.

Henson grabbed his arm and shook his head.

Jon narrowed his gaze at him. The last thing he needed was an argument with Henson in the heat of the moment. Despite his hesitation to trust Henson, Jon mouthed, "Together."

Chapter Thirty-Three

Hugh slammed back his sixth shot of scotch. The liquid burned his throat and numbed his senses, making the pain in his heart more tolerable. He opened the top drawer of his desk where he kept his weapons. The Smith & Wesson handgun would serve his purpose. Once loaded, he tucked it in the back of his waistband. Betrayal couldn't be tolerated no matter how much he loved her.

He strode toward the guest wing and knocked on the door. "Are you there, my angel?"

Her sickeningly sweet voice drifted out. "Come in."

Blood pressure medication couldn't keep his racing pulse at bay as he turned the knob and opened the door. The gun shook in his hand as he walked in the room and pointed it at her. "How dare you!"

Angel set her book aside, revealing a handgun in her lap. She scrambled out of the blue velvet chair and, with annoyingly steady hands, aimed the gun at him in one smooth motion. "What's this all about, my love?"

"You're a disgusting FBI agent! You want to betray me the same way Jon Kent did."

She pointed her gun at the ground and shook her head "No. Never. When we met, I was working undercover, but I quit. I fell in love with you. Hard. I'd never betray you."

He wanted to believe her and put his gun away, but

the evidence was damning. "I saw your phone records. You've been in communication with Dawn Chamberlain the whole time."

"She won't stop calling and begging me to work for her again. If you don't believe me, call her and ask."

"She'd lie to protect you. She knows the lengths I've gone to get revenge on Kent."

"No. Aunt Dawn is heartless and self-serving. She's never protected anyone."

Angel's words rang true, Chamberlain had betrayed her own organization to save herself, but Angel had already proven herself to be a fantastic, Oscar-worthy actor. She was a bombshell who could have any man she wanted and half his age. More than once over the past few months, he'd thought her too good to be true. Correction. She *was* too good to be true.

"Dammit, I love you, woman. Why couldn't you be who you said you were?" He wrapped his shaking finger around the trigger. Gazing into her emerald eyes, he couldn't shoot. She'd had plenty of time to shoot him and hadn't tried. Maybe she was sincere after all.

She sat in the blue velvet chair and placed her gun on the side table. "Come sit. Give me a chance to put your mind at ease. Please. I really do love you."

He took the chair beside her and placed his gun next to hers on the side table. "What's your real name?"

She reached for his hand, and he let her take it. "Karen Chamberlain."

"She's really your aunt?"

"Yes. She is." Angel pulled her phone out of the pocket of her robe and handed it to him. "Look through my photos. There are old pictures of me with Aunt Dawn and her brother, my father."

Hugh scrolled through the images. A much younger Angel stood between Dawn and a tall man resembling them both. *These could be fakes. An elaborate plan to save her life if I made her.*

"No!" Angel jumped out of her chair and dove in front of him as a shot rang through the air. She collapsed on the carpet at Hugh's feet, unconscious, with blood pouring from a hole in her chest.

"Angel!" *She took a bullet for me.* "Hang on, my angel. I'll call an ambulance."

Hugh grabbed his gun and fired two shots at the empty doorway. Security would hear the gunfire and come to their rescue. He ran to the doors and shut them. Angel moaned as he grabbed her under the armpits and pulled her into the bedroom. If the shooter returned before security arrived, he'd hear them coming.

He kneeled on the floor beside her, picked up her phone, and summoned an ambulance.

He took her hand. "Hold on, my angel. Help is on the way."

She opened her eyes and managed to squeeze his hand lightly. "I love you so much. You have to believe me." Blood trickled out of the corner of her mouth.

Tears filled his eyes. "I do. I believe you. I love you, too."

Her eyes went blank, her head dropped sideways, and the grip on his hand loosened.

"No, no, no. Angel wake up!" He shook her shoulders. "Wake up!" He wrapped his hands around her neck, finding not even a hint of a pulse.

He stared at the gun on the carpet beside his knee and sobbed. After a lifetime of never shedding a tear and killing anyone who got in his way, karma had come full circle. Life would be a hollow, empty shell without Angel's warmth and love. Nothing would bring her back. Not money. Not revenge. She was gone from this world forever, but he'd see her in the next.

Hugh rested his head on her shoulder, picked up the gun, and put the barrel to his temple. "I'm coming, my angel." He squeezed the trigger.

****

Jon stood in front of the double doors leading into the guest suite, blocking Henson from entering. "We need to get out of here. Hugh will call 911, and this is the ritzy part of town. The cops and the ambulance will be here fast. We'll regroup and come back later."

"Get out of my way. It'll take me a minute to finish the job." Henson mumbled, "Christ, I shot her. I came here to protect her, and I shot her."

"Come on. I'll get an update from the hospital in a couple of hours."

Henson held up his dart gun. "Move or I'll put you down."

Jon stepped aside. "Fine. I'm leaving."

A loud bang came from inside the guest suite.

Henson charged inside the room.

Jon followed with his gun at the ready. A huge puddle of fresh blood in the center of the lounge gave off a horrible, yet familiar metallic odor. That much blood could only mean one thing—death.

"I killed her." Henson stood, shoulders slumped, in the doorway to the bedroom. "By extension, I killed him, too. What a pair. A gangster version of Romeo and Juliet."

Jon's jaw dropped as he approached the bedroom and peered over Henson's shoulder.

Hugh Jones, a man who ordered hundreds if not thousands of murders over the course of a disgusting career, and one who'd never let himself get attached to a woman, didn't seem the type to take the easy way out. Yet he did. Part of the top of his head was missing and his blood and brains covered both him and his lover.

His lover. An FBI agent who fell for her mark, even after reading his file and discovering how despicable a man he was. As shocking as her behavior may seem to the average person, Jon wasn't surprised. During his seven years undercover, he'd learned how hard it was to retain your own identity behind the character you pretended to be. It was only too easy to cross the line and lose yourself to the criminal underworld.

Jon tugged on Henson's shoulder. "Come on. We did what we set out to do. I don't feel like answering questions about it. Do you?"

Chapter Thirty-Four

At sunset, sitting on the lanai, with the ocean breeze rustling her hair, Jessica swallowed her last mouthful of Sally's homemade honey lemon tea. She'd put Bryce to bed an hour earlier. After being forcibly separated from him, she'd never take tucking him in and reading him a bedtime story for granted again.

Trent occupied the chair next to her, and they sat in silence, waiting for an update from Jon. They'd told Debbie and Sally what had happened, but they'd kept Jon's plan to themselves. No sense worrying them needlessly, but Jessica couldn't stop twisting her rings around her fingers nor the butterflies from flitting around her tummy.

Thomas slid the patio door open, came onto the deck, and took the chair on Jessica's other side. "I finished searching Dawn Chamberlain's phone and email records."

Jessica asked, "And?"

"Under the circumstances, she's managing to juggle Hugh Jones well. He's blackmailing her for cooperation and information." Thomas took off his glasses and stared out at the ocean. "She helped to arrange for Jessica to be grabbed in the parking lot of the hotel, but she hasn't told him about the undercover agent. And she refused to look into where the FBI took Jess."

Trent said, "That doesn't mean she didn't tell Jones

where Jon was months ago, and I bet they met in person a few times. I would say it's safe to assume it was her."

Thomas nodded. "They did meet, and you're probably right, but I was hoping to find something more concrete."

Jessica cradled her stomach. "We're sure it wasn't Sam?"

"Cynthia caught nothing on her listening device, and she hasn't found anything in his records from around the time you first saw Greer in the cafe in Lewistown." Trent's phone rang. "It's Jon. I'm putting him on speaker."

Breathless, Jessica asked, "Jon, are you okay? Where are you?"

Jon's soothing voice came through the speaker of Trent's phone. "I'm fine, sweetheart. It's over. Hugh Jones is dead. Cynthia and I are packing, then we're catching the first flight. We're landing there in ten hours. We have permission to spend a week together in protective custody until everything is sorted out."

Jessica sighed as a weight lifted from her shoulders. "How did he die, Jon? Did you...?"

"No. I didn't have to. Henson shot at Jones, then the undercover, his wife-to-be, dove in front of him, took the bullet, and died. Jones, overcome with grief, I'm guessing, blew his own brains out."

Jessica said, "I feel awful for the bride, but at least Jones won't be around to send anyone else after us."

"This has to stay between us. Henson and I bolted after the shooting. We weren't exactly invited into the mansion. I feigned surprise when an FBI agent called with the news."

Trent said, "Of course. Were there any cameras?"

"No. Jones never allowed cameras. He was paranoid of implicating himself if the wrong person got the footage. I've got to run so I don't miss that plane."

Jessica said, "I'll sleep better tonight knowing you'll be here in the morning." *And not alone with Cynthia.* "I love you. Safe flight."

****

Jon's spirits soared despite not sleeping much during the past week. He vibrated with energy as he pulled up to the safe house in Hawaii early the next morning. With Hugh Jones dead, they'd be able to go home to Lewistown in time for their little one to be born and put this nightmare behind them. And Cynthia was alive, dozing in the passenger seat beside him. *What a crazy week.* The grief of believing her dead had weighed him down so hard for so long, and now that burden had also been lifted from his shoulders.

"Cynthia, wake up. We're here."

She stretched and opened her eyes. "Wow. The house is on the ocean. And there are palm trees and fruit trees. Oh my gosh. This is amazing."

"Let's go in. Guaranteed there's hot coffee and breakfast waiting."

"Is Jessica okay with this? Me being here?"

Jon climbed out of the car and pressed on his lower back to relieve pressure. "Of course. She likes you."

"You've got to admit this is awkward."

"Only if you make it awkward. Come on."

The front door opened. Bryce sprinted down the stairs and wrapped his arms around Jon's middle as Jessica stood in the doorway, radiant and smiling. Hawaii was paradise, but it paled in comparison to how amazing it was to be safe and together as a family again.

Jon held Bryce close and ruffled his hair. "I missed you, too."

Bryce said, "Thanks for sending Mom back to me like you promised. You always keep your promises."

Jon struggled to keep tears at bay. Never had he been more grateful for anything than being able to keep that promise to Bryce. "I always will, buddy. I love you and Mom so much."

****

Cynthia sat between Trent and Thomas at the breakfast table. They had indeed been greeted by hot coffee and a feast. Cynthia shuffled food around her plate, unable to eat. As much as she wished Jon and Jessica the best, seeing them together with Bryce wasn't easy. If Hugh Jones and Ed Henson hadn't intervened, she'd be sitting at a breakfast table somewhere with Jon and *their* children.

Trent took her hand beneath the table and gave it a gentle squeeze. "Want to go for a walk on the beach?"

"Yes, please."

Cynthia left her socks and shoes on the porch and sank her tired feet into the warm sand. The grains filled the gaps between her toes and refreshed her skin as she padded along the beach, inhaling the briny scent of the ocean and listening to the waves slap the shore.

Trent walked beside her in a pair of flip-flop sandals.

She pointed to them. "When did you ditch the cowboy boots for those?"

"Jessica and I went shopping in town on the way here."

"Without me?" She teased.

"If I had known you'd be joining us so soon, I

would've picked you up some stuff. Maybe we could take a trip into town when the stores open."

"That sounds nice."

He took her hand. "I could tell you needed out of there. How are you dealing?"

She clasped his hand, relishing his warmth, and friendship? No, this wasn't friendship between them. It hadn't been in a long time. His touch made her skin tingle in a delicious way. Wait, he'd asked her a question. What was it? Oh yeah. "I feel like we shouldn't be here. Like we're intruding on their family which I'm no longer a part of. And even though I've come to terms with my marriage being over, it isn't easy seeing Jon live the life we planned with someone else."

"I understand. This is a strange situation. But you don't have to keep any more secrets, and you get to be Cynthia again."

"I've been thinking about that. I'll never be who I was before. I'd like to fly to Maryland and visit my family and tell them what happened face to face, but I don't think I could go back to my old job and my old friends."

"Sounds like you need a fresh start."

"You're right, I think I do." She stood in front of him and wrapped her arms around his broad shoulders. The ones that held her up as she'd cried on them countless times. "Will you be a part of my new life?"

He smiled and leaned his forehead to hers. "I thought you'd never ask."

She brushed her lips against his for the first time and tasted warmth and a hint of delicious caramel from the creamer in his coffee that morning. He always smelled of caramel.

He nipped on her bottom lip and her knees buckled as his tongue caressed hers. *Holy heck! This man is making me swoon.*

She clung to him tighter. Warmth spread low in her belly. "How private is this beach?"

Chapter Thirty-Five

Jessica lay awake beside Jon in bed. Snoring softly, he rested on his side facing her, his hair stirred in the ocean breeze coming through the open window. No doubt, the craziness of the past week had worn him out. With the threat behind them, her worries about staying married to him evaporated. He loved her unconditionally, would do anything to keep their family safe, and she loved him just as much.

His bare arm lay on top of the blue cotton blanket covering them. She longed to run her hand along his taut muscles and soft skin. Maybe tomorrow after a good night's sleep. Only a week had passed since the day she'd been kidnapped. Yet, it felt like an eternity.

She adjusted her pillow and shut her eyes. Seconds later, cold hands shook her shoulders.

"Wake up, Jess. You have to wake up."

"Adam?" Her eyes flew open.

Adam's ghost stood on the other side of the bed shaking Jon. "Wake up."

Jessica bolted upright. Adam's form had never been this solid. If she didn't know better, she'd swear he was alive. His eyes were wide like saucers. "Adam. What's wrong?"

"Quick." Adam continued shaking Jon. "They're coming with guns."

Jessica asked, "Who? Who's coming?"

Adam's form flickered, then vanished.

Jessica ripped off the blanket and shook Jon's shoulder. "Wake up!"

His eyes flew open. "What's wrong, sweetheart?"

"Adam was here. He woke me then tried to wake you. He said, 'Quick, they're coming with guns.' "

Jon rubbed his eyes. "Who?"

"I don't know. He vanished."

"Get dressed. Adam hasn't been wrong yet." Jon jumped out of bed and grabbed clothes out of his travel bag. "Hugh might've set something in motion before he shot himself."

Jessica rifled through her bags and yanked out a baggy tee and leggings. "I had a bad feeling about us all flying out of Kansas City on Jones' turf."

"Wake Debbie, send her to wake my mom, then take Bryce to the basement while I wake the others. Whoever gets there first, starts loading all the guns."

Jessica flew down the hallway to her aunt's room and shook her shoulder. "Aunt Debbie, wake up!"

"What's going on?" Debbie scrambled into a sitting position and swung her legs over the side of the bed.

"Wake Sally, then come to the basement. There are people on their way here with guns. I need to get Bryce."

Not bothering to change out of her pajamas, Debbie followed her out the door and ran across the hall. "Sally! Wake up."

Jessica ran ahead to the next room, yanked Bryce's blanket off the bed, then tugged him into a sitting position. "Wake up, buddy. You have to wake up fast."

He groaned and tried to lie back down. In usual Bryce fashion, he slept like the dead.

Holding panic at bay by a hair, she said, "No, not

now. This time you *need* to wake up." She grabbed him under the armpits, yanked him into her lap, and slapped his cheek gently. "Wake up!"

His eyes fluttered. "Huh?"

She stood him up and took him by the hand. "Basement, now. Hurry!" He staggered behind her as she dragged him out the door.

Jon sprinted toward them and scooped Bryce into his arms. "I got him. The others are awake."

Jessica cradled her belly as she ran behind Jon. *We'll keep you safe, little one.*

Aunt Debbie and Sally were already in the basement when they got there. Jon settled Bryce on a worn couch and covered him with a throw blanket. Bryce rolled over and went back to sleep.

Aunt Debbie loaded the barrel of a shotgun with slugs. "Do we know how many are coming? What's the plan?"

Jessica sighed and sunk into a chair across from Bryce. "We don't have much to go on. And I'm not sure you'll believe me if I explain our source."

Jon handed Jessica and Sally each a handgun, then grabbed a shotgun. "Adam's ghost started visiting us in Cochrane."

Debbie snapped the barrel of the shotgun shut, leaned it against the wall, and grabbed another. "Come again?"

Trent and Cynthia hustled down the stairs, followed by Thomas. Jon gave Thomas a handgun while Trent and Cynthia pulled shotguns out of the locker and started loading them.

Jessica said, "I know how this sounds, but it's true. Adam has been a big help."

Cynthia's brow raised. "Who's Adam?"

Jessica steeled herself for skepticism. "The ghost of my first husband. He warned us to get out of the house in Cochrane. Because of him, we weren't there when those men showed up."

Aunt Debbie said, "And tonight you're saying he appeared to you again."

"Yes, it seems he can only say so much, or he loses his connection with this world." Jessica swallowed around a lump in her throat. "He was able to say men were coming with guns, then he vanished."

Thomas said, "The night in Utah, when you came flying out of your room in the middle of the night, screaming for me to help you drag Jon in from the cold. You knew what was wrong with him, which made no sense to me at the time. Was that the ghost, too?"

"Yes." *Thank God, they seem to believe me.* "And he warned me to be ready to help myself escape at Jones' mansion."

"Okay. An unusual source." Trent loaded a magazine in the rifle. "But we need to prepare in case the threat is real."

Jon fastened a weapons belt around his waist. "Trent, coming upstairs with me?"

"Of course."

Aunt Debbie asked, "What about the rest of us?"

Trent said, "Maybe Jessica, Bryce, and Sally should hide in the storage room."

Jessica said, "But I can shoot, too."

Sally said, "So can I."

Jon rested a hand on Jessica's shoulder. "But Bryce can't. If all else fails, you two are his last protectors."

"Cynthia, Thomas, and Debbie guard the

basement." Jon pointed to a small window. "Thomas, keep an eye on the window. It's small, but you never know. And Debbie, you guard the storage room door."

Cynthia said, "How about I stay at the top of the stairs in case you and Trent need backup?"

"Okay. But everyone else stays in the basement." Jon gazed into Jessica's eyes. "No matter what, until the coast is clear, do not go upstairs. Below ground, they can't shoot you from outside of the house. If we're outnumbered, we fall back to the basement. And if that doesn't work, retreat to the storage room and wait for help."

Jessica studied the somber faces of her friends and family as they nodded their approval of Jon's plan. She wanted and needed to believe they'd prevail over the enemies Adam predicted would come. But an ominous sense of doom hung over Jessica like a saturated storm cloud about to burst.

"Let's slide this couch into the storage room." Jessica wrapped her arms around Jon, needing his warmth to chase away her dark thoughts. "Bryce will probably sleep through the night without a clue anything happened."

****

Jessica followed behind Jon and Trent as they shoved the couch across the floor. Bryce didn't move a muscle.

Jessica lifted Bryce's legs, sat on the sofa, then settled his feet on her lap.

Jon kissed the top of her head. "I love you."

"Love you, too." A vibrating sound tickled Jessica's ear drums. "I think I hear an engine in the distance. Do you hear it?"

Jon stood still. "I do. That's an engine all right. I'll send Sally in. And don't worry. I'll protect you."

Jessica's empty stomach churned. "I know. Be careful. I need you to be okay, too."

Chapter Thirty-Six

Jon joined the others still huddled around the weapons locker. "Time to get in position. There's an engine in the distance. Maybe two." He stared into the locker. "There are only three bulletproof vests."

Debbie said, "Since I'm staying in the basement, I'll go without."

Thomas said, "I'm fine as well."

Cynthia touched Debbie's arm. "Are you sure?"

"Yes. You'll be closer to the action. Put on a vest."

Cynthia pulled on a vest. "I won't let anyone down these stairs. I promise."

Sally wrapped her arms around Jon. "Be careful. I'll watch over Jess and Bryce."

"I will, Mom."

Sally nodded, then hurried toward the storage area.

Jon grabbed the shotgun he'd loaded earlier to go along with the pistol in his holster. "Okay, Trent. Let's do this." He handed him a set of night-vision binoculars and hung another pair around his neck.

Trent kissed Cynthia's cheek. "Don't leave that staircase unless we call. You hear?"

"I hear. Don't worry about me. Focus on the bad guys."

Things had shifted between Trent and Cynthia since their morning walk, and Jon wholeheartedly approved. If they could just make it through the night alive, maybe they'd all live happily ever after.

Jon bounded up the staircase with Trent on his heels. He swung the basement door open, then turned off the light switch in the hallway, plunging the main floor into darkness. The moon streaming through the sheer curtains hanging in the windows provided the only remaining light.

Trent stuck his binoculars around the edge of the curtains in the living room window, looking onto the tropical forest to the left of the house. "No one on this side."

Jon went to a window on the opposite side of the room overlooking forest to the right. "I see three men trampling through tropical flowers with shotguns and night-vision goggles. Out of shape mobsters. By the cheesy, floral-print shirts, I would say from around here somewhere. Definitely a present from Hugh Jones."

"Hold on. I see plants bending in the distance. One, two—three men on my side. Similar getups and pot bellies."

Jon maintained his watch. No other men surfaced besides the three he had eyes on. "Any more on your side?"

"Just three."

"Same here. We're outnumbered three to one. Shouldn't be a problem."

Trent asked, "Do we call the local police?"

"It'll take them at least forty minutes to get here." Jon pulled out his phone. "I'll text Assistant Director Pruitt. It's early morning in DC."

"Okay, I'll take a peek out back." Trent strode to the sliding doors and lifted the binoculars to his eyes. "Nothing. I didn't expect there to be. The ocean is choppy. I don't think anyone is sneaking up on us that way."

"Didn't hurt to check. You never know." Jon's phone pinged. "Pruitt says she's sending help. Doesn't say what kind."

"Help is good, but I think we've got this."

Jon lifted the binoculars and shifted the curtain. "All six men are at the end of the gravel laneway huddled together. Huffing and puffing as they chat and smoke cigarettes."

Trent joined Jon at the living room window and stuck his binoculars around the edge of the curtains on the opposite side. "Could they be waiting for something?"

"Maybe. These mobsters are a conceited bunch. But to only send six guys when they know there are two feds?"

"They're expecting to take us by surprise. Shoot us in our sleep."

Jon shivered as the hairs on his arms stood on end. "You're probably right."

"I'm getting antsy waiting for these guys to make their move. In an ideal world, I'd creep behind them and blow their brains out."

"No time for that now. You'd be exposed in the open space between the house and the forest. Those guys might be out of shape, but they probably know how to use those guns. What I wouldn't give for a sniper rifle."

Trent said, "I know, right?"

Outside the window, one of the six men turned and pointed toward the house. The other five climbed the steep, half-mile rocky path leading to the front door, and the sixth man who'd given the order followed behind them.

"Seems they're all coming to the front door," Jon said. "Keep watch. I'll fortify."

Jon dragged the large, rectangular wooden dining table across the room and flipped it on its side, facing the front door. He knelt behind the table with one knee on the floor and the other leg bent to anchor. He positioned the shotgun on his shoulder and aimed for the front door. "What are they doing?"

Trent moved the curtain back into place and came to kneel beside him. "All six are on the porch. The one in the lead has a lockpick."

"Okay. We keep quiet and let them break in. You want the first man through the door?"

Trent nodded and placed his shotgun on his shoulder.

Silence stretched between them as the seconds ticked away. Then metal scratched and ground in metal, and the deadbolt turned, disengaging the lock. The knob twisted, and the door cracked open.

Jon took a slow, deep breath, fighting to tamp the adrenaline threatening to speed his heart and breathing. Calm was essential to get off an accurate shot. And he couldn't miss. Their lives depended on it.

The door opened, and one man walked in on sock feet with another at his heels.

Jon aimed for the second man through the door and pulled the trigger as a shot exploded from Trent's gun. Both bullets hit their mark. The two men collapsed in a heap with the top of their heads missing.

Another man stood frozen inside the doorway covered in blood and brain matter. Before he gathered his wits enough to flee, Jon aimed and fired. The bullet penetrated the space between the man's eyes and propelled him backward out the door.

On the porch, a fourth man yelled, "Three men down. Fall back."

Trent ran to the window and moved the curtain aside. "I see two men running toward the forest. There should be three."

Jon grabbed a decorative mirror off the wall and sprinted to the front door. He angled the glass outside in both directions. The porch was empty.

****

Two gunshots erupted in quick succession over Jessica's head on the floor above them. She flinched with Bryce's feet still in her lap, then held still and stared at Bryce's face, waiting for him to open his eyes. After a minute passed, and he didn't stir, and no other gunshots went off, Jessica released the breath she'd unconsciously held.

Sally paced and wrung her hands. "I felt so useless after passing out on Debbie when her house got broken into, and hiding in here now isn't making me feel any better."

Jessica's voice squeaked after being silent for so long as they waited for the inevitable confrontation. "Someone had to keep Bryce safe. And trust me. When guns are going off, it's no place for someone to be who doesn't know what they're doing. I was lucky to survive the shooting in the hotel parking garage."

"You're right. I know you're right."

One thunderous bang echoed through the small storage room, followed by a second, then a third.

Jessica's stomach churned. She recited prayers in her head, pleading with whomever listened her loved ones would survive unscathed, and she wouldn't need to use the loaded handgun resting on the arm of the sofa.

Those shots hadn't come from upstairs, but outside the storage room door.

****

At the top of the basement staircase, Cynthia peeked around the corner into the living room with her shotgun ready in case things went sideways. The deadbolt turned, and her body vibrated, anticipating violence.

Her heart pounded a rock drummer's solo as the front door opened and two men came in. Before she took a step forward, Jon and Trent's shotguns exploded, unleashing a deafening boom. At the same time, glass shattered.

The ringing in her ears made it difficult to process what was happening. Her eyes burned, then watered from the acrid taste of gunpowder and the coppery scent of blood.

Wait, the glass shattered behind me! She spun and headed down the stairs. Three more blasts assaulted her eardrums. She ignored the throbbing now accompanying the ringing and kept her feet steady as she descended with the shotgun resting against her shoulder.

At the bottom of the staircase, a man lay beneath the window, unconscious with blood spurting from his chest. She scanned the room for Thomas and Debbie. *Oh no! Thomas!* She strode toward him, then stopped and gagged. No one could help him. He was only recognizable from the clothes he wore, most of his face was missing.

Debbie said, "Get ready. He came through the window. Thomas wasn't fast enough to shoot before he got hit. I shot him, but there may be more men behind him."

Cynthia spun around. *No!* Debbie sat against the wall with her bloody hands pressed to her side. She knelt beside her and stammered. "Debbie, you got shot."

"I know, dear. Don't worry about me. Make sure none of those men get my niece and nephew."

Cynthia reined in the panic and spoke with conviction to reassure herself as much as Debbie. "I will."

Cynthia ignored the man bleeding out on the worn area rug, pushed a chair beneath the broken window, and scrambled on top of it. She braced her shotgun on the windowsill and against her shoulder and peered through the sight.

A man in a horrible floral shirt looked over his shoulder as he ran around the side of the house toward her. She cleared her mind, calmed her breathing, aimed for his head in case he wore a bullet proof vest, and pulled the trigger. He toppled on the ground with the side of his face missing. A second man came around the corner. She squeezed the trigger again and the man's neck exploded.

The rage and pain simmering under the surface boiled over, and she unleashed a cry of triumph. She turned and hopped off the chair. Debbie's body was slumped forward.

"No!" Cynthia dropped to her knees in front of Debbie and put pressure on the wound. "Help!"

Footsteps pounded on the stairs, and Trent appeared "What's wrong?"

"One of the men tried to come in the basement. Debbie shot him, but he shot her, and killed Thomas."

"You're doing right keeping pressure on her wound.

Jon contacted the FBI for help already. They should be here any time. I'll keep an eye out for the other two men."

"They're dead. I perched in the window and killed them before they could get in here."

He stood and crossed the room to the window with the phone to his ear. "Do you hear that?"

"What? My ears are ringing. I can barely hear you."

"Blade slap from a helicopter. Jon texted Assistant Director Pruitt for help a while ago. We'll get Debbie to a hospital fast." He sprinted up the stairs.

The storage room door cracked open.

Jessica said, "I heard screaming, then talking, and now a helicopter. What's going on out there?"

"It's safe to come out but keep Bryce in there."

"Why?" Jessica swung open the door. "What's..." Her eyes widened and she scrambled to her knees beside Debbie. "Aunt Debbie. Wake up. Please, wake up." Jessica's shoulders shook as she dissolved into tears.

Sally came out of the storage room and stood behind Jessica. "Oh no, Debbie. And poor Thomas." She kneeled and put a hand on Jessica's shoulder as her eyes swam with tears.

Cynthia's own eyes filled, and the bulletproof vest she wore became a hundred pounds heavier. She wanted to hug Jessica, but she had to keep pressure on Debbie's wounds. *Hang on, Debbie. Please hang on.*

Jon and Trent came flying down the basement stairs followed by two men wearing FBI gear carrying a stretcher.

Jon lifted Jessica from the floor and wrapped her in his arms. He whispered in Jessica's ear, but whatever he said didn't slow down her crying jag.

One of the FBI men kneeled beside Cynthia. "It's okay, ma'am. You can let go. I'll take over."

Cynthia stood. Trent took her by the shoulders and steered her away to a corner. She stripped off the vest and dropped it on the floor. "I should've given one of them that vest. Then they wouldn't be…"

"Don't go there. You didn't shoot them." Trent pointed to the shooter who had perished while she tended Debbie. "That scum did."

Since her hands were full of Debbie's blood, Cynthia wiped her tears with her sleeve. She watched as the two FBI men strapped Debbie to the stretcher and carried her up the stairs.

Chapter Thirty-Seven

Jessica climbed out of the car outside the emergency department at the hospital and rushed inside while Jon and Sally parked. A grey cloud hung over Jessica's head with the tiniest beam of sunlight shining through. Aunt Debbie had a pulse when the FBI transferred her to the hospital's care, but she'd lost a lot of blood, and the medic suspected internal bleeding and possible organ damage.

Jessica rushed to the reception desk. She couldn't stop tapping her toe and clenching her hands as she waited.

A receptionist with kind brown eyes asked, "How can I help you, ma'am."

"My aunt, Debbie Johnson, was flown in by the FBI. Do you know where she is?"

"Let's see here. Debbie with an 'ie'?"

"Yes, that's right."

"What's your name?"

"Jessica Kent."

"She's in surgery on the fourth floor." The receptionist handed her a clipboard and a pen. "You're listed as her next of kin. We'll need you to sign forms. Her doctor will look for you in the surgical waiting room when Mrs. Johnson is out of surgery."

"Any idea how long until we hear something?"

"Check in with the desk upstairs. They might be able

to tell you more. You can submit those forms there as well."

Jessica waited by the doors for Jon and Sally to come in from the parking lot, then they got on the elevator. The doors opened on the fourth floor and the antiseptic odor of bleach and the tiled, yellow, institutional hallway sent her pulse into a frenzy. Her feet froze in the middle of the hallway, and the clipboard shook in her hands.

Jon grabbed the clipboard as it slipped from her grasp and wrapped an arm around her shoulders. "This isn't Utah. I'm not unconscious, and no one is taking you from me ever again."

It never failed to astonish how easily Jon could read her. "I know. I don't know what came over me. I was focused on Aunt Debbie. The incident in Utah never even crossed my mind until we stepped off the elevator."

"It's to be expected after the kidnapping. You, okay?"

Sally said, "I could stay and call when she's out of surgery."

Jessica said, "It's okay. I want to be here. I'm fine now. Besides, I have to get past this before the baby comes."

****

After they checked in, a trauma nurse stepped out of the operating room. She informed them the bullet had punctured Debbie's liver. The surgeon was working to cauterize the surrounding vessels and repair the organ.

Three long hours passed. Debbie was still in surgery, and they hadn't gotten any more updates. Jessica stood by the window, cradling her growing stomach. Beyond the tall city buildings and condominiums, the ocean met the sky. She stared at the undulating, turquoise waves, fighting to keep panic at bay. Was there any worse fate than waiting for a loved one to come out of surgery?

Sally touched her shoulder. "Do you need anything?"

For the tenth time Jessica told her, "I'm fine. Thank you."

Sally sat next to Jon. "What about you, son?"

Jon shook his head.

An unfamiliar voice called, "Jessica Kent."

Jessica pivoted from the window. "I'm Jessica Kent."

A man in scrubs approached them. For better or worse, he'd have the answers she needed, putting an end to the agonizing wait. With a surgical mask covering his face, she couldn't read his expression.

Jon scrambled out of the chair and wrapped his strong arm around her shoulders. She leaned into him, drawing strength from his familiar musky scent. Sally stood on the opposite side of Jessica and took her hand in both of hers, as the doctor stopped in front of them.

"I'm Dr. Graham. I operated on your aunt."

Jessica nodded, but said nothing, wishing he'd rip the bandage off, and say what needed to be said.

He continued, "She came through surgery, but her condition remains critical. The bullet did significant damage to the right side of her liver. Only time will tell if her liver can regenerate, or if she'll need a transplant."

Jessica's knees wobbled as the surgeon's words dealt their blow. If they hadn't selfishly invited her and Sally to the safe house in Utah, Debbie would be home, safe in her beloved farmhouse, instead of fighting for her life in a Hawaiian hospital.

Jon asked, "Do you have an inclination one way or the other?"

"Well, for a sixty-six-year-old woman, she's in remarkable shape. Her vitals improved immediately after we gave her blood transfusions. If that's any indication of her body's ability to heal, I would lean toward her recovering, but I don't want to make any promises."

Jon kissed the top of Jessica's head. "See? Don't lose hope."

Jessica met the doctor's gaze. "Thank you, Doctor, for patching her up and giving her a chance." Aunt Debbie was the strongest woman she knew. If anyone could pull through something like this, it was her.

"You're welcome. Debbie will be moved to the ICU for observation. You can visit her briefly once she's there. She needs her rest."

Jessica nodded.

The doctor turned and left the way he came.

Jessica said, "Thank God, she made it through surgery, but I wish it had been all good news. What if her liver doesn't grow back?"

Sally picked up their purses and slung them over her shoulder. "This is your Aunt Debbie we're talking about. No matter what, she'll fight."

"Come on. First things first. We'll wait to visit Debbie." Jon took Jessica's hand and led her to the elevator. "Then, if you'd like, we can make arrangements to medivac her to a hospital back home when her condition is stable. The FBI will take care of it."

A kinder, more considerate husband couldn't possibly exist. Jessica squeezed his hand. "Yes, I'm sure that's what she'd want. To be closer to home. We'll need to call her sons to let them know what's happening."

"I already thought of that," Sally said. "I texted Sheriff Hank, and he sent Ken and Kevin's phone numbers. I figured it best to wait until we had more to tell them. I'll call them after we see Debbie."

Jessica grasped Sally's hand. "Thank you. I don't know what I'd be doing without you guys."

****

Once her aunt was settled, Jessica tiptoed into the room with Sally and Jon behind her. Aunt Debbie's face was ashen from her ordeal, yet peaceful in sleep behind her oxygen mask. She'd been connected to an EKG and vital signs monitor, but thankfully no extra tubes or wires added to her discomfort besides her IV fluids.

Jessica touched Aunt Debbie's hand and spoke softly. "I don't know if you can hear me, Aunt Debbie. But I'm here, and so are Sally and Jon. You're going to be okay. Rest and heal. We'll take you home as soon as we can. I love you."

Jon took Jessica's hand and tilted his head toward the door.

Jessica followed him and Sally to the desk in the hallway. "What's the plan? Should we get a room somewhere and take turns sitting with Debbie?"

"I booked a three-bedroom family suite at a hotel a few blocks away," Jon said, "Why don't we go check in, and you can get some rest? We barely slept last night. Trent and Cynthia are meeting us there later with Bryce."

Jessica said, "But what about Debbie?"

"She'll be out of it for quite a while after surgery," Jon said. "I'll call Assistant Director Pruitt and ask her about a flight for Debbie. Then I'll grab a quick nap, and we'll come back here. Okay?"

A man walked by them with a chair tucked under his arm. He set the chair by Debbie's door, sat, then pulled a paperback out of the inside pocket of his blazer.

Sally's brow raised. "Who's that?"

"I'm guessing the FBI posted a guard." Jon said, "I'll go introduce myself."

A guard. While worrying about whether her aunt lived or died, she'd pushed the shooters to the back of her mind. Bryce was safe with Cynthia and Trent for now. But what if it wasn't over? What if there were more men coming for them?

Sally looped her arm through Jessica's. "At least we know she'll be taken care of while we rest. Jon's right. You and that baby need sleep. No pregnant woman should be dealing with all the craziness you have in the past few months."

"I know. Crazy doesn't even begin to describe it."

Jon strode toward them. "There will be a guard in place until the FBI finishes their investigation into the shooting. They want to be sure those men were the last of the threat."

Jessica asked. "Why didn't they come talk to us after the shootings?"

"They got statements from Cynthia and Trent," Jon said, "Assistant Director Pruitt asked them to give us a day before requesting ours. By then they're hoping to have more to tell us."

Sally said, "That was considerate."

"It was." Jessica sighed. "But answers would be nice. I want someone to tell us we're safe."

Chapter Thirty-Eight

Later that afternoon, Jon fired at the car in front of Bryce's motorcycle as they played video games in their suite with the volume muted.

Bryce giggled. "Thanks, Dad."

"You're welcome, buddy."

Playing with Bryce proved to be the best therapy. Although Jon didn't pull the trigger, the burden of Thomas' death landed on his shoulders. Sadly, Jon had no one to send Thomas' body to. Both his parents had died of cancer, and he had no siblings or other close relatives, but he had tons of friends from freelancing for the FBI, plus the ones he'd met online.

To honor Thomas' memory, Jon planned to host an online memorial service after they returned to Lewistown. Afterward, he'd take a trip to Thomas' hometown in Telluride, Colorado, to scatter his ashes over the Bridal Veil Falls.

"Is Mom gonna wake up soon?"

"I don't know, but she needs her sleep."

Jessica and Sally hadn't roused since they'd gone to bed three hours earlier. And since Trent and Cynthia dropped Bryce off at the hotel, he hadn't heard from them either. Jon yawned. He wouldn't be able to put off sleeping much longer, even if it meant dozing in a chair at the hospital while Jessica visited Debbie.

Bryce crossed the finish line in first place, cheered,

and fist bumped Jon. "Dad?"

"Yes."

"What happened to Aunt Debbie? Trent said you and Mom and Grandma were at the hospital with her."

Jon winced as his mind raced to come up with an answer. Amid all the worry and shock, they'd never discussed what to tell him. "She's hurt, buddy. She needed an operation, but she should feel better soon."

Bryce set his remote aside. "Can I see her?"

"Later, okay? She's sleeping a lot right now for her body to heal, so she wouldn't even know you were there."

Bryce pouted. "Why did we have to leave another nice house and come here?"

Another doozy. "We're closer to Debbie here. Besides, once she's better, we get to go home."

Bryce jumped into his lap and smiled. "Home? It's safe again?"

Jon ruffled his hair. "I think so. The FBI is making sure."

"Good. I miss Daisy."

"Me too. She's a good horse." Jon's phone vibrated in his pocket with an incoming call from Georgia Pruitt. He shifted Bryce out of his lap. "Keep on playing. I have to take this call. Okay?"

"Okay."

Jon hit the accept button as he stepped onto the balcony and slid the door shut.

Assistant Director Georgia Pruitt said, "I wanted to update you on the shooting at the safe house."

"I'm listening."

"We identified the shooters. They belonged to a suspected prostitution ring on the main island. All the key players were killed during the shooting."

"You don't foresee anyone else from the Kansas City mob coming after us again?"

"Highly unlikely. We raided their warehouses and arrested them all a few hours ago. Without Hugh's protection, we feel confident we can make the charges stick this time."

"That's wonderful news. Thank you so much."

Jon hung up and shoved the phone in his pocket. The elephant he'd carried on his back for months climbed off and walked away. He rolled his shoulders and sighed as he lifted his face to the sky and soaked in the Hawaiian sun. With any luck, they'd be leaving the warmth behind and returning home to winter by the end of the week.

The sliding door whooshed open behind him, and Jessica came outside, rubbing her eyes. There couldn't be a more welcome sight than the woman he'd loved his whole life. The dark circles under her eyes had lightened, and her skin had regained its healthy pregnant glow.

Jessica wrapped her arms around him and kissed his cheek. "Your eyes. They don't look haunted anymore. Did something change?"

"I just got off the phone with Georgia Pruitt. The Kansas City mob is behind bars. It's over."

"That's amazing news." Jessica beamed for a few seconds before the smile fell from her lips.

"I know. It's bittersweet with Debbie in the hospital."

"And Thomas dead because we involved him in our mess. Let's tell Aunt Debbie when we visit. Who knows? Maybe some good news and the promise of home will spur her liver along."

"That's the spirit, sweetheart."

****

Jessica glanced up from her book every so often at her aunt's face. Over the course of the past two days, Debbie's skin had morphed from the pasty color of an egg white to a healthier light pink. The gradual transformation made it easier to stay positive about her recovery.

Debbie had woken a few times for long enough to eat and FaceTime with her sons for a few minutes before the pain meds knocked her out again. The yellow Afghan and daisies Sally had gotten her from the gift shop had brought a weak smile to Debbie's lips the first time she woke enough to be aware of her surroundings. Debbie loved yellow. She referred to it as a little bit of sunshine in places the sun couldn't quite reach.

Even though Debbie had to be in pain despite the meds, she didn't complain. She only wanted to know when the drowsiness would pass, and when she could get out of bed and walk around.

A light knock sounded on the door.

Jessica called, "Come in."

Dr. Graham entered with a chart in his hands and touched Aunt Debbie's foot.

Aunt Debbie's eyes fluttered open.

Dr. Graham's eyes crinkled. "Good afternoon, Mrs. Johnson. How are you feeling today?"

"Drowsy. The medication you're giving me for the pain is too strong. I'd rather be awake even if it means more pain."

"Okay. Most patients beg for a higher dose, but we can try lowering yours. Sound like a plan?"

Debbie nodded.

"I have some good news," he continued, "I've read

the results of your latest tests."

Jessica perched on the edge of her seat and held Aunt Debbie's hand. "Well, don't leave us hanging."

He chuckled. "Your liver count dropped, which means it's healing. I've given the go ahead for your transfer to Montana."

Aunt Debbie's face lit up like she'd gotten a new gun. "We're going home, Jess. Can you believe it?"

"Yes, I can. And you're going to be okay. No transplant for you, which doesn't surprise me either. You're the sweetest and toughest woman I know. And I love you."

Debbie squeezed her hand. "I love you, too."

"Dang these pregnancy hormones." Jessica's eyes filled with tears, and she brushed them away with her sleeve. "I'll call the others and let them know we're Montana bound."

****

Three days later, Jessica stood between Jon, Bryce, and Sally on the tarmac at the airport as two paramedics wheeled Aunt Debbie onto a deluxe medivac plane. Once they secured her bed, the rest of them boarded. Assistant Director Pruitt had wanted them to fly together as a family and spared no expense. No doubt due to Pruitt's guilty conscience over all the times the FBI had failed to protect them.

Trent and Cynthia had left the day before, bound for Maryland, to visit her family and explain her disappearance in person. As much as she liked Cynthia, spending every day with her and Jon in close proximity was the definition of awkward.

Jessica sank into her plush leather seat with Jon and Bryce on either side of her. "I never thought I'd be happy to be trading hot beaches for snow."

Jon said, "Don't worry. In three months, it'll be summer in Montana. And we may not have palm trees, but we have even bigger mountains."

Bryce groaned as he crossed his arms. "Three months is a long time. And there's no ocean in Montana."

"We'll find a lake and a beach when it warms up." Jessica stroked his hair and employed an important tool in any mother's arsenal— redirection, and distraction. "I bet your friends will be happy to see you."

Bryce sat up straighter. "Can we have a big play date at the ranch next weekend?"

She chuckled. *Well, that backfired, but the smile on his face will be worth the effort.* "A house full of little boys. What could be better?"

As they flew toward Washington State, the clear skies revealed a line of rocks in the distance growing taller and taller. At dusk, they neared Montana. The sun descended in the sky in a blaze of fire and glory, giving the Rockies a golden hue. The mountains stirred love deep in her heart as they called her home.

Jon kissed her hand. "Another glorious Montana sunset spent together."

"One of many more to come."

Chapter Thirty-Nine

As spring turned to summer, the hay stalks grew along with Jessica's baby bump. And after a few months of rehabilitation, and taking it far easier than she'd wanted, Aunt Debbie was slinging hay and mucking stalls in her new barn. Jessica's everyday life had returned to its glorious and normal routine.

Enduring loss, fear, and being forced from her home twice in the past year had bestowed upon Jessica a special gift—an appreciation for every moment and all the small things in life she'd previously taken for granted. She valued each smile and carefree laugh because they signified her family's joy.

One evening in August, the dog days of summer, Jessica rocked in a new porch swing Jon had built that spring. The temperature had dipped, and a refreshing cool breeze carried the sweet smell of hay, swept her ponytail off her neck, and rustled her skirt against her shins.

Jon came out onto the porch and handed her a mug of chamomile tea. "Feeling any better?"

"The heartburn is easing off some, but my lower back is still aching." No matter how or where she sat the last few days, her back throbbed. "The joys of pregnancy. It'll be worth it when our little boy or girl is born."

He leaned on the wooden porch railing. "Want me

to massage your back or run you a bath?"

"Both, please." She set her tea on the side table and reached out her arms. "Help me up?"

"Of course, sweetheart." Jon took her arms and lifted her to her feet.

She took a few steps toward the door, then a gush of liquid trickled down her legs. "Jon."

He turned from the front door to face her. "What?"

"Never mind the bath. Wake Bryce. My water broke."

Jon's stood still, and his face drained of color. "It's time?"

"Yes. You aren't about to faint, are you? You're white as a ghost."

He slapped his cheeks and pink returned. "I'm fine. A bit surprised and nervous is all. You get in the truck, and I'll get everything else." He sprinted in the house as if the wind was at his back.

Jessica chuckled despite the pain in her back which she now identified as early labor. Killers, gunfire, and fleeing for their lives hadn't incited this kind of panic in Jon. For a change, she was calm and collected and he wasn't.

Jon's voice carried through the front door he'd left open. "Bryce! Wake up! Baby time!"

Jessica waddled to the truck and climbed in the passenger seat. Rubbing her tummy, she said, "I can't wait to meet you, but please wait until we get to the hospital to be born. I'm not sure your daddy is in any condition to deliver you himself."

****

Ten hours and five pushes later, Jessica held a pink-skinned, chubby, seven-and-a-half-pound baby girl in her arms. Jon stood beside the bed with his arm around Jessica's shoulders. Jessica gazed into her healthy newborn's dark blue eyes, and her heart swelled, making room for another precious child. After all they'd survived together throughout her pregnancy, all was finally right with the world.

Jon kissed her cheek. "You did good, sweetheart. She's beautiful, like her mother."

"I think she looks a little like you."

Jon held their daughter's tiny hand. "Maybe. Either way, she's the prettiest baby I've ever seen."

"I don't think the name we picked suits her."

"No. She doesn't look like a Hailey. What should we name her? You did all the hard work so it's only fair you choose."

"Remember when Bryce said we should name the baby Chase?"

Jon chuckled. "We might have to adopt him a dog and name it Chase."

"Oh, he'd love a dog." Jessica brushed a finger over her baby girl's tiny nose and chubby cheeks. "And your big brother's going to love you, too."

She lifted her gaze to meet Jon's. The most magnificent smile lit up his face. Being a father suited him. Much had changed since the first time they'd laid eyes on each other again after fifteen years apart. The darkness in his eyes that day on Aunt Debbie's porch no longer had a hold on him. Since returning home from Hawaii, the carefree Jon she'd known and loved from their younger years had returned, and she was lucky to have him.

She said, "I think an older and more traditional name would suit her. Maybe Cassie, short for Cassandra."

"Cassandra Kent. It has a nice ring to it."

"I think so," Jessica said, "She's in a deep sleep. Can you put her in the bassinet?"

Jon slipped a hand under Cassandra's head and cradled her in the crook of his arm. "She's so small." He tiptoed to the bassinet and set her down as if she was a feather that could blow away in the wind.

A gentle rap on the door interrupted their quiet moment with their new addition.

Jon opened the door. "What are you guys doing here? I thought you were in Colorado."

Jessica recognized Trent's voice in the hallway. "Assistant Director Pruitt sent me. I need to talk to Jessica."

"Now? Couldn't it wait until Jess and the baby are released tomorrow?"

Jessica took a deep cleansing breath. *This can't be anything good. May as well get it over with.* "Let them in. They came all this way."

Cynthia looked in the bassinet and smiled. "She's adorable. Congratulations."

"Thanks." Jon crossed his arms. "What's up?"

Trent said, "When our crew searched Hugh Jones' mansion after the shooting, they recovered some bugs planted by Karen Chamberlain. The one in Jones' office was a mess of static. It's taking weeks to unscramble each call."

Jon sighed. "What was on the bug that's so awful you were sent in person."

Trent frowned. "This might also explain how Hugh Jones found you in Lewistown. Maybe it's better if we play the recording. We think we know who Jones was talking too, but we need confirmation."

The part of the brain responsible for sensing danger prickled at Jessica's consciousness and her stomach churned. "From me?"

"Yes." Trent handed Jessica his phone. "Hit play when you're ready."

They'd been through so much. No matter what this was, they'd deal with it. She touched the screen and braced herself.

"Are they dead yet, Mr. Jones? The name from the hotel shooting hasn't been made public. Is Jon Kent the agent who died?"

"No, it was Agent Gardner. The assassin I sent, Ed Henson, failed."

"Leave them to me. After the heat dies down and they drop their guards, I'll take care of them myself."

"Good. I'll enjoy my honeymoon a lot more knowing they're in your capable hands. Don't fail me."

"Fail you? Let's not forget you promised to take care of it yourself. You failed me. You owe me now, Mr. Jones."

Jessica's hands shook as the recording ended, quieting the dark, menacing voice in conversation with Hugh Jones. The voice that haunted her nightmares. The hairs on the back of her neck prickled. *It can't be. The hotel shooting happened long after he died.*

Jon's brow furrowed. "Jess, what's wrong. Do you know who that is?"

Her voice trembled. "He isn't dead." She clung to Jon's arm. "How isn't he dead? He fell off the cliff."

Trent said, "I have to hear you say his name."

Jessica said, "It's David Hayes. The serial killer who used to live next door to me."

"Are you absolutely sure?" Jon wrapped his arms

around her.

She leaned her face against his chest and fisted Jon's shirt. "I'd know that horrible voice anywhere. It's him. And he's coming for us. What are we supposed to do? We can't go on the run with a newborn."

"I know you're both in shock. The FBI is going to throw all their resources at figuring out what happened after he fell off the cliff, his real identity, and where he is now," Trent said. "Since you and Sam connected him to so many crimes last year, he's been added to the most-wanted list."

Jon snapped, "After everything that's happened, we're supposed to trust the FBI?"

"Not them." Cynthia sat on the edge of the bed. "We knew you wouldn't want to run again. If that rental house across the street from the ranch is empty, Trent and I want to move in. We'll help keep your family safe."

Jon said, "Jess just gave birth. She's exhausted. Can we talk about this and let you know later?"

"Of course. We'll leave you." Trent followed Cynthia into the hallway and shut the door behind them.

Jon sat in the chair beside Jessica's bed and held her hand. "What do you think?"

"If we let them stay, they'll end up in danger again. The same way they did with Hugh Jones." She sighed and rubbed her eyes. "But I don't see any other choice. I'll be busy with the baby and Bryce, and you have the ranch."

"Trent's an active FBI agent. Security detail is part of his job, and Cynthia seems determined to stick with him. We can't feel guilty accepting their help."

"I'm exhausted and overwhelmed. Can you watch Cassandra while I sleep?"

"Of course." Jon squeezed her hand. "Don't worry. I'll protect you and the kids. While you sleep, I'll call the security company and have more equipment installed."

"I'm not falling apart over David. I'm okay. Better than okay with this little sweetheart." Jessica turned on her side to face Cassandra, then reached in the bassinet and held her tiny, perfect hand.

Their sweet daughter slept peacefully, the way only a baby can, oblivious to the bomb dropped on the day of her birth. Jessica refused to let David's evil cloud this miraculous day. Cassandra was a blessing.

For the sake of her family, Jessica vowed to keep herself together in a world where a monster lurked waiting to pounce. Even if it meant living across the street from Jon's sort of ex-wife until they managed to slay the beast.

A word about the author...

Growing up as an only child in a small town, I dreamed of becoming an author. My father laughed and said okay, but you might be broke. I shrugged my shoulders and kept clacking on the keyboard of our home PC, delighted when my words appeared on the small monitor, a staple of early '90s technology.

In high school, when it was time to decide on a future career, I chose to pursue an Honours Degree in Criminology at the University of Ottawa, but at the back of my mind, the dream of writing for a living persisted.

Fast forward fifteen years, and as a happily married woman and proud mother to two children, four dogs, and a cat, my dream came true.

For information on upcoming releases please visit my website: michellegodardricherauthor.wordpress.com